THE CHARMING MAN

A Q.C. DAVIS NOVEL

LISA M. LILLY

While River City, where most of The Charming Man is set, is a real apartment complex in Chicago, this book is a work of fiction. The fictional events that take place there are just that — fictional, as are the community organizations and associations based there. The managers and residents of the apartment complex are entirely products of my imagination.

Indeed, all names, characters, places, and incidents in the book are either products of my imagination or are used fictitiously. Any resemblance to actual events, locales, or persons, living or dead is purely coincidental.

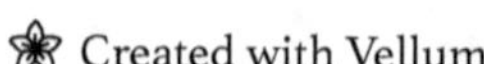 Created with Vellum

1

———

Oh love is handsome, love is charming
And oh so pretty when it's new
But love grows old and waxes cold...

The Water Is Wide (Trad.)

December 13, 1:50 p.m.

"I won't go." My friend Joe's baritone voice rose in pitch.

I rested my forehead against the rough interior brick wall of my office. Outside, snow coated Dearborn Street, including the driving, parking, and bike lanes. I imagined lying on a smooth white swath of it. Feeling snowflakes fall on me, blanketing me in their icy beauty.

"A trip to Aruba's a really nice gift," I said. "And expensive."

"No big deal. I'll pay her for the airfare."

"It is a big deal. I'm sure she went to a lot of trouble to plan it."

Though I wanted to, I couldn't ask Joe to turn down the early

Christmas gift from his girlfriend. Especially in a year when the temperatures in Chicago had started dropping below freezing in mid-October. He was too good a friend for me to be selfish about this. And he'd been a rock since Marco's death.

A little too much of a rock, I guessed. His girlfriend and I got on well. But she quite reasonably expected a little more alone time with him than she'd been getting.

"Q, seriously, I don't mind. I'll tell her I promised you I'd be here for Christmas. She'll understand."

Joe's the only person not officially family who gets away with calling me Q on occasion and, less often, Q.C. He was also the only person I could imagine viewing the holiday windows on State Street with this year or eating Frango mint pie under the two-story Christmas tree in what had once been Marshall Field's.

Since Marco's death I found myself understanding at last why my mother ignored Christmas. Normally I love the winter holiday season, but relentless cheer makes loss that much harder. Unlike most people, though, Joe never acted like I ought to be over Marco's death by now. He never shot me sidelong, worried glances if I didn't appear as merry as the season demanded or said too little.

I grasped the window ledge. The ridges of its bricks pressed into my fingertips. What sky I could see between the buildings across the street looked slate gray.

"I'll be fine," I said. "Go to Aruba. I'll feel a lot worse if you don't."

Blizzard conditions were predicted for the next twenty-four to forty-eight hours. It looked like nearly two inches had fallen since I'd started running invoices half an hour ago. Most businesses had sent their employees home early or told them not to come in at all today.

I worked for myself, so I never got the day off.

"You'll still go to Carole's?" Joe said.

"I'll figure something out."

I didn't want to tell him that a family emergency had drawn our friend Carole's husband back to Paris for the rest of December. She'd be joining him a few days before Christmas, so having a holiday dinner with them was out. If I believed in fate, I'd have thought its idea of fun was to force me to choose between the proverbial rock of spending the holidays with my sister and the hard place of spending them alone.

"You're sure."

I cleared my throat. "I'm sure. And I've got invoices to get out the door. See you at rehearsal."

We sang in an a cappella trio together. At least Joe wasn't leaving until after our last job. It was at a private law firm holiday party on the upper floor of Gibson's, one of Chicago's most well-known steakhouses. The food promised to be excellent. The pay was pretty good too. So long as I had no more than a glass of wine, I'd probably be all right.

I sank into my desk chair.

A click of a button populated my time and hourly rate for a case involving two brothers suing over who got to control the family business after their dad's death. The invoice total wasn't bad — over three thousand dollars. But I was sending the bill later than usual, which meant I'd get paid later. Possibly not until next year. Not bad for tax reasons but not good for my bottom line. Despite all the hours I'd been spending in the office, my firm, still new, had earned less than the year before.

I had five invoices left to run when my phone rang again.

"Quille Davis," I said.

"I need your help," Carole Ports said.

～

December 13, 2:01 p.m.

I'm convinced the chain coffeehouses and cafés in Chicago purposely redesigned their seating this year to be as uncomfortable as possible to move people along. Most of them feature tall tables and chairs where the only options for a purse are hanging it over the seat back — an open invitation to thieves and pickpockets — or clutching it awkwardly in your lap. The few tables of normal height are surrounded by backless stools so narrow they threaten to topple if you shift your weight.

Café des Livres, though, on the first floor of the building where I work, still has a corner with couches and overstuffed armchairs near a fireplace. Its bookcases overflow with books, and dark, rich chocolate scents the air. Since Marco's death I'd spent nearly every other evening here. Often working late, but sometimes just staring at the fire.

Usually the café buzzes with people. But today its small marble tables — all with real cushioned chairs — sat empty. The proprietor, Carole, and I sat across from one another in front of the fireplace, and only one customer waited at the counter for his café au lait.

"How long has she been missing?" I asked Carole.

After apologizing again about having to go away for Christmas and making sure she wasn't taking me from anything vital, Carole had told me that her neighbor Rani Singh was missing.

"Her sister last saw her yesterday evening." A sixtyish French-woman, Carole favors flowing skirts and colorful scarves and looks serene in the face of the rudest customer. But now she clutched her delicate teacup so tight I feared it would break. "I got an email from her early this morning confirming our appointment, and she never appeared. No one's heard from her all day."

"Has anyone talked to the police?" I said.

"It is too soon, *non*?" Carole said.

"There's no set time requirement," I said.

In Chicago, police don't necessarily wait twenty-four hours to look for someone. They start investigating after a reasonable amount of time, which depends on the circumstances. I'd learned that when I wrote a paper on child abduction instances in Illinois for a criminal justice class in college. I'd learned a lot of things working on that paper, including about my own family, so it had been burned into my brain.

Carole sighed. "Police are not a good option. Rani overstayed her student visa. She would be deported."

Rani had come to the United States four years ago from India to live with her sister and attend the University of Illinois at Chicago. I'd earned my undergraduate degree there. Carole had introduced us and asked me to help Rani settle in, which I'd done my best to do. I hadn't seen her much since then, but I remembered her being a friendly, happy girl.

"But if she's in danger—" I said.

Carole shook her head. "Her sister, Shanda, thinks Rani is irresponsible and simply decided to skip the meeting without telling me."

"But you're worried," I said.

Carole glanced at her wristwatch. "It has been over four hours. She was supposed to be here at ten this morning to interview me and take photos. She's writing an article about local immigrants who run businesses. Rani is not one to miss a meeting."

Four hours isn't forever, but I'd never known Carole to worry unnecessarily. I couldn't dismiss her concerns the way I might if my mother called anxious about something. Not that my mother calls me.

"And you've tried to reach her?" I said.

"I left three voicemails and texted her. Repeatedly."

"Any chance she's stuck at school with her phone turned off or out of juice?"

Outside the café's plate glass window snow blew sideways, creating a sort of translucent drape across the street.

"I checked. No classes today. The entire University shut down."

"I can refer you to a private investigator," I said.

"Shanda will never talk about family to a stranger," Carole said. "You, as my friend, she will talk to."

"But I don't know what I can do." I sipped my Chai latte, comforted by the spicy sweet taste. In the month since my birthday I'd fallen back into a bad habit I'd developed after Marco's death — caffeine with a side of sugar several times a day. It got me through, but made it harder to sleep at night. Which made me more tired and more in need of caffeine, a tea company's dream.

"You discovered the truth about Marco," Carole said.

"I don't know Rani the way I knew Marco. And I'm not sure my acting or lawyering skills will help find a missing person."

I worked as a professional stage actor from the age of eight all through college. The ability to change my appearance and adopt different personalities had helped me learn more from the people surrounding Marco than the police had, but some luck had also gone into that. Plus, I could hardly have made things worse for Marco, he was already gone. A missing girl needed a professional to find her.

I told Carole that.

Carole set her empty teacup on the side table between us. "If you don't help, she'll have only me. *Je suis sur* there is a better chance of finding her and making sure she is safe if you are with me."

I still had doubts. And Rani might walk in the door at any moment. But there was no question I'd try to help. Since I'd met her, Carole had offered me a listening ear and solid advice, and she'd never asked for anything in return.

"What are you most concerned might have happened?" I said.

~

December 13, 2:18 p.m.

"Rani takes a lot of photos from the Harrison Street Bridge. What if she slipped? Or she went climbing around outside River City and fell?"

"Does she take a lot of chances when she takes photos?" I stood and started layering on my winter gear.

No one in Chicago bothers with fashion when the wind chill drops under zero degrees Fahrenheit, and today it was twenty-five below. But I'd had a client meeting in the morning, so I'd worn a charcoal gray blazer to dress up my jeans and V-neck long-sleeved T-shirt, my standard office uniform. I struggled to pull my zippered fleece sweatshirt over the blazer as Carole and I talked.

Carole fumbled with the top button of her long wool coat. The fabric strained, as she wore two sweaters under it. "No, no. Rani is not — *qu'est-que c'est le mot juste* — a daredevil. But there are many out of the way places and alcoves."

River City, the aging apartment complex where Carole and her husband live, was one of the first residential buildings in the Printers Row area of Chicago. In the late eighties it was heralded as part of the wave of the future. Its serpentine towers and rounded windows gave it what was considered a space-age look at the time.

Now it loomed at the end of Polk Street about four blocks from the café, its splotched curving concrete walls a sharp contrast to the shiny glass high-rise that had recently sprung to life across the street in what had once been a field.

If Rani had slipped outside the complex in an out-of-the way nook freezing to death was a real possibility. Each year the news reports multiple deaths in Chicago due to extreme weather.

"Did Shanda check hospitals or ERs?"

"She did finally send her assistant to do that, I badgered her so. Rani wasn't at any of them."

I crossed a wool scarf over my fleece, put on my parka, and wrapped another long green scarf around my neck, doubling it so it covered my mouth and nose as well. I could barely turn my head to look at Carole.

"So why assume the worst?" I said.

"That article last year. The one about Chicago architecture luring photographers to take shots from high places. It talked about that man who fell from the twentieth floor of the London House along the river while taking photos. And then the 2012 death. They had to cut the photographer out of the chimney. That image, it stays in my mind."

2

———

December 13, 2:20 p.m.

River City stands on the edge of the Chicago River's south branch. The walk there from the café would be nothing on an average day, but only for Carole was I willing to do it in high winds, bitter cold, and snow.

I wore earmuffs under my wool hat and light knit gloves under my mittens. That morning I'd secured my long dark hair, which is wavy and thick, with a tight ponytail holder and lots of gel. It was tucked under the back collar of my coat, but still the wind whipped strands into my face and eyes. I blinked against the sting as I struggled to shove the hair under my hat.

Carole had wrapped two brightly colored wool scarves over her face. Her long wool coat, like so many women's coats, had buttons that stopped a foot above the hem. The two sides of the coat ballooned in the wind, leaving her knees and lower thighs exposed. She grabbed it with both hands and pulled it shut.

It's one of those ludicrous things fashion designers do — assume that a woman who buys a long, heavy wool coat with a fur collar has no interest in keeping her legs warm.

A thick layer of snow coated the parked cars we passed, and

fresh snow was quickly filling in tire tracks in the street. We stopped a few yards short of the intersection of Polk and Clark. There wasn't much traffic, but I didn't relish being pushed into the crossing at an inopportune moment. It had happened to a woman who worked at the Sears Tower back when it had been called that. She'd been killed.

On the opposite corner stood Sociale, a local wine bar and restaurant. The rows of glass doors that made up its north and east walls folded open in good weather so the interior tables flowed into the outdoor seating. Through them I could see the bar area circled by dangling icicle lights. I was supposed to meet my friend Lauren and two male realtor friends of hers there for drinks at 7:00 p.m. if the blizzard wasn't as bad as expected.

Usually I love fall and early winter in Chicago. The snow falls white and glistening, the air feels brisk but not yet frigid. The lingering warmth of summer keeps Lake Michigan from freezing, and its water keeps downtown less chilly than the rest of the city.

This year, though, I wished instead I could slink away and hibernate. I'd lost track of the number of men Lauren had introduced me to in the last three months in an effort to keep me busy, if not happy. My jaw ached at the thought of plastering on a smiling face and sitting among glowing lights hearing holiday music and glasses clinking all around me. I'd started to feel other people were pushing me to "get back to normal" less out of concern for me and more because they didn't want to feel bad during the holidays.

And then there was my sister. I'd looked into her husband's activities because she'd asked me to and learned things she now wished she didn't know. He didn't seem to blame me. He appeared relieved the truth had come out.

My sister, on the other hand, had spent Thanksgiving in full shoot-the-messenger mode. Or at least shoot-the-messenger-dagger-eyes-while-pretending-to-be-fine mode. Much as I loved seeing my Gram and my niece and nephew, I had no desire for a repeat performance on Christmas.

I looked away from the restaurant to check the traffic light. The wind shifted again, smacking my face. At least the light had changed.

Eyes watering, I stepped into the street.

⁓

December 13, 2:26 p.m.

Carole and I stamped our feet on soggy mats inside River City's glass-walled lobby. A giant pine tree decorated with white lights and pinecones towered over worn leather couches in a small seating area. Trails of slushy footprints and puddles of water led to the resident elevator bank and two nonfunctioning escalators. I guessed not many people from maintenance had made it in today.

The wide open space smelled faintly of disinfectant.

A lone security guard stood at the circular check in counter, but she was on the phone. Carole waved as we unwound our scarves and shook the snow off them.

We walked down one escalator. I stepped carefully to avoid slipping or stumbling on the uneven stairs. My boots were designed to keep my feet warm and dry but were a bit clunky.

"This looks different." I pointed to a newly-painted wall with a glass double door. It closed off what had once been a health club and pool with glass walls that allowed passers-by to see people working out on treadmills and stair machines inside. It had also made the Lobby and Marina Levels smell of chlorine and later, after a major flood closed it down, of mildew.

"Supposedly we will soon have a health club again," Carole said.

We passed two darkened offices.

Shanda's office stood across from a third vacant space.

Gold letters on Shanda's door said Singh Recruiting LLC and below that, Singh Aid and Services (SAS), which Carole told me was Shanda's non-profit. Rani's interview with Carole had been meant for the SAS e-newsletter.

The small reception area had no windows, but a glass panel on the wall provided a view of the hallway. A man I guessed to be in his mid-thirties, so maybe a couple years older than me, typed on a laptop on a durable-looking wood and metal desk.

From the side, his most noticeable feature was a chin receded so far it almost appeared absent. When he turned to greet us, though, his large brown eyes and long dark lashes dominated his face. Combined with his perfectly-shaped, symmetrical nose, he had nearly cover model good looks if you added the chin.

He smiled as if thrilled we'd walked into the basement office. "Carole, good to see you."

"This is Quille," Carole said. "Quille, this is Aidan, Shanda's assistant."

Aidan had broad shoulders and looked tall sitting down. When he stood to shake hands, though, he was barely an inch or two taller than me, making him 5'9" at most.

"Good to meet you," Aidan said. He shifted his gaze to Carole. "Shanda tells me you're worried about Rani."

"She was supposed to meet us at ten," Carole said. She and I had agreed to tell everyone, other than Shanda, that the meeting was with both of us. It was simpler than explaining over and over why I was there.

"I checked the Northwestern and Rush ERs and she's not there," Aidan said.

"Would she go anywhere else?" Carole said.

"Doubt it," Aidan said. "I checked with a friend who's a paramedic. That's where they'd take her if anything happened downtown or at U of I's campus."

"When's the last time you saw her?" I said.

He sat with his arms on the desk, his back straight, and his head tilted up slightly. Giving us his attention, taking our concerns seriously, but not overly worried. "Yesterday. We meet here for coffee most mornings before I start work, but she didn't come today."

"Were you concerned?" I said.

He shook his head. "We don't meet every day, so no. I was a few minutes late. I figured I'd missed her and she'd headed to school before the snow started." He looked at Carole again. "I'm sure she's fine, just got caught up in something."

"So you don't call each other if you aren't going to make it?" I said.

"No, no, no. It's not a formal date."

"You said you meet most days," I said, switching into deposition mode where you parse out the words a witness chooses. "Does that mean every other every day? A few times a week?"

Aidan tapped his index finger on the desk. "Two, maybe three times a week."

"What time?"

"Seven-thirtyish." He glanced at Carole. "Are you sure she didn't forget your meeting?"

"I am," Carole said. "She confirmed early this morning — at 5:30 — then failed to appear."

I shuddered. I'm a morning person, but not that much of one.

Aidan nodded at me. "Too early for me, too."

"You said you saw her yesterday," I said. "Did she meet you for coffee then?"

"Yep. Monday, too."

"How early do her classes start?" Carole said.

"Maybe nine? She likes to study in the library before them."

I wanted to write down his answers or note them in my phone, but sometimes that makes people less comfortable talking. "And where do you go for coffee?"

If Rani had gone without him we might at least trace her movements that far.

"The grocery store. Here in the building."

Another desk, also wood and metal, sat behind Aidan's. Stacks of cardboard boxes from Amazon and Zappos lined the wall behind it. Its top was bare other than a stapler, a stack of what looked like bills, and a mug with the words Save The Parks emblazoned on it. The mug was filled with pens, highlighters, and a pencil with an orange and black pumpkin-shaped eraser on it.

"Is that her desk?" I said.

"Sure, sure, sure. She uses it if she wants to study here or to put together things for the newsletter. I use it for some projects as well. When I need to spread out."

The light for the top line on the three-line phone on Aidan's desk blinked off. "If you want to talk to Shanda, she just wrapped up her call."

3

———

December 13, 2:32 p.m.

Shanda took off her headset as we entered. She wore her straight black hair wound into a bun at the back of her head, but otherwise looked like the photo I'd seen.

Her office was about twelve by twelve, the size of a small spare bedroom. Smooth gray built-in counters set at desk height ran the length of three walls, with two sleek armless chairs against the fourth wall. Matching shelves above the counters held bins, color-coded file folders, books, and plants, though I didn't see any source of sunlight to keep them alive.

She waved us toward the chairs and we perched side-by-side on them.

"It's nice of you to come," she said after Carole introduced us. "But it really wasn't necessary, especially with this weather. I'm sure Rani forgot her meeting. Just like last week."

"Last week?" I glanced at Carole. She hadn't mentioned anything about Rani disappearing another time.

Shanda nodded, her hair shining in the overhead light. "She nearly gave me a heart attack. Missed the newsletter deadline and was hours late for dinner. She was holed up at the library at

UIC. Claimed somehow she had the deadline wrong on her calendar. And swore she told me she'd be at the library late, but she hadn't."

Carole compressed her lips, deepening the fine lines that curved around her mouth. "I did not know that. But she confirmed her appointment with me. There's no date confusion."

"Did you try reaching her last week?" I said to Shanda. "When she didn't show?"

I couldn't imagine being so nonchalant about a sister's failure to appear. My sister Kendra was unhappy with me these days, but she'd raise an alarm if I'd been missing half a day. Still, we had reason to know what a truly awful thing a missing person could mean. Maybe tragedy had never hit Shanda's family.

Shanda took off her reading glasses and set them on her desk next to the phone. "Of course I did. She said her phone ran out of batteries and she didn't have a charger with her, so she didn't get my texts and didn't know I was worried."

I took out a small pad of lined yellow paper from one of my large parka pockets. Carole had given me the notepad from her café office. I could have used my phone to take notes, but I hadn't charged it since this morning. If I ran out of power, I didn't want to lose anything. "Does Rani usually answer texts?"

"She does unless she turns off her phone when she studies. Or maybe she tells me she does and ignores me."

"She can't be in the library now," I said. "Carole told me the UIC campus is closed."

"She could be at the Harold Washington," Shanda said.

Chicago's main library branch is about six blocks from River City. A cavernous building with high ceilings, endless rows of metal shelves, and tile floors, there's nothing particularly cozy about it that makes anyone want to linger. But it was close by if Rani wanted to study away from home.

"The Harold Washington is closed as well," Carole said. "I saw it on the news this morning. All the Chicago library branches are. And it has been very quiet today. My counter clerk checked the other nearby universities for me."

DePaul University, Columbia College, and Roosevelt University had multiple buildings in or within a mile of our neighborhood. If they were all closed, it was unlikely Rani was hidden away somewhere studying.

"I suppose you checked Find My Phone or other locator services?" I said to Shanda.

Given her lack of concern I wasn't sure she had, but it was a better way to phrase it.

"I did. Just in case. But she's not connected to the office computer system, only her own iPad, and she must have taken it with her. It's not here or in our apartment."

"When she missed dinner last week, was that a surprise?" I said. "Or does Rani tend to be absent minded?"

"Very, at least lately," Shanda said. "She says she'll meet me for coffee at two, and she wanders in at two-thirty. She tells me she'll finish something over the weekend, and she doesn't do it until Monday morning."

That explained why Shanda wasn't quick to assume something bad had happened to Rani. But the appointment with Carole had been for an interview, not a coffee date.

"Never has she missed any meeting with me," Carole said.

Shanda frowned. "It's good to hear she's more responsible with other people."

"You said lately," I said. "Since when?"

"Always, really. But it's gotten worse recently." Shanda glanced at the ceiling. "Maybe four or five months? Maybe more."

"So since early summer?" I said.

Shanda shook her head. "I'm not sure when I started noticing, but the weather was turning warm."

It had been a cold, rainy spring, suggesting the change in Rani's behavior had started closer to summer. Though Chicago has had snow as late as June 1, and it's been as high as sixty-five degrees in January.

"Is she having trouble in school?" I said.

"Not that I know of. But this overstayed student visa, I don't know how she let that happen. Why she didn't stay on top of that."

"If she's still in school, why wouldn't her visa still be good?" I said.

"She must have dropped below full-time status. She's in her fifth year, picking up credits she needs. Maybe she didn't know she couldn't drop below a certain number of hours."

"Does Rani have a boyfriend?" I said.

My friend Danielle, the alto in the a cappella trio I'm in with Joe, is also a criminal defense attorney. Danielle always tells me that when a woman is dead, injured, or missing, the first person police look at is the husband or boyfriend. And for good reason. Fifty-five percent of the time when a woman is murdered it's by a man she knows. Men, on the other hand, are more likely to be victims of the types of stranger violence I'd grown up fearing.

"Not since a couple years ago. She was seeing someone — she tells me no one calls it dating now — her second year of college. They broke up for about nine months, then got back together for a few months. Then no one."

Shanda didn't have contact information for the ex-boyfriend. I asked for his name to try to track him down. Because I sometimes need to research defendants, I subscribe to a database that makes it easier to find people. I also figured there would be a lot of information on social media. I sent the name to my assistant. She lives in another state and works for me from home, and she's a great researcher.

I thought back to the types of questions the detective who'd investigated Marco's death had asked me. Not that he'd been a model of perfect investigative technique, but I figured he'd followed standard procedure.

"Is there anyone you can think of who was angry with Rani?" I said.

Shanda laughed. "Rani? No. Everyone loves Rani."

My reaction had been similar after Marco's death, but I'd been wrong.

4

December 13, 2:40 p.m.

"Anyone who had a disagreement with her?" I said, hoping the more mild word would prompt a response.

"Some people in the building dislike Save The Parks, and she's very involved," Shanda said.

"Save The Parks?" The name sounded vaguely familiar.

Carole shifted on her chair, angling her body to face me. Her gold bangle bracelets jingled as she moved. "STP began when the developers started planning the Roosevelt Collection. It pushed to ensure enough green space and a designated park."

The Roosevelt Collection, a U-shaped apartment and shopping complex, stands a block southeast of River City. You need to climb steep stairs beside a private school to get to it, as Wells Street is about one story below Roosevelt Road in that area. The plaza area features a coffee shop, outdoor eating and sitting areas, fire pits, a giant chess set with pieces as tall as small children, plus a playground. A multi-screen movie theater anchors the development at the base of the U.

Last year Marco and I had strolled through it more than once in December and January. We'd loved the white light displays that looked like leaping reindeer and dancing snowflakes.

I hadn't gone yet this year. Probably I wouldn't.

It was one of many new developments and luxury apartment buildings displacing fields and corner parking lots in the Printers Row area of the city. The old saying that there were only two seasons in Chicago, winter and construction, no longer made much sense. Construction noise and dust had permeated the neighborhood year-round for the last two or three years and was projected to continue for over a decade if people would keep moving in.

"Rani's involved in the organization?" I said.

"She's a member," Carole said. "She takes photos for the website."

"And who doesn't like it?" I said.

"Ty Hudson," Shanda said.

Carole shook her head. "He's a developer who lives in the building. He clashes with Rani at the meetings, but I can't imagine him harming her. He's a lovely man."

I wrote the name on my yellow pad.

"What do they clash about?"

Carole frowned. "Ty claims the cost of his development on State Street shot sky high because Save The Parks convinced the city to make him double the green space."

I put a star by Ty's name. "Anyone else unhappy about Save The Parks?"

"Some neighbors feel STP members are too hysterical," Shanda said. "Or they think opposing development is pointless and self-defeating since more people makes the neighborhood more vibrant and safer."

I had mixed feelings myself about the influx of luxury apartments — and their residents — in what had been a quiet, roomy sort of neighborhood featuring hundred-year-old converted warehouses and lots of open space. I always felt more relaxed near my home than downtown, though it was only blocks away.

More people meant I felt safer walking at night. But I wasn't sure I actually was safer. More people with money had increased break ins and muggings, as residents now had things worth stealing. I did my best to protect myself by keeping my smartphone out of sight when walking and using cross-body purses or keeping my wallet in my pocket to make me a trickier target for grab-and-run crimes. The twenty-somethings shuffling along listening to ear buds and holding their thousand-dollar smartphones out in front of them, though, were low hanging fruit.

"Anything else Rani's involved in where she butts heads with anyone?" I said.

"No butting heads that I know of, but she attends Tenants Association meetings." Shanda glanced at the clock on her shelf. "I'm sorry. I have a pitch with a major IT company in fifteen minutes. We can talk more later if Rani hasn't surfaced."

College, Shanda's newsletter, Save The Parks, the Tenants Association. I'd thought I juggled a lot between representing clients in lawsuits, handling tax preparation, and singing, but Rani had me beat if she managed to take part in two organizations, work for Shanda's non-profit, and pursue her degree. Maybe that was why she'd switched to part-time at college.

"You mentioned her calendar," I said. "Any chance she keeps it here at the office?"

"Part of it. Take a look. Quickly."

~

December 13, 2:50 p.m.

I stood behind Shanda as she clicked a few keys. She wore a light, citrusy perfume. A calendar appeared on her screen. "Our shared office calendar. The meeting with Carole is listed. I don't see Rani's personal appointments, though, so I don't know what else she might have going today."

As I glanced over Rani's listings, I wondered if the sisters liked working together. I could only imagine Kendra and I trying to do that. It would be a disaster. And my clients in family businesses did nothing but argue and sue one another. Though, to be fair, the ones who got along didn't come to see a litigation lawyer.

"So if she were studying at the library, that wouldn't be in here?" I said.

"Probably not. Unless it was a formal study group meeting."

"And if she made plans for dinner with a friend?"

"She'd probably mark that private," Shanda said.

Despite her calm words and tone, Shanda's fingers drummed the gray counter, and she held her body stiff. She might be nervous about her upcoming conference call, but according to Carole she'd been an IT recruiter for over a dozen years. It seemed more likely she wasn't admitting to herself how worried she felt about her sister.

I pointed at the entries for tonight. "So after the appointment with Carole, her next place to be is at six?"

"Yes, the Tenants Association meeting, then the Save The Parks meeting. She always attends both, and the Tenants Association has its holiday party tonight. I'm sure she'll turn up then."

December 13, 2:57 p.m.
Carole and I decided we'd make a quick stop at the grocery store, then look around outside before the storm worsened.

The store was on the Marina Level, too, but far down the hall from Shanda's office. It had more space and products than a convenience store, but was nowhere near a full grocery store. We talked with Niu, the young woman at the checkout counter in front. She was the daughter of the owners. She said Rani came in often, alone or with Aidan.

"Did she today?" Carole said.

Niu straightened candy and gum on the racks near the register as we talked. "Didn't see her. She might have gone through when my mother was checking people out. We were both here all morning. Lots of people stocking up. Finally quieted down half an hour ago."

"How late are you open tonight?" I said.

"I'm closing in half an hour or I'll never get home. Even my mother agreed. She doesn't want me driving later."

"Won't residents be unhappy?" I said. The store's posted hours indicated it stayed open until nine-thirty p.m. on weekdays.

"Not much left anyway." She waved toward the empty deli case along the south wall and the bakery shelves that held only a couple loaves of bread and a squished coffee cake. "But the office has keys and codes if things get desperate."

"Your family no longer lives on site?" Carole said.

"New rent's too high."

Carole asked when she'd last seen Rani, and Niu said a few days before.

"Did she seem upset about anything?" I said.

"She didn't say much, but she never does."

"*Vraiment?*" Carole said. "She talks with me all the time."

"Not with me." Niu pulled a small stuffed elf from behind a magazine, frowned at it, and dropped it in a basket full of other abandoned items. "She doesn't like me. I kept trying to be friendly and finally came to the realization that nothing I did or said would make a difference."

5
___

December 13, 3:05 p.m.

"The Harrison Street Bridge first," Carole said as we stepped out of the lobby into the turnaround driveway that fronted the complex. "We will probably be unable to cross later."

"This feels like looking for a needle in an infinite number of haystacks." I wound my second scarf over my face. It felt damp and smelled of wet wool from our previous walk.

"*Mais non*," Carole said. "Rani takes many photos from the bridge. It is her favorite place, and if she took photos today she would have wanted shots from there of the river, downtown, River City, and the old post office with the snow and gusts."

A roof covers the circular driveway in front of River City, but in the half hour we'd been inside the wind had blown over an inch of snow in from the street to cover the asphalt and the sidewalk. Now I felt grateful for my wool socks and Hunter rubber boots, which had made my feet and calves sweat while inside. The boots rose to my knees and had removable fleece liners that cost an extra sixty dollars.

Last November that had seemed like an unnecessary luxury, as the previous two winters had seen little snow. This year,

25

though, we'd had the most precipitation of any year in Chicago in the last decade — over fifty inches of rain or snow. It had also been one of the coldest autumns on record, with over twenty days below twenty degrees. And it wasn't officially winter yet.

Beyond a glassy new skyscraper that housed luxury apartments, skeletons of two more buildings rose. Blue tarp flapped in the wind where it had come loose from its fastenings, hitting the metal fencing around the construction sites. A sign on the fence proclaimed No Gate Hiring. Another said Proud Union Workers.

Sirens wailed in the distance but overall the city seemed unnaturally quiet, with far fewer horns than usual and no squealing brakes. A few SUVs and one taxi drove along Wells Street, normally jammed with traffic at this time of day with parents and nannies collecting their kids from the British School down the street.

Harrison Street rose on a grade toward the bridge over the Chicago River. My foot slipped on a patch of ice beneath the snow layers as we approached. I grabbed Carole's arm and the two of us teetered a few seconds before righting ourselves.

We paused in the center of the bridge, gripping the railing, to look over the frozen river. The construction sites stretching along the river were eerily empty of workers, but dump trucks, steam shovels, and other earth moving equipment stood waiting to be called into use when the wind and snow stopped.

The east side of the river had once been an encampment with different colored tents where homeless people lived. Eventually the space would become part of Chicago's River Walk, connecting to the current pedestrian walkway that ran north and east along the river all the way to Lake Michigan.

As with any other development in the city, I felt conflicted about this one. The part of me that had grown up fearing strangers had prompted me to keep a sharp eye out the rare times I passed the makeshift settlement. Yet I felt for the people who'd once created a community behind heavy foliage, all of it gone now.

When I'd been fifteen, my parents had moved back to Edwardsville without me to be near my middle sister's grave. I'd hardly been homeless. I'd moved across the hall into my Gram's apartment and lived with her until I finished college. But the loss of home, of the place where you keep your things and that you feel is all your own, struck a chord with me.

The wind shrieked, cutting through all my layers. I stared down at the river. It looked like a rough sheet of ice under a layer of white. Had Rani fallen onto it, I didn't think she would have broken through. But if she had, we'd never see her now.

~

December 13, 3:22 p.m.

At the main entrance to River City again, Carole led me up a metal staircase two stories above Wells Street. We followed a snow-covered walkway past storefront businesses. A narrow path of packed down snow suggested someone had shoveled earlier, but fresh snow had already nearly leveled out the area.

We passed a daycare center, an accounting firm, and a legal aid clinic with an American flag in the window that advertised help with immigration issues. On the east side rows of offices with large windows and drawn blinds looked deserted. Another metal staircase at the end led to the street level again where we passed a covered parking area and a large open parking lot.

I gestured toward the snow-covered cars. "Should we check?"

I had to shout in Carole's ear to be heard over the wind.

"No, no." Carole waved her hands in front of her, almost like an umpire's Safe motion. "Rani has no car. She walks."

"She could've used someone else's."

I don't own a car, but frequently use my friend Lauren's. We live in the same building. She owns a car and I own a parking space so we share.

Carole cupped her hand around her mouth and spoke directly into my ear. "She doesn't know how to drive."

Another set of stairs rose to our left. Stepping gingerly after discovering the snow hid ice underneath, we made our way to the top and entered a landscaped park. It's off the fifth floor of the complex. I'd been there in the summer when Carole and her husband hosted their annual barbeque. Today, ice glazed the tree branches, making them shiny and beautiful if they hadn't been whipping about in the wind. A long oval walking path surrounded trees and shrubs and a concrete patio area. Snow covered its wrought-iron tables and chairs. A cylindrical building housed the resident clubhouse.

The snow made it hard to pick out the sidewalk from the grass except where bushes and shrubs poked through. Apartments faced most parts of the park, including some with patios fronting it. I hoped if Rani had been taking photos here and had slipped and fallen, someone would have seen her before the snow came down to cover her. To be sure, though, Carole and I inspected every snowdrift large enough to hide a person underneath. My fingers, hands, and wrists grew numb halfway through. My nose ran under my scarf, making it damp and sticky. The wet wool smell filled my nostrils.

"Only one more place," Carole yelled over the howling wind as we circled back to the staircase.

It was tempting to suggest we go inside for a while, but that would mean braving the bitter cold another time after getting used to warmth again. After fumbling out a tissue to wipe my nose, I settled my scarf around my face once more with numb, aching fingers. I wanted to be finished with the outdoors for the night. I decided when we were done I was cancelling the date for drinks and hitting up Carole for a spot in her guest room tonight rather than fighting through the storm to get home.

As we traipsed around the back of the building toward the marina I crossed my arms and put my hands under them to help warm my fingers.

I was surprised to see a dozen or more snow-covered boats docked in the marina. They were all sizes, the largest looking equal to some of the small yachts I saw cruising along Lake Michigan in warm weather. The other harbors in Chicago empty by early November and stay that way through early spring. Checking out the lakefront in March and April is a great way to find out if boaters are expecting a warm spring.

Also surprising was that the water in the marina hadn't frozen, though the river beyond it was a sheet of ice.

A handful of outbuildings stood along the concrete area fronting the marina. We opened the door to the building that housed the garbage bins. A rat bolted out, startling me. It made me grateful again for my knee-high rubber boots, though it took one look at us and darted in the opposite direction. It brought my rat sightings since moving to Chicago to three.

Not bad.

Throughout our tour I'd mentally mapped the building and its outcroppings, visualizing it as if it were a model for a stage set. Joe and I had met when I'd acted in my first play at the age of eight, and he'd taught me the technique to help me remember my blocking. River City with its multiple levels and indoor and outdoor spaces posed more challenges than the most complex stage set, though.

All the same, when Carole led me up concrete steps beyond the marina I guessed we'd emerge near the front resident elevator banks and the security desk and I was right. We stamped our feet on the sodden gray mat again to clear some snow from our boots.

Carole fished out more tissues from her cross-body bag. I checked my phone. A message from Lauren full of snowflake and Santa emojis reminded me about tonight's drinks, saying since everyone lived in the neighborhood we'd be fine to meet regardless of the blizzard. With clumsy, cold fingers I typed a short, emoji-free answer that I couldn't make it and why.

Carole's red and orange silk scarf fluttered as she gestured toward the lone security guard. "Novia Jones, meet Quille Davis."

"You should get a medal for making it in," I said. My hands were burning from the switch to heat after cold.

"A medal for foolishness." Novia tucked a strand of dark hair, which had come loose from her braids, behind her ear. She wore navy dress pants and a navy blazer over a long-sleeved gray collared shirt with River City emblazoned on it.

"Roads very bad?" I said.

"Not when I left home. But halfway here I came to realize how foolish I'd been not checking the weather. The wind practically blew my car into the next lane on the expressway."

"You're welcome to stay the night with me," Carole said, and turned to me. "Novia lives in Blue Island."

Blue Island is a south suburb. The storm must have started in the north, but I suspected within the hour the entire Chicago area would be under siege.

Something Novia said nagged at me, but I wasn't sure what. Maybe the failure to check the weather before she left, though I'd been guilty of that myself. I relied on Gram to text me about serious warnings. She'd texted three times this morning.

Novia shook her head. "Thanks, really, but I called the property manager and told her I may need to turn around and head back home before it gets worse. I feel bad leaving, but I don't want my mom alone all night if I'm stuck here."

Carole asked if Novia had seen Rani today, and she hadn't. She remembered seeing Rani yesterday or the day before when she'd left for school, but they hadn't talked.

"Maybe you should check River Road," Novia said.

6

December 13, 3:31 p.m.

River Road hadn't worn well. Designed to look like an expansive indoor version of an outdoor main street, the apartments along it had round picture windows that looked out as if onto a real street. Originally it featured old-fashioned street lamps, lush green trees and shrubs, and conversation areas with sofas and armchairs. Its beauty, along with the landscaped outdoor park, had been a huge part of why Carole and her husband had chosen River City as their home.

No couches or chairs stood there now, only faded squares of dulled bronze tile where they'd once been. Discolored splotches on the floor marked where rain had leaked from the atrium twelve stories above.

But vestiges of beauty remained, including something I love about Chicago overall — random artwork. A bronze sculpture of a fine-boned woman stood in the middle of one former seating area. Another bronze-sculpted face with hair streaming out like a sunburst around it jutted from a wall near the elevator. A few deep green peace lilies in bronze pots decorated the edges of the walkway.

Carole and I walked the circular road, checking the alcoves near the elevators and the laundry room. I'd unzipped my parka and both fleeces and unbuttoned my blazer, but I felt hot and sweaty underneath all the layers and in my knee-high boots.

No sign of Rani.

I hadn't really expected it. Probably a dozen people passed us while we were on the indoor road. If Rani had gotten hurt here, surely someone would have seen her.

~

December 13, 3:43 p.m.

On the third floor, which was known as the Upper Level, Carole and I split up to check a series of office suites, including the ones we'd seen from outside.

The first four offices nearest the stairwell had no names on the doors and no one answered my knocks. Small holes in the wall about eye level to the right of two of the doors suggested there had once been plaques listing inhabitants.

The vacancies made me wonder about the complex's future. People in the neighborhood often talked about whether the group of developers who'd recently bought River City meant to spruce it up and turn it into luxury rentals or ask the city to let them tear it down and build anew. The complex had begun as high-end rental apartments. It turned condo in the late 1990s.

About a decade later it had both figuratively and literally gone underwater. In the 2008 recession owners who'd hoped to flip the units became stuck with them without a way to cover the mortgages. A couple years later heavy rains and overflow from the Chicago River flooded units, the parking area, and most of the businesses on the lower levels.

I'd been doubtful when Lauren told me about the rumors that developers wanted to buy it in bulk and turn it into apartments again, but she'd been right. Some residents moved out after the bulk sale. Others, like Carole and her husband, Frery, stayed, hoping for renewal.

If the developers were aiming for upgrades, they hadn't started here, as it took another three offices before I found one occupied. Its door had a frosted glass window with Elizabeth Driscoll, Attorney At Law stenciled on it in gold cursive letters.

Ms. Driscoll's rectangular waiting area smelled like cinnamon and apple. A row of white lights glowed around the coffee table's edges. Modular chairs sat on either side of a water cooler. A door on the left led to an office that held a conference table stacked with paper and cardboard boxes. Black metal file cabinets lined the walls.

A tall brunette woman with broad shoulders and a single silver streak running from her part to the ends of her bobbed hair emerged from the office on the right. She wore black-framed glasses, a red blazer over a lilac print blouse, and a black skirt. The color combination suggested to me an attempt to appear both sympathetic and aggressive. That plus her being a solo attorney made me guess she did family law or estate planning and related litigation.

"Elizabeth Driscoll?" I extended my hand. "I'm Quille Davis. A friend of a resident here, Carole Ports."

We shook, and she told me to call her Eliza. Her grip was firm and her hand warm. "Carole's a lovely woman. How can I help you, Quille?"

"Carole's neighbor Rani Singh missed an appointment this morning. No one's heard from her all day, and Carole asked me to help track her down."

Eliza pressed her hand over her heart. "Little Rani's missing? That's terrible."

The "little" made me pause, though if I had to guess I'd have put her around 5'3", as I felt a bit tall around her. She was also thin, though I didn't think strikingly so. Eliza, however, being broad-shouldered and close to six feet, might see Rani as quite petite.

Eliza waved me into her office. Her desk faced forward, a plate glass window overlooking the walkway above Wells Street behind her.

"You know Rani well?" I said.

Eliza's monitor blocked our view of one another. She pushed it aside. "She often walks outside in the morning and pops in to see me if she has time."

"Did she today?"

"Not today, no." Eliza waved toward the window. "I thought she might have decided to stay home."

Outside, snow had blown against the railings around the outer walkway, obscuring the bottom half of the metal bars. Heavy falling and blowing snow made it look like a thick, white cloud had descended on the street. Through it I could barely make out the outlines of the Paper Place Lofts, a former paper and printing warehouse across the street that had been converted into condominiums. The new three-story apartment complex and private school to the south weren't visible.

It was as if the world simply ended at the edge of the Paper Place Lofts.

Eliza asked where we'd looked for Rani so far and I told her. Short of walking the entire neighborhood block by block, she had no other suggestions.

I took out my notepad. "When's the last time Rani stopped in to see you?"

Eliza adjusted her glasses, then folded her hands in front of her on the desk. "Yesterday, I believe."

"But you're not sure?"

"Possibly the day before. But definitely this week."

"So yesterday or Monday?"

"Right."

"How often does she stop in?" I said. "And what time?"

"A couple times a week, usually around seven-thirty or eight in the morning. She walks inside or outside a mile nearly every day, but sometimes I have a client so she doesn't come in."

I added walking daily to my mental list of Rani's activities along with school, studying, working on Shanda's newsletter, and community organizations. I could only think she had a machine that manufactured extra hours in her day.

"Are you surprised Rani missed an appointment?"

"Oh, yes. It's not at all like her."

"Shanda told me it is."

"Oh, maybe Rani's different with her sister. Most youngest siblings are way more responsible with other people than with their own families, don't you think?"

"Maybe," I said. "So Rani's the youngest?"

I'm the youngest in my family, but I was pretty sure everyone thought of me as the most responsible. My mom would say it's because I had the least trauma, at least until Marco died. Also because I was more or less raised by Gram, who still works as a bookkeeper though she's in her late seventies. She's adamant about keeping commitments and reaching goals.

My parents, on the other hand, sort of drift through life. My sister Kendra always tells me they were different before our middle sister died. I have to take her word for it. I've never known our parents to be any other way.

"Yes," Eliza said. "There are two or three other sisters between her and Shanda, I think, but Rani's the baby."

I tapped my pen on the notepad. "Do Rani and Shanda get along?"

"Oh, I think for the most part."

The contrast between Shanda's and Eliza's experiences with Rani might be only about the difference between a sister and a friend. But it also fit with Shanda discouraging Carole from asking questions or worrying about Rani, suggesting an idea I didn't want to consider — that Shanda might not want her sister tracked down.

"And when they don't?" I said.

"Well, I'm seeing it from Rani's point of view, of course, as she's the one I visit with. She tells me Shanda's very critical. Such as she complains if Rani isn't twenty minutes early to everything the way she is."

I scribbled that in the margin of my notes about Rani's family. If Shanda tended to get to everything early and Rani was regularly on time or a few minutes late, that could account for Shanda's view of her as unreliable.

"How long has Rani been stopping to talk with you?"

"Since I moved into this office. So about three years."

A frenetic version of Jingle Bells with blaring horns and a throbbing bass filtered in from the hallway. Someone had forgotten to put headphones on. And to choose better music.

"And do you see her otherwise?"

"Almost never. I don't break for lunch, and I leave early—by six or six-thirty at the latest. I've got a long drive home." She nodded toward the brown leather couch along the wall. "I may sleep here tonight, though."

Only attorneys think they're slacking off if they leave the office before seven at night.

"Has Rani been upset about anything lately?"

Assuming Rani hadn't slipped and fallen in some out of the way place, she might be so upset about something that she needed time to herself and had forgotten to tell Carole.

"No offense, but you're asking a lot of questions, and I don't really know you." Eliza took out a smart phone. "I need to check with Carole."

I nodded. "Of course."

Until Carole responded we chatted about the last blizzard, which had been in 2014. I'd had a bad cold and had been working from home, but Eliza had gone to her office. It had taken her two and a half hours to drive home on the expressway.

After getting a confirming text from Carole, Eliza stowed her phone in her top desk drawer. "So there's nothing I can think of that Rani was *upset* about. But she was very interested in this little homeless man who's been hanging about."

"Homeless man?" I grasped both the chair arms.

"He hangs around outside the building. Inside too."

I let my hands drop into my lap, reminding myself that just because a stranger who might be homeless had been in the complex didn't mean he'd harmed Rani. Joe sits on the board of a non-profit that does job training for homeless youth. From attending its benefits I knew that people who live on the street are at least as likely, if not more so, to be the victims of violence as the perpetrators.

"Have you seen him?" I underscored "little" on my notepad. It was the second time Eliza had used the word.

"Not personally, no."

"How would someone who doesn't live here get in?"

Setting aside my personal fears about strangers, if a non-resident could enter easily that undercut the security pretty seriously.

"To the common areas? The back door to the parking lot, the one near the grocery store, is unlocked until ten p.m. For the apartments you need a keycard, but he could follow someone in."

A rumbling sounded in the distance. It might be a Metra train. The Rock Island railroad line ran only two short blocks away. But it sounded more like thunder.

"How long has the man been hanging around?" I said.

Eliza tapped her fingers on her desktop. "A month or so, I think. I feel like that's when Rani first mentioned him."

"What made Rani think he was homeless?" I said. "Did he tell her he was?"

"I'm not certain. But she mentioned the way he was dressed.

Jeans and a trench coat and a lot of layers. You know, scarves, gloves. And a cap with ear flaps."

I gestured to my double scarves and fleeces. "It must be more than layers."

As a former actor, I'm always conscious of how much the way I dress and appear influences people's perceptions. It's made me wary of assuming too much based on how a person looks. It's also helped me in my career.

"Layers today, no, wouldn't be enough. But I think he dressed that way no matter what the weather. And the trench coat was dirty and too short and looked too tight."

"And did he tell her he was homeless?"

I'd learned from years of questioning and cross-examining witnesses to be sure I got my original question answered. It's easy to lose track. Conversations meander.

Eliza rubbed the bridge of her nose with her finger, bumping her glasses. "I don't think so."

"Was she worried about him hurting anyone?" I said.

"She said he was harassing people. Asking for money, standing too close, stepping into their path when they tried to go past him. But she didn't seem worried he'd hurt someone, more that he might get stuck outside with how cold it's been this year. In fact, she'd found a glove in the hall that she thought was his, and she wanted to find him and return it."

"Why did she think it was his?"

"It was very distinctive. Black with yellow stripes around the palm. She showed me."

"She was carrying it with her?" I said.

"In her backpack. In case she ran into him."

It was a nice thing for Rani to do, to try to track down the man to return his glove. I hoped it hadn't put her in danger.

Living in Chicago is a daily balancing act between being kind and staying safe. When people ask me for money on the street, if I have change in my pocket I'll usually hand it to them. But I won't stop and open my wallet. It's like asking for someone to steal it. Likewise, if a car slows and someone leans out to ask directions, I'll do my best to give them, but I don't come within arm's length of the car.

Given what happened to my sister, Gram thinks I'm crazy to talk with strangers at all. But when I'd moved into the city ten years ago I'd promised myself I wouldn't let fear rule how I interacted with people.

I didn't want to live like my mother.

"When did she show you the glove?" I said.

Eliza leaned back, elbows on the chair arms, and glanced at the ceiling. "I want to say a week or two ago."

I flipped pages on the notepad, reviewing notes the way I do after I interview a client or depose a witness. I hoped that experience would help me find Rani, but as I struggled to read my handwriting I couldn't help thinking again that Shanda ought to talk to a real police detective. I supposed that was easy for me to say, though. I didn't need to worry about anyone I loved being deported.

The underscored word *little* jumped out at me.

"He was a small man?" I said.

"Small?" Eliza's eyebrows rose. "No, Rani said he was tall. Maybe a foot taller than her."

So "little" was a verbal tic. Probably one Eliza wasn't aware she used.

"Does Rani have a boyfriend?" I said. Shanda had told me no, but Rani might not tell her older sister everything. I certainly didn't.

"Not lately. Which is such a shame. She's such a cute little girl."

I held back a frown. It annoys me when people assume there's something sad about being single and somehow it's worse if the person is attractive. Before Marco, I hadn't dated anyone for more than a year, and I'd been happier than when I'd been with any of my previous boyfriends.

"Do you know Shanda's assistant, Aidan?"

"Oh, yes. Lovely young man. Helped me out one day when I had to take boxes to storage."

"So you like him?" I said.

"Very much. He has a nice sense of humor. And he always stops to see if I need anything taken to UPS if he's doing a run for Shanda."

Lightning flashed outside the window, and the rumbling sounded again. Definitely thunder. Until 2011, I'd had no idea a thunder and lightning storm could co-exist with snow. But the 2011 blizzard had included thundersnow.

"Do you think he might have harmed Rani?"

"Aidan? I can't imagine it. But I can't imagine anyone harming her, so I suppose that's not very helpful."

"Do you know if Rani visits any other offices along this stretch?" I said.

I was trying to decide if we ought to try to reach tenants in offices that looked occupied but were empty today because of the weather.

Eliza waved her hand. "I doubt it. Right now, they're almost all empty. They had a heckuva time renting space for a long time. Seems like it's starting to change with new management, but we'll see."

Going back to my first notes about Eliza, I spotted a gap.

"So when Rani stopped in yesterday or Monday was that the last time you saw her?"

"Oh, no, I saw her this morning. Didn't I tell you?"

7

———

December 13, 3:58 p.m.

  I bit my lower lip. I'd had this happen with clients, too. You can spend an hour on a topic, but if you don't ask exactly the right question in exactly the right words you miss out on the information you need.

"You saw Rani this morning?" I said.

"Yes. She ran by in a rush maybe five-thirty or six a.m."

"And that's earlier than usual?" I said.

"Oh, yes. I called out hello and she didn't pause."

I checked my notes to see what Carole had said earlier about Rani's email, squinting to read my own printing. Rani had passed Eliza's office either right before or right after sending the email to confirm with Carole.

On the last page of the pad I started sketching out a timeline as we talked.

"Do you always get in that early?" I said.

"More like sevenish. It's the only time to get things done before clients start calling or I have to be in court."

I usually made it to my office by seven-thirty for the same

reason. Other lawyers I knew stayed late. Lately, I'd been doing both.

"But today was different?"

Eliza's bobbed hair swung as she nodded. "I've got a very complex trial starting next week. Judge wouldn't give us an extension until after Christmas, can you believe it? Scrooge. So I've been in very early all week."

"What direction was Rani going?" I said.

"Toward the east elevators. She can take those to Shanda's office. I figured she must have an early appointment or something."

I twisted in my chair. From Eliza's office you could see the suite's front door, but the window was frosted. Eliza couldn't have seen more than a silhouette. "How could you be sure it was her?"

"She has a very distinctive way of walking, this little wiggle, especially when she's in a hurry. I'm guessing it drives the boys crazy."

"And she didn't come back your way?" I said.

"If she did, I didn't see her. But I was absorbed in my case file, I might not have noticed."

That Rani, or someone who walked like her, had headed toward Shanda's office didn't mean much. But it fit with Aidan's guess that Rani might have come in early, not found him, and gone on her way.

"Anyone else you think Carole and I should talk to?"

I heard the door open and shut behind me and turned again. Carole had just walked in.

Eliza rocked her chair back for a moment. "The head of the Tenants Association. Debbie Stillwell. She knew Rani, and I'm sure she'll know about the homeless man. Rani told me people in the building complained about him at the last meeting."

"*Mais oui*, we should talk to Debbie," Carole said. "I should have thought of her myself."

~

December 13, 4:02 p.m.

Eliza told us we were welcome to use her side office, which smelled of dust and old paper, to call Debbie.

I shut the door, moved some boxes so Carole and I could sit side-by-side, and filled her in on what Eliza had said. Carole told me she'd talked to several other office tenants. No one knew Rani or had noticed a woman matching her description in the last day or two.

Carole had never seen or heard about a man who looked like the one Eliza had described asking for money or hanging around inside or outside River City. I called Shanda's office to ask her or Aidan about the man, but got voicemail. Carole dialed Debbie Stillwell's work number and put the phone on speaker.

After introducing me, Carole told Debbie about the missed appointment.

"Oh, no," Debbie said. "You think something happened to Rani?"

Her words came quickly and her voice, which otherwise sounded like an alto, rose into soprano territory at the end of each sentence.

"*J'espère que non,*" Carole said. "But we are looking for her. With the weather so bad."

"It's horrible," Debbie said. "Horrible. I'm leaving my office in a few minutes and I'm so afraid the Red Line won't be running or will stop in the middle."

I stifled a sneeze. The dusty room was getting to me.

"Are you coming to the party tonight?" Carole said.

"If the Red Line trains don't freeze."

"And have you seen Rani today?" Carole said.

"No. Probably last time was in the laundry room Sunday."

"Someone mentioned a homeless—" I said.

"That homeless man? He hangs out near the entrance by the grocery store. But I've got to go, my boss is heading my way. Sorry! I'll talk to you at the Tenants Association party. Hopefully Rani'll be there."

～

December 13, 4:08 p.m.

Niu was locking the front glass door to the grocery store when Carole and I got there.

Other than a few security fluorescents, the lights inside had already been shut off. Niu said she hadn't seen the supposedly homeless man hanging around the complex, but a few tenants had mentioned him. She didn't remember exactly who.

"Rani?" I said.

She paused midway through zipping her puffy coat and waggled her hand back and forth. "Maybe. Maybe not."

She'd heard the man was tall and hefty-looking and approached people in the parking lot at night. She didn't know anything else.

～

December 13, 4:14 p.m.

I decided we should talk to the neighbors without Shanda. If Rani was upset with her sister and had taken off because of it, they might feel freer to speak without Shanda listening in.

The first five people who answered their doors had little idea where Rani might be, but I formed a better picture of her. They described her as upbeat and happy. She played with the neighborhood kids in the park in summer, and she put flyers under everyone's doors about what happened at the Tenants Association meetings, as she knew not everybody checked their email.

One neighbor had heard about but not seen the homeless man, and she'd heard it from Debbie Stillwell. No one had seen Rani in the last couple days, but they all said that wasn't unusual. People came and went at different hours. Everyone said that Rani hadn't seemed troubled about anything.

One young woman who looked about Rani's age, though, glanced at Carole and hesitated before answering that Rani hadn't seemed concerned about anything. When I pressed her, she insisted she had nothing else to say.

I mentally noted her apartment number so I could return alone. If she were holding something back, maybe she'd be more comfortable if Carole weren't there.

Though the opposite issue might be the problem. If she still wouldn't say anything to me, I'd send Carole back alone.

8

————

December 13, 4:34 p.m.

Shanda was hanging up the phone as we walked into her office. I filled her in on the talk with Eliza. She said Rani hadn't mentioned seeing anyone homeless around the building. I asked if I could look through Rani's things at home and in her desk.

"It's been six hours since she was supposed to meet Carole," I said.

"I'm all right with the desk," Shanda said. "All three of us use it at times. But I can't let a stranger go through her personal things. Not when I still think she'll show for tonight's party."

I didn't completely disagree. I wouldn't want someone rifling through my personal possessions because I missed a meeting. But I didn't tell Shanda that workspaces sometimes reveal just as much.

For some of the cases I handle I review emails and texts of employees of businesses. It's amazing how many personal things people use their work email for, including sending detailed health information, describing meetings with their kids' school

46

counselors, and sending their lawyers and friends information about divorce proceedings.

I opened Rani's middle desk drawer.

"When do you expect Aidan back?" I said. "I'd like to ask him a few more questions."

"Soon. I hope. I sent him to UPS. If we want anything out this week it's our last chance. He texted that he got there fine, but they're having connectivity issues, so it's taking longer than usual to fill out the forms."

Shipping probably would become impossible within the next hour or two. Gram had just texted me to say blizzard conditions would worsen throughout the night and most roads and sidewalks would be impassable.

The only personal item I found in Rani's desk was a four-year-old day planner with a cover showing a spray of daisies. The pages emitted a faint citrusy scent, as if Rani had handled it recently with perfume or lotion on her hands.

I keep a paper calendar to back up my online calendar. My legal malpractice insurer requires it in case the electronic version gets deleted. Each year I write notes on the back page to carry over from one year to the next.

Rani's back page had no notes, but she did list four combinations of letters, numbers, and characters that looked like passwords. I didn't know what they matched, but they might come in handy. I snapped a photo of the page and also asked Shanda if I could hold onto the calendar. I hadn't brought the leather shoulder bag I usually use in place of a briefcase, but my parka had four inner and four outer pockets, all wide, all with Velcro seals.

Shanda said that was fine and suggested one of the passwords might be for Rani's Singh Aid and Services email. After experimenting a bit using my phone to access the Internet, I discovered the third password on the list worked on gmail with user name RSinghSAS.

All I found, though, were emails forwarding possible newsletter photos and articles to Shanda. Rani must have a personal email address, too, or she communicated only by text or social media.

I popped my head into Shanda's office to ask about a work laptop. She told me Rani didn't have one, only an iPad she used for school. So far as Shanda knew, Rani's iPhone backed up to the iCloud, but not to any other device.

Unfortunately, I'd already tried. Either the password for iCloud wasn't included in Rani's list, or Rani had a user name not based on her actual name, as I hadn't found anything.

"Do you have a shared file server so you can access her photos or articles?" I said.

I hoped Rani's collection of photographs might include something beyond what she'd posted on social media. That could tell us more about places she went or what she did in her free time.

But Shanda shook her head, clicking her mouse and staring at her monitor as she spoke. "I don't worry about those things. The newsletter, the photographs, that's all Rani. It was her idea to send something out monthly to keep in touch rather than only running the website."

It seemed far too risky to have no way to access that information in the event Rani was out sick or on a trip. I've found, though, that a lot of small business owners don't have the type of backup they ought to, and they often don't have a second person to step in if something happens to them or a key employee.

Carole, who'd been sitting at Aidan's desk on FaceTime with her husband, called out to us to suggest we finish talking over dinner at her apartment.

As Shanda texted Aidan to join us there when he got back, my iPhone buzzed. Lauren was upstairs at the security desk.

9

December 13, 5:05 p.m.

Lauren stood at the security counter, which was otherwise deserted. Ice crusted her rabbit fur hat, fur-lined gloves, and cashmere scarf and glistened throughout her long blond hair.

I hugged her, but quickly let go when ice slid down my neck. "I hope you're not here to drag me to the bar."

Lauren shook the snow off her hat. "Hardly. Since drinks got canceled, I figured this is my perfect chance to get a closer look at what's been done since the conversion back to apartments."

Lauren's a real estate agent who focuses on Printers Row, the larger South Loop, and downtown. When River City had been condos and I'd been shopping, she'd steered me away from it as inexpensive but too risky. Some people had done well in the bulk sale to developers, but many had paid more than they got back, so I counted myself lucky to be out of it. Plus I loved the loft Lauren had found for me, which was in the same building where she lived.

"Makes sense," I said.

She petted the front of her dark blue, nearly floor-length shearling coat. "What do you think?" she said to Carole. "My mom gave it to me last spring for my birthday. She said staying warm in winter is no reason to sacrifice style."

"Stunning," Carole said.

I'd seen and admired the coat when Lauren had gotten it, though I couldn't imagine how any coat, no matter how pretty or warm, could be worth four times my monthly mortgage payment. Unless I were planning to live in the tundra, something not on my To-Do list.

I filled her in on Rani and what we'd learned as we headed for Carole's. Lauren had helped me sort through quite a bit about Marco's death, and I figured her insight as someone who'd never met Rani could be useful.

"Did you check the roof?" Lauren said. "In case she went up there to take photos?"

"It's closed from November on," Carole said.

"Not really," Lauren said. "Almost every time I've gone up in winter I've been able to show it."

I texted Shanda, who'd stayed in the office to finish a few things, to let her know we'd be delayed.

When I hit Fifteen in the elevator, the amber gemstone on my citrine ring caught the light.

Lauren stared at it and frowned. "You were going to wear that tonight?"

"Yes."

I wore the ring all the time. It made me feel closer to Marco. It also was my birthstone, and one of my favorite pieces of jewelry.

Lauren raised her eyebrows. "Ever figure that's why your dates don't work out?"

"I thought it wasn't a date." She'd pitched the evening as friendly holiday drinks.

"Please," she said.

Thankfully, the elevator doors opened.

A set of metal stairs led to the roof. As Lauren predicted, Carole's keycard unlocked the door, but it took all three of us pushing to get it open against the wind. Snow obscured our vision. With our arms linked we inched forward.

Guardrails kept us in the center of the rooftop. Blocked-off sections on either side served as gardens in the summer and held a foot of snow now. I held on tight to Carole and Lauren. The building must have been designed so that no one could actually be blown off the roof, but I didn't love testing that.

We made our way to the south end of the area open to tenants and back.

It took all three of us to shut the door again once we got inside. We left a trail of ice and slush along the floor on our return walk to the elevator. I felt satisfied that Rani wasn't out there, at least not now.

I tried not to think about all the places she could have fallen if she had been.

~

December 13, 5:25 p.m.

I suspect most men I know, including Carole's husband, who'd gotten Carole to start tuning in, watch ABC meteorologist Cheryl Scott's forecasts as much because she's pretty as for accuracy. I like her because she always seems upbeat without being annoyingly cheerful. Also, I like to see women draw enough of an audience for the networks to pay them the types of salaries usually only men command.

Tonight, though, Cheryl looked worried. Staring straight into the camera, and with none of her usual gestures toward the map behind her, she warned against driving or walking outside.

Conditions would continue to worsen, she said, through late tomorrow and possibly the following morning. Lakeshore Drive had been closed for hours, the city not wanting a repeat of the 2011 blizzard when hundreds of cars were trapped on the winding road along the lakefront.

Carole had drawn the blinds to try to keep more of the chill out. After helping Lauren set out small plates and wine glasses on the polished dining table, I parted the blinds and peered out. I saw swirling white over bright spots that must have been lights inside the buildings across the river. It was like an impressionist painting except in black and white.

Its beauty felt almost peaceful despite the faint sound of sirens from somewhere in the city. I pressed my forehead against the frigid glass, imagining myself floating out into the silence among the snowflakes pirouetting in the night.

Carole's warm hand on my shoulder drew me from the view. *"Aidez-moi, s'il te plait."*

Shanda walked in as I was helping Carole assemble a tray of cheeses, crackers, grapes, and mixed nuts. The odor of rich French onion soup filled the kitchen and made the apartment feel cozy despite the howling wind.

The four of us gathered at one end of the table, avoiding the seats near the glass sliding doors to the balcony. The air for about a foot in front of them felt ten degrees colder than the rest of the room.

Shanda reported that her packages had gone out at last. She'd invited Aidan to join us for dinner, but he'd said he had work to do on his own blog, where he wrote about financial issues for teenagers.

"You'll have plenty of chances to talk to him after the party," Shanda said. "He's staying in the office tonight. He lives in Berwyn, and the Eisenhower and Stevenson have both been shut down, and so has the Burlington Northern."

Berwyn is a near west suburb along the same train line as LaGrange, which is where I grew up. The two expressways and the railroad line Shanda had mentioned were the best ways to get to those suburbs. A lot of people were going to be stuck in the city tonight.

"What's Rani do in a typical day?" I said to Shanda as Carole set a warm loaf of brioche in front of us. "After her morning walk and coffee?"

Shanda sliced a triangular section of brie and spread it on a chunk of bread. "If she has no class, she might come to the office to study or go to the library at school. Or see friends, maybe. I don't know everything she does. We both have busy schedules."

I helped myself to a handful of grapes. "How often do the two of you spend time together? Not working on something but to catch up? Talk, relax?"

Shanda laughed. "Relax? My recruiting business took off, happily, soon after I started it, which is why I can pay Rani's tuition. But it means I work a lot."

Lauren sipped her wine, a medium-bodied Bordeaux Carole had taken from the wine rack on her marble kitchen island. "She doesn't get financial aid?"

Shanda unwound her hair from its bun and let it fall around her shoulders. "There are almost no scholarships or aid packages for international students. What little there is goes to graduate students. Some schools waive application fees, but that's about it. It's hard for people like Rani, but it makes sense. Plenty of U.S. citizens are seeking places at colleges. There's no reason the government would fund students from elsewhere."

"Are you hoping Rani will join your business someday?" Lauren asked.

It was a good question and something that ought to have occurred to me. I represented enough people with family businesses, either handling their tax issues or when they sued one another.

But it was so outside my personal experience that I hadn't thought to ask. The only person in my close or extended family with a business was my brother-in-law, and he mainly had a series of schemes that drove him deeper into debt each time. My dad was self-employed repairing guitars and other stringed instruments, but he wasn't in a position to hire family or anyone else. Part of the reason Gram hadn't been able to help Kendra or me pay for college was that she'd already been providing a lot of support for my parents.

Lauren's dad, though, owned several auto parts stores and commercial and residential properties all over the country. Lauren's first commission, a month after she'd gotten her license, had been for selling her parents' large Barrington home when they'd downsized to a Lincoln Park condominium.

"I used to hope so," Shanda said. "I thought she'd work in the computer field for a few years and then if, like me, she preferred to be more people-focused she'd think about becoming a recruiter. There's so much I can teach her. But she seems less and less interested each year, and she spends more time taking pictures." Shanda spread her hands wide. "Pictures."

Carole moved into the open kitchen area to stir the soup. "She's quite talented."

"But unfocused." Shanda frowned. "No pun intended. She tried to convince my parents after her first year of college that she ought to switch to Columbia College and major in photography. Photography. People can take photos for free. Quille, you must understand. Didn't Carole tell me you used to be an actor or singer or something like that? It's no way to make a living."

"I still sing," I said. "I don't act anymore. It's not the main reason I quit, but you're not wrong. In any type of art it can be a challenge to earn enough to survive."

I didn't love Shanda's dismissive tone about creative pursuits, but I understood why she wanted something more sure for Rani.

Joe, whom I'd met in theater, had gone back to school for an MBA in finance. We both knew talented actors, directors, and designers in their forties and fifties who worked regularly in theater and still needed day jobs to supplement their income. Some of them had nothing set aside for retirement and no health insurance.

"But someone has to take photos for your newsletter, *non*?"

Carole said as she ladled the French onion soup into bowls. "And you work late so often already. You have no time."

Shanda waved her hand. "I don't really need them."

"But they make your materials eye-catching and lovely," Carole said. "It is part of why I read every month."

I helped Carole carry the soup bowls to the table, inhaling the rich scent.

"There are stock photos I could buy or get free," Shanda said. "It's what a lot of bloggers do."

"So Rani didn't transfer to Columbia?" I returned to my seat next to Lauren.

"No. She wants to stay here, and if she can't get a job there's no way she can even if she gets her student visa straightened out. Though I suppose you'd know better than me about that."

"I don't," I said.

People think lawyers know everything there is to know about the law. In reality, most of us know a lot about a few areas, and enough about a lot of other areas to refer people to someone else.

I don't know how to fix a parking ticket, whether you can force your neighbor to trim the tree hanging over your lot line, or how to get Medicare to pay for medical transportation for your aging grandparent. But if you need help figuring out your taxes or fighting the IRS, or you're a small business owner who just got sued, I'll be there.

Lauren finished her wine. "Couldn't you sponsor her to stay?"

"No," Shanda said. "I'm not a citizen, only a permanent resident with the green card."

"And *c'est difficile* even for citizens," Carole said. "Frery has dual citizenship. It's the only reason we were able to come here and open our business. If we had to rely on his sister who lives here, we would have been refused."

I spooned soup into my mouth. As with all Carole's creations, it was rich and perfectly spiced. "So isn't it odd Rani let her visa lapse?"

Shanda took a long drink of wine. "Sometimes she drops the ball. In a major way. Her first year here she got a credit card. One of those banks that markets to students directly. She ran up a giant bill on everything and nothing. My parents paid it, but they refused to continue paying her room and board, though they'd been covering that and I'd been paying her tuition. That's when I let her move in with me."

"Where'd she live before that?" I said.

"A studio apartment in University Village. With two other girls."

I spread soft goat cheese over crackers and added black olive tampanade on top of it. Carole had introduced me to the combination at the café and I loved it. "Have you contacted those girls?"

"Between my conference calls I texted some of Rani's friends, including them. Just in case." Shanda wiped her lips with her napkin. "No one has seen or heard from her today. Or this week."

10

December 13, 6:00 p.m.

The Tenants Association holiday party was being held in the clubhouse, the cylindrical building in the southwest part of the park. We didn't need to go outside to get there, though. Carole led us on a circuitous route that took us to the Lobby Level, up one level on the frozen escalators, and to a separate set of elevators which opened directly into the clubhouse.

Shanda was surprised. She'd never gone to the clubhouse any way other than by walking outside through the park.

The Party Room itself stood beyond the restrooms and opposite a sink with cabinets above it that were missing two of their handles.

Lauren, Shanda, and Carole headed right in. I hung back and scanned the crowd for Rani two or three times, though I could tell at first glance she wasn't there.

The room was half full. White and blue lights sparkled along the edges of folding tables that held plates of cookies, red and green napkins, and wine, beer, and soda in clear plastic cups. Tinsel draped the tall cocktail tables scattered around the room. A two-foot Christmas tree with tiny gold ornaments sat on a table right inside the doors, an electric menorah with flames illuminated next to it. Christmas songs with too many instruments vying for attention beneath manic-sounding singers blared from the back of the room.

A woman with long dark hair wearing a heavy wool coat brushed past me. A long purple scarf hung around her neck, and matching purple mittens had been stuffed into her pockets. Her eyebrows curved in well-kept lines over her dark eyes.

She hugged Shanda and then Carole. "So good to see you. Have you heard from Rani? I took the long way around the building, too, hoping I might run into her. No luck."

Carole turned to me, gesturing that I should join them. "Debbie Stillwell, this is Quille Davis. You met her on the phone today. And this is her friend Lauren Hughes. They're stuck here with us tonight."

"This weather is insane." Debbie shrugged off her coat. Underneath she wore a red turtleneck sweater and dark pants. "I'm so glad I made it here. The Red Line stopped twice, and I got trapped in a car with this guy who reeked of whiskey and insisted on singing Jingle Bells repeatedly at the top of his lungs. Public transportation."

"Seriously," Lauren said. "On the bus this dufus wearing a backwards baseball cap and covered with snow and ice stamped on the toes of my boots. I told him if he did it again he'd owe me fifteen hundred dollars, but he didn't know Christian Louboutin from Crocs."

Debbie looked down at Lauren's designer navy blue leather boots. "Oh my God. Those are fantastic. But why would you wear them in a blizzard?"

Lauren glanced at me. "We were supposed to be going out."

"No one would have made it tonight," I said. I turned to Debbie. "You're the head of the Tenants Association?"

"I am. And condo board president before that. I thought I was going to get stoned at every meeting when we were debating the sale of the building."

"What was the issue?" I said. I had a pretty good idea, but I like to hear people's own words and thoughts.

"A militant group of resident owners opposed it. Mostly people who'd bought high and were afraid they'd get a bad deal, but some who just wanted to stay," Debbie said. "Prices have gone up so much. A lot of them couldn't afford to live here anymore after the sale."

I took a plastic cup of Coca Cola from the table, not wanting to drink any alcohol beyond the glass of wine I'd had at dinner. I was already feeling blue with the holiday season. I didn't need anything that might make me feel lower.

"Did Rani have a view about it?" I asked Shanda.

It didn't seem like the type of conflict that would cause Rani to become so upset she'd want to disappear for a while, but you never know what will set someone off. In my first year of solo practice I'd had a case where my client paid me fifty thousand dollars in legal fees over an eight thousand dollar dispute. His sister, who had sued him, must have spent double that, as she'd had a big firm lawyer.

"She didn't care so long as she still had somewhere to live." As she spoke, Shanda looked past me, her eyes trained on the doors.

Debbie shook her head, setting her long hair swirling around her. "Not true. She desperately wanted the deal to fall through. She said River City was one of the few places people with limited income could afford to buy in this area. She figured buyers would rehab and jack up the rent to match all the new luxury high rises."

Rani probably wasn't wrong.

It was what was happening in the neighborhood overall. At the moment the part of Printers Row where I lived was still one of the more affordable neighborhoods within walking distance of downtown. If you didn't mind a hundred-year-old building that stood within half a mile of the federal lock up, you could get a two bedroom for less than a one bedroom cost in River North or farther south in the South Loop. But the taller, newer buildings, which also stood farther from the prison, charged double the rent for less space, and they were crowding out the aging converted warehouses and lofts.

Shanda shifted her gaze to Debbie and frowned. "I didn't realize you knew Rani that well."

"We had some good talks in the laundry room when everyone was buzzing about it," Debbie said.

"You mentioned people against the sale. Who was for it?" I said.

"Ty Hudson for one. He owned three units, and he bought all of them at bargain basement prices so he stood to profit a ton," Debbie said.

She gestured toward a tall black man talking with a few other residents near the holiday cookie table. He wore a charcoal suit and light gray shirt unbuttoned at the collar. His mustache was thin and neatly trimmed, and he was otherwise clean-shaven. Gram would have admired his posture. He stood with his shoulders back, chin lifted, arms relaxed at his sides.

Carole had mentioned him as having clashed with Rani at Save The Parks. Apparently he'd had good reason.

"What did you think about the sale?" I asked Debbie.

"I bought my unit cheap, so it worked out fabulously. Now I'm hunting for something in River North."

"What about this homeless man?" Shanda said. She had a death grip on her briefcase, and though she was talking to Debbie, her eyes kept flicking toward the entrance behind me. "Did Rani tell you about him?"

"I've seen him," Debbie said. "Twice in the parking lot. The last time was a few days ago. I called out to him, but he took off."

"Management better do something about that." The voice was low, somewhere between a baritone and bass.

I turned and saw a man taking off an ice-crusted knit cap. Underneath, he had salt-and-pepper hair. His forehead had lines in it, though not heavy ones, and I guessed him late forties or early fifties.

Snow covered his boots and jeans up to his knees.

Carole gestured toward me and then him. "Quille, Patryk Kaja. He used to live here, but after the sale he and his wife moved across the street to Wells Place."

Patryk's handshake was firm and not too tight, which I appreciated. I'd had an opposing counsel who seemed to want to crush my fingers when he shook hands to show how tough he was. I'd taken to wearing a cubic zirconia ring with sharp edges on my right hand when I knew I'd see him. That way it dug into his fingers if he squeezed too hard.

Before I could ask why someone who didn't live in the building would come out on a night like this for a party, Debbie said, "You've run into him too?"

Patryk shrugged off his leather jacket. Under it, he wore a long sleeved olive-colored shirt with a brown sport coat. No tie, but he looked far more dressed up than anyone else here other than Ty Hudson. Most of the tenants wore some variation of jeans and sweaters or sweatshirts.

No one other than Patryk and Debbie wore coats. They must have all gotten to the clubhouse through the same out-of-the-way method that Carole had shown us. We'd left our winter gear in her apartment.

"Not personally," Patryk said, "but Janelle has. In the parking lot. It makes me nervous every time she comes here alone."

He brushed the snow off his jeans.

"Janelle's his wife," Carole said.

"And business partner," he said. "Janelle Byerly."

"Oh," I said. I'd seen the name on the door to the offices next to the neighborhood drycleaner. "Byerly-Kaja Investment Advisors. You're right down the street from my office."

"On Dearborn? What do you do?"

"Lawyer," I said. "And singer."

I added the second part because in downtown Chicago you can spit and hit a hundred lawyers. So unless you do murder trials, like my friend Danielle does, no one really wants to hear about it. Most people are a lot more interested in the musical part of my life.

"Sounds like more fun than law," he said. "And less stressful. You know the joke about the lawyer who complains to St. Peter that he died too young?"

"And St. Peter says 'according to your billing records, you're two hundred years old,'" I said.

I've heard every lawyer joke in the book, mostly from my family members. Everyone makes fun of lawyers. Until they need one.

"I'm surprised you came over on a night like this," Debbie said.

"For a minute there with all the snow blowing around I couldn't see anything but white. But I like to stay in touch. It's good networking," Patryk said.

I asked if he knew Rani, and he said he did, but he hadn't seen her for a few weeks.

I asked where his wife had seen the homeless man, and Patryk said near the back entrance by the grocery store. He had little to add to what I'd already heard.

Shanda glanced at the time on her phone. "I can't believe Rani didn't show. I think it's time you go through her things."

11

———

December 13, 6:32 p.m.

The walls of Shanda's pie-shaped apartment angled outward. In the living room area a couch ran along the windows, and a narrow daybed against a side wall, a stand with a flat screen TV across from it. A counter separated the kitchen and living room areas.

Shanda set her purse, a small Coach clutch, on her kitchen counter.

I took out my phone. We'd agreed that first I'd call my office mate, Danielle, and ask her about the visa issue. She's a criminal defense attorney, former prosecutor, and former cop, and some of her clients have immigration issues. Her insights into police procedure had been invaluable when I'd been trying to figure out what had happened to Marco. She could provide information. And, I hoped, a second voice to encourage Shanda to talk to the police.

On speaker, I explained the situation and asked if the police would check Rani's immigration status if we reported her missing.

"Probably," Danielle said. "Didn't used to be that way, but

from what I'm seeing now almost any interaction with the police prompts deportation proceedings."

"I don't understand why you want to involve the police at all," Shanda said to me. "Carole told me they were next to no help to you after your boyfriend's death."

I was surprised Carole had said that. She so rarely criticized anyone. "I wouldn't say no help. I might be dead if the detective I contacted hadn't listened to me."

"But you were the one who found out the truth."

"With my friends' help, and it took time," I said. "If there's a chance Rani's in danger, better a whole police force trained in solving crimes looking for her than one actress-turned-lawyer who's good at asking questions."

Shanda's lips tightened. "But if she's safe and just can't reach us, we risk her being out of the country forever."

"Is that right, Danielle?" I said. "Because who would ever report a crime in that situation? There must be some exception."

"There is," Danielle said. "Officially. Crime victims can apply to return to the U.S. But you've got to prove you're a victim, so if your friend is stuck on a bus with a dead cell phone and you send the police after her, the exception won't apply. And last I heard that docket was so backed up it could be five or ten years before she could get back into the country even if she was a crime victim."

Shanda face crumpled. "Five or ten years?"

"I'm sorry," Danielle said. "It's not news anyone wants to hear."

"But with her missing this long — " I said.

"Most missing people turn up, Quille. Your family's experience — it's not typical. Anyway, unfortunately, it might be a moot point. Hold on." Keys clicked in the background. "Yep. You'd need to go to the police district in person to make a report. You're in the First District on State and 18th. All the roads between you and there are closed. I barely got back to the office from Bridgeview."

"They won't help over the phone?" I said.

"It's the policy. You have to go in person to report a missing person. You can try calling. Though, in my experience, someone who's been missing for less than a full day probably won't be a priority."

"Even in this weather?" I said.

"It's a worry, for sure. But she's young and healthy and it's more likely she forgot her appointment this morning and got stuck somewhere. Like at a friend's house. Keep in mind, all those people marooned on the CTA bus that one year eventually got home no worse for the experience."

After Danielle and I hung up, with Shanda's permission I called the general police number to ask how to report a missing person. I didn't mention Rani. It took a while to get through to the right person, and then we learned only what Danielle had already told us. I also got the impression weather-related emergencies had the police force stretched to its limit already.

So I was it.

I asked to see where Rani kept her clothes.

A mirrored wall hiding a coat closet separated the galley kitchen from the entryway. On the opposite side of the door to the hall stood the bathroom. It was laid out in a way I'd only seen in hotels. The tub/shower and toilet were in a small room with a door, but the sink was in an open area between the bathroom and bedroom, with a closet opposite it. That was where Rani kept her clothes and things.

Shanda's were in an armoire in the bedroom, which was where she slept.

Rani's hanging clothes had been sorted by length and color, and the built-in drawers held neatly folded and stacked T-shirts and jeans. None of it seemed to fit with Rani being absentminded and disorganized about her schedule.

The closet otherwise gave few clues to Rani's personal life. As Shanda had said, her phone and iPad were nowhere to be found.

Her blue nylon backpack was missing as well, as was Rani's wool winter coat, her heaviest black fleece, a pair of gloves, a hat, and a scarf. Two extra hats and a pair of mittens lay in a bottom drawer, plus a gray scarf that had a bit of blue plastic tarp stuck to it, no surprise given the construction throughout the neighborhood. These days it was hard not to get construction dust in your eyes, gravel in your boots, and debris in your hair in this part of Chicago.

I looked through the laundry basket, which was half full of clothes to be washed next time around, the coat closet, and all the drawers again.

"Anything else that could be missing?" I said.

Shanda shook her head. "I can't say I know every piece of clothing she owns. But this is pretty much how full her closet is day-to-day."

All Rani's possessions seemed to be stored in the closet. She hadn't left anything lying on the kitchen counter, coffee table, or couch. I marveled that two people could live in such a small area and keep it so clean.

My own condo was a one bedroom with a sleeping loft above it and far more floor space. I'm fairly organized and clean, but when Marco had been on the verge of moving in I'd been concerned I wouldn't be able to keep it neat enough for him. He'd kept his own space in very precise order.

"Rani's very considerate that way," Shanda said when I mentioned it. "She feels I did her a favor letting her live here, so she tries to be as unobtrusive as possible."

That added to my unease. If Rani was considerate about her belongings and Shanda's space, I doubted she'd purposely leave Shanda in the dark as to her whereabouts.

My phone buzzed. Danielle had confirmed with a friend who did immigration law that her recollection of the victim reporting exception was correct. She sent me the friend's home and cell phone numbers in case we had other immigration questions, adding that it was okay to call her late, as she was a night owl.

We were about to leave when Aidan knocked on the door. He'd finished his personal work and suggested he and Shanda call all the clients on Shanda's newsletter list in case Rani had gotten close to any of them personally and might be with one of them.

It seemed like a long shot, but I didn't see any point to all three of us going to the Save The Parks meeting.

I left them to it.

~

December 13, 7:04 p.m.

Thirteen people, most of whom looked familiar to me from the Tenants Association party, gathered toward the far end of the room for the Save The Parks meeting. Most of the holiday decorations had been put away, and the space looked more like a bland conference room.

Debbie Stillwell stood in front, reading from notes on her tablet.

I supposed it made sense that she was running this meeting. It reminded me of the different bar associations I belong to. You run into the same attorneys and judges at most of them because those are the people who make time for professional associations or who find them useful in their businesses.

The sparkling lights remained around a couple tables in back. A percolator with hot water, pots of coffee, and sturdy white mugs, plus a pitcher of ice water, had replaced the holiday food. I filled a mug with water and drank it down. It was looking like it might be a long night, and staying hydrated mattered if I didn't want one of the migraines that often plagued me to kick in.

In low voices, Lauren and Carole told me no one at the party other than Debbie had personally seen the homeless man. But they guessed fewer than fifty people had attended, and the number of tenants in the building totaled well over five hundred.

I told them about my call with Danielle and about what Shanda and Aidan were doing.

"I can do nothing else here," Carole said. "I already told Lauren who everyone is."

She decided she'd knock on the doors of neighbors who hadn't been home when we'd tried earlier.

After Carole left, Lauren pointed to Ty Hudson. Because he and Rani had clashed, I'd asked Lauren to see what she could find out about him. Now he stood near the last row of folding chairs, a plastic cup of wine in one hand.

"He was working the room," Lauren said. "So was I, and I made sure we crossed paths. You should totally talk to him."

"Did he confirm he and Rani argued over the sale?"

"No. That is, yes." She took my arm and spoke into my ear. "He's good-looking, no ring, employed, and based on when he graduated college, which I looked up, in your ideal age range."

"And what did he say about Rani?" I said.

"They argued, but the same way you do in court. Not personal. My guess after chatting with everyone? Rani's got a boyfriend she's not telling her sister about and they're at his place enjoying being snowed in."

"Why think that?" I said.

She rolled her eyes. "Please. You seriously think she was at the library that other time with her phone out of batteries? Everyone says Shanda's super controlling. Rani's just trying to get some space of her own."

I refilled my mug. "Maybe if she'd been gone an hour or two. But she has to know Shanda's really worried now."

"My point exactly," Lauren said.

A man seated in the front row droned on about his role in pushing the developers to create the park behind the movie theater at Roosevelt Collection. A sort of apathy seemed to have settled on the group. The building shuddered with the wind, but the party room itself was warm, and it smelled like freshly baked cookies. All the residents presumably would be walking inside the building to get to their apartments, not out in the snow, so they had no reason to put off going home. Yet none showed any sign of hurrying the man on, answering him, or cutting him off so they could leave.

An eerie series of notes that sounded like the beginning of an old sci-fi television show echoed throughout the open space.

Debbie, who'd been leaning on her elbows on the podium, her eyes glazed over, reached into her purse.

"Sorry, sorry. The normal rings are so boring. I'll turn it off."

The man resumed his droning.

"This guy's going to go on all night," I whispered to Lauren. "I think I'll go talk to Rani's neighbor, the one who seemed like she might have more to say."

A rapid-fire series of pings came from the front. Debbie glanced at her phone. "Oh, no."

The man paused, blinking as if he'd immediately become so immersed in his speech again that he didn't know who had spoken. "What?"

"It's Janelle," Debbie said. "Patryk never made it home."

12

December 13, 7:15 p.m.

Debbie split people willing to help into groups to trace Patryk's route out of River City.

Over the phone Janelle had told her Patryk usually stopped at the ATM in the grocery store after Tenants Association meetings, then left by the south exit, cut through the parking lot, and crossed the street to their apartment complex. Ty Hudson volunteered to go with Debbie, taking two elevators down to the Marina Level.

Lauren and I agreed to walk down the five flights of stairs with the thought that Patryk might have chosen them. We didn't find him, which was a relief. I'd worried he'd slipped and broken a limb or had a heart attack in the stairwell.

But when Lauren and I rounded the curve on the Marina Level and came within sight of the grocery store, I saw Ty squatting near the opposite wall. Beyond him lay a man with salt-and-pepper hair clad in jeans and a leather jacket.

Lauren grasped my hand as we walked closer. Patryk lay face up. A purplish bruise had swelled under his left eye. His brown leather gloves were on, and his coat was unzipped and his olive shirt unbuttoned to show a chest with black and gray hair. His knit hat lay a few feet from him as if it had flown from his grip when he'd hit the floor.

Ty's right hand rested on Patryk's chest. He looked up as we approached. "I started CPR, but he already felt cool."

Debbie stood near the glass door to the grocery store, clutching her phone. Her face looked pale, almost as white as Marco's had been when I'd found him dead in his living room. "He had no pulse when we found him," she said.

"911?" Lauren said.

"I was just going to try again. Can you believe I couldn't get through?" Debbie dialed with shaking hands.

I leaned sideways against the wall. It felt cool against my cheek. Debbie's voice rose and fell but I didn't hear her words. White noise like crashing ocean waves filled my ears. I smelled plaster dust, probably from work in one of the empty offices.

"Hey." It was Lauren's voice in my ear. Her hand, warm, held my upper arm, which otherwise felt like ice. "Quille? Let's have you sit."

I let her guide me to the floor. The tile chilled my legs through my jeans.

I put my forehead on my knees. The rushing in my ears grew faint.

"What?" Debbie said. "That can't be right."

I lifted my head, propping my elbows on my knees and my chin on my hands. I needed to pull it together. Patryk's death was not only tragic and frightening on its own, if it somehow related to Rani's disappearance I had to stay clear about what was happening.

Ty had moved to stand next to Debbie.

"What are we supposed to do?" she said into the phone.

Breathing slowly and deliberately, I studied the area as

Debbie listened to the 911 dispatcher. Trails of slush ran between Patryk and the glass double doors that led to a vestibule and to the outer doors fronting the parking lot. I saw no weapons anywhere. Patryk's body was angled in a way that made it possible he'd slipped and hit the back of his head on the wall, then fallen and bruised his cheek, assuming Ty moved him before performing CPR.

Debbie's arm dropped to her side. "Unbelievable. They may not be here for hours. The only advice is to not touch anything, to block the area off if we can, and to take photos."

"Hours?" Ty rubbed his hand over his face. "How many?"

"Four or five. It's ridiculous. The police station is so close," Debbie said.

I got to my feet, keeping one hand on the wall in case the dizziness returned. "I talked to a friend earlier who said all the roads that way are closed."

Ty's fingers flew over his phone. "True. Downed power lines to the south and east of us. Plus a lot of first responders out on Lakeshore Drive. Somehow part of it didn't get closed in time. The city didn't learn much from 2011."

That year hundreds of vehicles had been stranded, including a CTA bus, during a blizzard. Passengers had waited six hours on it before abandoning it. With that history, I would have thought the city would have closed Lake Shore Drive today when the first snowflake fell.

"Let's take some photos," I said. From years of vocal and acting training I was able to keep my voice steady, but it took all my effort.

Edging along the wall opposite Patryk, Lauren and I took photos. As we neared the double doors to the vestibule I saw something laying near the gray outer door to the parking lot. Not wanting to disturb any possible evidence, I stayed where I was and zoomed my phone's camera.

It was a glove. Black with yellow stripes across the palm.

Lauren looked at me, a question in her eyes. I knew we were thinking the same thing. This glove might be the one Rani had been carrying around to return to the homeless man. Or it might be that glove's mate.

13

———————

December 13, 7:29 p.m.

"The building office must have some tape," I said, "to block off the area."

The others had noticed the glove, but not knowing its possible significance hadn't connected it to Rani.

"But it'll be locked, won't it?" Lauren said.

"I've got keys," Debbie said. "From when I was board president. For emergencies."

"Why don't you and Lauren go check the office," I said, thinking it would give me a good chance to talk to Ty alone. "Get paper and markers, too, to make signs, or print them out if you can get on the computer."

Lauren studied my face. "You're okay?"

I nodded.

As she and Debbie headed for the escalators, I shifted to look at Ty and keep Patryk's body out of my sightline. Ty confirmed that he'd found Patryk on his left side and turned him onto his back for CPR.

I pointed at the double doors. "Those are unlocked until ten?"

"Right. Inner and outer sets," Ty said. "A lot of people complain about that, but the grocery store wants easy access."

"Did Patryk park in the lot?" I said. "Do you know?"

My knees shook. I resisted locking them, which can lead to passing out, as I'd learned in my first dress rehearsal for a musical at the age of ten. I concentrated on Ty's face. As Lauren had said, he was attractive, with nice cheekbones and expressive eyes, but I was more interested in his demeanor. He'd volunteered to take the fastest route to the grocery store. That didn't mean he was guilty of anything, but it was something to keep in mind.

"I'm sure he walked over," Ty said. "He and Janelle have been renting across the street since the sale. All he needs to do from here is take a left, pass the covered parking, cross the street and be at his building."

"So it's closer than going out the main entrance upstairs," I said.

"Yeah, if he stops at the ATM."

I'd never make a habit of getting cash before walking alone into any parking lot at night. The possibility of getting attacked is always a factor when I choose which block to walk, whether to take a shortcut through a plaza at night, and where to stop for cash. But men probably don't think about the risks as much as women do. Especially a man like Patryk who'd been tall and in good shape.

"Does he come back to River City a lot?" I said.

"For the Tenants Association meetings." Ty nodded to a cushioned bench down the hall outside an MRI Center. "Mind if we sit? I'm not feeling too steady at the moment."

The center had a grand opening sign with a balloon bouquet next to it. The balloons sagged, their strings drooping toward the floor.

We sat side by side. Ty clasped his hands, which were shaking, together. "Patryk gives — gave — talks at the Immigration

Rights Center, too. A lot of his clientele are immigrants new to the city."

I remembered the public aid agency with the United States flag in the window. Ty confirmed that was it.

"Have you run into a man asking for money?" I said. "One who might be homeless?"

Ty's eyes widened. "No. You think he might have done this?"

"Patryk said the man hassled Janelle. And other people saw him in the parking lot." I retracted my hands into the sleeves of my blazer. We were far enough from the doors that I didn't feel drafts from outside, but my whole body felt chilled.

"You think Patryk might have confronted him?"

"Maybe. Though Patryk might have slipped on the slush and fallen."

The glove suggested otherwise, but as an attorney I'd learned to keep an open mind and look at all angles. You can't refute the other side's case if you don't truly understand it, and you can miss a lot about your own facts if you form a theory too soon. I guessed examining all the possibilities would be important for a detective, too, so I didn't want to jump to conclusions.

I also knew both Joe and Danielle would warn me against reflexively blaming the homeless man.

Joe because he hated stereotypes about the homeless. Danielle because her years of experience as a police officer and criminal attorney bear out the statistics that while men are more likely to be victims of stranger violence than women, the most likely person to kill anybody at all is a romantic partner or family member. That hadn't been what had happened to my sister, but in my head, if not my gut, I understood that my family's experience had been unusual.

"Have you seen Rani Singh today?" I said.

Ty tilted his head. "Rani? No, not today. I told your friend Lauren that."

"But you know her?"

"Sure." His voice came out evenly, no vibrato or change in pitch.

I kept my eyes fixed on Ty's, which helped keep me from staring at Patryk's body on the floor twenty yards away. When I'd found Marco dead in his living room, I'd sat with him until the police came. All the emptiness and loss I'd felt then flooded back when I looked at Patryk, along with sadness for his wife. Though I'd never met her, I knew she'd now lie awake wondering about his last moments and whether anything she could have done might have changed what happened.

"And you've seen her recently?" I said, forcing my thoughts back to Rani.

"Last night. In the laundry room. She still hasn't turned up?"

That made him the next to last person to have seen Rani if Eliza had been correct about who'd hurried past her office door this morning.

"She hasn't. Did she seem upset about anything when you saw her?" I said.

"I was taking clothes out of one dryer and she was putting them in another. I was on a conference call at the same time. She seemed fine, but it's not like we talked."

Years of theater training make me pretty good at reading people's expressions, which also helps me as a lawyer. But I can't tell for sure if someone's lying. Mostly because a good liar is good at not acting like one.

I started to ask Ty how long he'd known Rani, but Debbie and Lauren returned with printed Do No Enter signs, tape, and green sticky notes. Debbie and Ty volunteered to brave the outside, hugging the wall opposite Patryk and exiting through the heavy gray side dock door in the vestibule so they could tape Do Not Enter signs on the outside of it and the two glass exit doors. They locked all the doors when they came back in. I didn't like the idea of people needing to go around to the front entrance in the storm, but it seemed wiser to block this entrance after what had happened.

Lauren and I strung masking tape from one side of the hall to the other, fastening neon green Post Its onto the tape to make it more visible.

"With the ATM in the grocer, there must be a security camera," I said. "It might have a view of the hall through the door."

"The cameras have been on the fritz," Debbie said. "Some glitch in the system."

I put my phone in my inside blazer pocket. "All the cameras?"

"All the ones on this level," Debbie said. "I was on my way out and heard an IT guy arguing with one of the security guards about it. It's been out for days."

I'd met people like Debbie in theater and in the firms where I'd worked before starting my own practice. They knew all the gossip and got involved in every drama. Or created drama if none existed. But it was starting to bother me how much Debbie knew or claimed to know about everything and everyone, especially in such a large complex.

"Someone needs to tell Janelle," Ty said.

14

December 13, 7:48 p.m.

"We can't just call," Debbie said as we headed for the elevators. "We've got to go there. So she's not alone."

Without discussing it we'd passed the escalators, skipping the climb to the Lobby Level. Maybe the others, like me, felt worn out now that some of the adrenalin and fear of finding Patryk had dissipated. Our footsteps echoed through the deserted halls.

"In this blizzard?" Lauren said.

"It's only across the street," I said.

"I'll go," Debbie said.

"In seventy-mile-per-hour winds and white-out conditions?" Lauren said. "You could get blown smack into a building. Or be run over by an SUV because the driver doesn't see you."

We'd reached the elevators. I pressed the Up button.

"I'll go with," Ty said. "We can hang onto each other to keep from getting blown around. And I doubt anyone else is driving around here if police can't get through."

"Do you both know Janelle well?" I said, wondering again about the combination of Ty and Debbie. Together they'd found Patryk, and now they were offering to go see Janelle together. I'm not much of one for conspiracy theories, but there could be something happening that wasn't obvious to outsiders.

Or I just needed to think about something, anything, other than seeing Patryk's dead body.

"I met her and Patryk at a networking event when I first moved here from Milwaukee," Ty said. "They're as good of people as you'll find anywhere."

"What if that homeless man killed Patryk?" Lauren said. "He could still be out there, and you could run into him."

Debbie jabbed the elevator button as if it would make it come faster. "Oh my God, you're right. We need to tell everyone. They need to know there's a homicidal homeless man out there. Or in here."

"It could have been an accident," Ty said.

Debbie slapped her hand against the wall next to the call buttons. "Could have been? That'll help if someone else who lives here comes face to face with a violent crazy man."

Groaning sounded from inside the walls as if an elevator were lumbering to life somewhere above.

"And he might be mentally ill," Lauren said. "That whole deinstitutionalization thing."

"That doesn't mean everyone on the street is mentally ill," I said.

"But it's a higher than average percentage," Debbie said.

"That's also true of lawyers," I said. "But since we mostly can afford to own homes, no one categorizes us as a group as crazy."

Ty ran his hand over his hair, though it was too short to have become disheveled. "We should notify everyone regardless. In case people go downstairs to the store. We don't want them stumbling onto Patryk."

Lauren folded her arms over her chest. "Right. That'd be absolutely awful."

I didn't disagree. Finding a person dead is not something you ever forget. For the first few months after Marco's death, every time I'd tried to call on a good memory of being with him the sight of his face, chalk white in death, intruded instead.

"Is there a global building email list? Or text list? Maybe Lauren and I can send something while you go see Janelle," I said.

"In the office," Debbie said. "But it's stored on the system, and I don't have passwords."

I refrained from expressing surprise that there was anything Debbie hadn't finagled access to.

The elevator finally arrived with a hollow ding. We stepped in. Ty pressed RR, I assumed for River Road. "Need to get my coat."

I hit LL for the Lobby Level.

A second after it started to rise, the elevator jerked and froze. The doors slid open a few inches, and the lights went out.

～

December 13, 8:02 p.m.

The elevator's oval window usually provided a view of the floors as the elevator rose, but now I saw only blackness. The elevator shaft might be blocking the window. I edged away from the corner where I stood. I kept my elbows out a little at my sides the way I do on crowded street corners to keep a little distance from everyone around me.

I'm not claustrophobic. But being crammed in this small space in the dark after seeing Patryk dead didn't exactly make me feel comfortable.

"Power might be out for the block," Ty said.

In the closeness of the elevator his voice sounded warm and resonant. My shoulders dropped a little.

"Or it's just River City," I said.

I'd lived in the Printers Row neighborhood for over six years.

While other parts of the city often lost power during that time, we never had.

"There should be light filtering in from the street," Ty said. "Whether we're at Lobby Level or River Road."

He had a point. It's never really dark in downtown Chicago, which is why you can rarely see stars at night. The lobby elevator bank had glass doors, and the lobby itself had glass walls, so ambient light from streetlights and traffic ought to filter in. The atrium over River Road also let some light in even at night. Though if the falling snow were thick enough, it might block it.

Rustling came from my right. A light shone from Debbie's cell phone. She turned the flashlight beam on the opening between the elevator doors. They'd frozen about six inches apart. At least the elevator had stopped nearly at floor level.

I pressed the emergency button and braced myself for a loud bell. Silence.

Debbie texted the property manager to ask about emergency procedures and got no response. I pushed the sleeves of my blazer to my elbows and wiped my forehead.

"The manager might be stuck somewhere with no cell service," Lauren said. "Remember how many cell phone towers got knocked out in 2011?"

"We should be moving in a minute," Ty said. "They're supposed to have a back up generator that'll operate the elevators and turn on emergency lighting. Every high-rise has to. It's in the city codes."

"If it doesn't we could squeeze out one-by-one," Lauren said.

"Squeeze out?" Debbie said. "Are you insane? Get chopped in half is more like it if the power goes back on."

"There must be sensors," Lauren said. "Otherwise people's yappy Pomeranians and toy poodles would get smooshed all the time when they race in at the last minute."

Lauren and I had bonded early on in law school over our mutual dislike of dogs. In Chicago, disliking dogs makes you almost as much of a pariah as if you hate babies. Maybe more so. I'm baby neutral, but I'd been terrorized as a child by a neighbor's bulldog, so I'd never come to like dogs and never wanted to.

Lauren just found them annoying.

Debbie clicked off her flashlight. "We should conserve."

I rubbed the back of my neck. The tight muscles were becoming sore, which often sparked a migraine. Three Ibuprofen usually heads one off if I take them early. But my small bottle of Ibuprofen, plus Imitrex if it got worse, was up in Carole's apartment in my parka pocket.

Distraction is the best bet when I start feeling pain, and I might never have Debbie and Ty in such close quarters again. So I asked why Ty was involved in Save the Parks.

"You can't be a welcome guest there," I said. "Not as a developer."

"You're not wrong," he said.

"He's involved in all the developments Save The Parks opposes," Debbie said.

"Not all," Ty said. "But most. As I told Lauren, Rani and I have had many a debate about it."

His tone made it sound like a friendly, almost fun debate, if such a thing existed in the world anymore.

"They argue all the time," Debbie said. Though I couldn't see her, I imagined her with her hands on her hips, tossing her long hair back in indignation.

"Disagree." Ty's tone remained calm. "Rani understands development can be good for the neighborhood. She wants to make sure there's enough green space, but unlike most people running the group, she's not a hypocrite."

There was a shuffling sound. "You're calling me a hypocrite?" Debbie said. Her voice sounded louder, and I guess she'd moved closer to Ty and me.

I rolled my shoulders backward hoping to loosen my muscles.

"Not you. Not anyone at River City," Ty said. "This place has been here for decades. I'm talking about the board member from Vetro. Vetro, which was built in 2010, and he's complaining about the new developments changing the character of the neighborhood. Hello? He had no problem moving into a brand new high rise building that changed the neighborhood, and now he doesn't want anyone else to be able to."

Before Vetro had gone up, the stretch of Wells Street between downtown and Roosevelt Road had been mostly parking lots, barely-trafficked businesses, and an empty field along the river. I'd usually avoided walking that way.

Now it was one of the safest streets, with doorpeople in every building along the way and lots of light. But it had lost the hidden enclave feel and looked more and more like downtown with tall buildings and lots of cars and trucks. When I returned to the old low-rise warehouse-style buildings in the blocks around my condo I felt more at ease and at home.

"So the Save The Parks people dislike you," I said.

"We don't dislike him," Debbie said. "But he can't get around that he's pro-development."

Next to me Lauren's phone glowed as she typed texts. I couldn't see who they were going to, but I guessed every number she could think of to complain about us being stuck.

"Of course I'm pro-development," Ty said. "I'm a developer."

"Why go to the meetings?" I said.

"Spying," Debbie said.

Ty laughed, though Debbie's tone had sounded borderline hostile to me. "Sure, I like to see what they're up to. Know what sort of protests are coming down the pike."

Lauren clicked her phone off and we plunged into darkness again. "I'm surprised they let you attend."

"Can't stop him," Debbie said. "We use the building common area, and management says if we do that we have to let any tenants attend. But he won't be a tenant much longer."

"Maybe we should think about squeezing out," I said. I felt far too warm, and the back of my head throbbed.

"Actually I will," Ty said. "I'm moving out of my apartment, but my boat will still be docked here. I checked. That's enough to be a tenant."

"Boats shouldn't count." Debbie flicked her flashlight on again, shone it over the elevator panel, and hit the emergency button. Still nothing. "Unbelievable. This has to violate every building ordinance in the books."

Lauren took out her phone again. "The northern suburbs lost power hours ago, and two cell phone towers there went dark. They're calling it the storm of the century." She rolled her eyes. "Seriously. Try some originality."

The amount of hyperbole in the news these days drives me crazy, but this time I feared it might be accurate.

"We can't stay in here all night," I said.

15

December 13, 8:06 p.m.

Turning sideways, I clamped my arms against my sides. I figured as long as I moved my whole body in between the half-open doors, rather than sticking a far more breakable arm or a leg through first or last, at worst I'd get bruised. An elevator couldn't have the strength to chop a whole human in half.

I hoped.

I held my breath, stepped quickly sideways, and was out. My exhale came out in a loud rush of air.

The other three followed. Using the light from Debbie's phone we made our way to the glass doors enclosing the elevator bank. We were at the lobby.

We gathered near the glass wall that fronted the circular drive. No lights were visible from Wells Street. The buildings across the street, kitty corner, and to the north all must be dark, though it was hard to be sure with snow flying everywhere. The glass shuddered. I stepped back from the frigid air.

Debbie's keys jingled as she struggled with the lock on the management office door. I held my phone, shining the light on her hands.

Darkness surrounded us.

Once the door finally swung open, Debbie handed me the keys in case Lauren and I needed them later. She and Ty headed for the stairs to River Road where his apartment was.

The computers and laptops in the management office had battery power, but all were password protected. The only thing I could access was an Internet browser, but the connection was out.

"Must be wireless," Lauren said, "and it went out with the power. I could create a hotspot with my phone."

"Let's see if we can find a password list first," I said. "We could be out of power for a while, and I don't want to waste your battery."

I hoped someone had written down passwords the way Rani had, but we rifled through hanging files and drawers and found nothing.

Debbie had forwarded from her phone to mine the email addresses she had for Save The Parks and the Tenants Association. Combined that totaled over three hundred addresses. Some were duplicates, so if we emailed about Patryk we'd reach maybe half the residents at best.

"Carole might have more addresses," Lauren said. "She seems to know everyone, and we need to tell her about Patryk."

Lauren called on the office landline. Carole must have answered right away because Lauren started talking about finding Patryk.

I walked out to the security counter so I didn't need to hear what I'd just lived through. I'd had too many conversations like it after Marco's death. To stay busy, I searched through the drawers and files there by the light of my phone. No password list turned up, but I did find a cinnamon-scented candle and a book of matches.

Using the landline, I called my assistant. She'd found a phone number and email for Rani's ex-boyfriend. He was willing to talk with me, but hadn't heard from Rani in several months.

As I thanked her and hung up, footsteps and voices sounded from deeper in the building. I recognized Debbie's hurried tones. She and Ty emerged from the hall a moment later, buttoning coats and pulling on hats and gloves.

Ty shoved the emergency exit door hard.

"Good luck," I said, and immediately recognized it was a ridiculous thing to say. There was no luck involved in giving Janelle news. Though I supposed it could apply to getting through the storm safely.

"Thanks," Ty said.

Lauren's voice still murmured from the office.

Between the candlelight's reflections on the glass wall and the snow flying outside, almost the instant they stepped outside Debbie and Ty disappeared.

December 13, 8:11 p.m.

Dear Residents of River City:

I'm very sorry to tell you that there's been an incident in the hallway outside the grocery store. It's not clear what happened, but Patryk Kaja, who was visiting for the Tenants Association holiday party, was found on the floor near the south exit from the Marina Level.

It appears his head was injured. He did not survive.

Police are on the way, but due to severe weather may not arrive for several hours. Please avoid the grocery store (which is closed anyway) and the exit. The police asked that we not disturb anything.

I've also learned that several residents have seen a man who may be homeless both in the outdoor parking lot and in the hallways on the Marina Level. While it's not known if he is dangerous, given that we don't know the cause of Patryk's death please be cautious if you see the man or anyone else unfamiliar to you in or outside the building.

On an unrelated note, Shanda Singh has not heard from her sister Rani at all today and is concerned she is caught somewhere in the storm.

If you spoke to, saw, or heard from Rani today, please respond to this email or contact Shanda directly. Her contact information is below.

Sincerely,

Your neighbor Carole Ports

~

December 13, 8:15 p.m.

After Lauren proofread the message, which I'd written on her phone, she sent it to Carole to review, add Shanda's information, and send out.

"How do you feel about climbing some stairs?" I said to Lauren.

16

December 13, 8:25 p.m.

Lauren and I sat at a small glass-topped dining table in the studio apartment of Rani's and Shanda's neighbor, Vina. She poured us spicy black tea made with Bergamot root. She'd made a pot right before the power had gone out, and it was still lukewarm. I wrapped my hands around my cup.

She also had Advil, for which she had my undying gratitude, as somewhere between Café des Livres and Carole's apartment my bottle of pills had gotten lost. My head felt like a giant had placed his hands on either side of it and squeezed. On the upside, at least those hands didn't hold ice picks. There might be time for the three Advil I'd swallowed in one gulp to work.

A stubby vanilla-scented candle on the dining table and a row of tealight candles in glass holders on the coffee table near the daybed provided flickering light.

"When's the last time you and Rani studied together?" I said.

Vina, a college student, was the neighbor who'd seemed hesitant to speak when I'd knocked on her door along with Carole. The email about Patryk's death had convinced her Rani might be in real danger, though. Vina attended Roosevelt University, not U of I, so she and Rani had no classes together, but they met for study sessions.

"Used to be every week." Vina brushed her short, wavy dark hair away from her eyes. "Rani liked coming over here for a change of scene. But it's been months. Three or four at least."

"Because?" I said.

"I don't know." Her hands flew up and toward the sides in frustration as she spoke. "She wouldn't tell me anything except she was very busy. Or behind on a project, but she didn't say what project. I started to think she was mad at me for something, but she said no."

"So I think you said you last saw Rani Saturday," I said. It was too dark to check my notes, but I remembered that from the last conversation.

"Yes. Saturday morning. We ran into each other at Dollop over in the Alta."

The Alta, a block away, was one of the newer high rises in the area. Dollop, a local coffee chain, had a café on its ground floor.

"When I was here before I got the feeling there was something else you wanted to say. Maybe not in front of Carole?"

Vina looked down at her hands, which she'd folded in front of her on the table. I sipped my tea. It had gone cold.

"Rani loves Carole," Vina said. "Wants Carole to think well of her, and I don't know anything for certain. I don't want it to tarnish Rani's reputation or upset anyone."

Lauren pushed her teacup aside. "More upsetting would be something terrible happening to Rani if we don't find her."

Vina grimaced. "Of course. But you must understand. An Indian woman's reputation is vital. It's not like here, where it doesn't matter."

"I wouldn't say doesn't matter," I said, "but I understand what you're saying. We won't share anything you tell us unless it's absolutely necessary."

Wind raged outside. The windowpanes rattled.

"All right. If Rani's in trouble — " Her dark eyes darted around the room, as if checking to be sure no one else could be listening. "Rani may be seeing someone Shanda would disapprove of."

Lauren sat back in her chair abruptly, making the table shake. "We figured that. I can't imagine Shanda liking anyone Rani dates."

Vina rubbed her fingers in a circle around the rim of her teacup.

"You think it's more than that," I said.

"Yes. Maybe — perhaps — someone married." Vina dropped her chin, practically speaking into her tea.

"What makes you suspect that?" I said.

"Her being so busy but not telling me why. She doesn't need to tell me everything she does but we used to study together regularly. Then suddenly she's saying she's got no time but there's nothing new in her schedule. In fact, last year she said it'd be easier this year because it's her last and she's just making sure she hits a last couple courses and has enough credits."

"Could she be mad at you about something?" Lauren said.

"I finally asked. By text since I hardly see her. Like I said, she insisted no, and said she could explain everything soon, just not yet."

"How long ago was that?" I said.

"A month or so."

I bent my head toward my left shoulder to loosen the muscle tension on the right. The Advil was kicking in, and I felt only aching along my neck muscles on each side and up through my temples. No throbbing and no pressure.

The lighter school schedule fit with Rani switching to part-time. Explaining everything soon might mean she was seeing someone married who would soon be separated. Or it could be something else entirely.

"And she wouldn't say more?" I said.

"No."

Lauren went to the kitchen sink, rinsed her teacup, and filled it with water. "If she is seeing someone, any idea who?"

"None."

"Any man she talks a lot about? Admires? Has a close friendship with?" I said.

"Admiring a married man doesn't mean having an affair."

That suggested Vina had someone in mind. I resisted the urge to fish my notepad from my inner blazer pocket. If I started writing, she might stop talking.

"No, but it would help with who else to talk to," I said. "Anyone who knew Rani well might have an idea where she is or what happened to her."

"She's still friends with her ex-boyfriend, the one she stopped seeing a year or two ago."

"He claims he hasn't seen her." I'd spoken with him before we'd made our climb to the fifteenth floor. He'd sounded genuinely worried for Rani but hadn't had anything helpful to offer.

"And she and Aidan, Shanda's assistant, are friends." Vina stirred her tea with a tiny silver spoon though she hadn't added sugar or milk to it. "And there's Jeff Chang, the head of the Immigration Rights Center. He lives in the building."

"Immigration Rights Center?" I frowned, thinking back. Someone had mentioned the organization to me recently. Ty Hudson. He had said Patryk gave talks there.

"She volunteers there," Vina said. "Once a week for almost two years. She always says how dedicated Jeff is and how hard he works for the clients, but that doesn't mean anything's happened between them."

Rani volunteering at the Immigration Rights Center made her having a visa issue especially strange. She'd likely be more aware of the pitfalls than most people here on a visa, and she had a quick source of advice if she did get into trouble. I wondered why Shanda hadn't mentioned this volunteer work.

Lauren had resumed her seat, and she shifted her chair to stretch her legs out sideways. "Is there chemistry between her and Jeff?"

"I've never seen them together," Vina said.

"But she talks about him a lot," I said.

Vina poured herself more tea from the ceramic teapot, draining it, and set it back in the center of the table. "I wouldn't say a lot."

"Jeff's married?" I said.

"Yes. He and his wife live here in River City."

There was a loud snap and one of the tealight candles on the coffee table flared. The vanilla scent grew stronger.

I asked if Rani knew Patryk, and Vina said she wasn't sure. The possibility that Rani was hiding a relationship with Patryk and that was the connection between the two seemed like a stretch. He had to be at least two decades older than her. That didn't rule out a relationship — stranger things have happened — but nothing else suggested the two were involved.

"Anything else?" I said. "That made you think Rani might be seeing someone?"

"She seemed a lot happier," Vina said. "The few times I saw her."

Lauren's eyebrows drew together. "And that makes you think she's seeing a married man?"

"No, no." Vina waved her hand, making the flame of the stubby candle in front of her flicker. "But her happiness, it's like joy and excitement and tension all at once. The way you feel when you first meet someone and can't wait to see him again. That's how she strikes me. It makes me think she met someone though she doesn't want to tell me about it."

It was how I'd felt about Marco, and we'd never gotten beyond that phase. I hadn't known him long enough. I liked to think we would have been happy together a long time. What I'd seen of relationships in my family didn't give me much reason to believe that, but I hoped we would have been different.

"Any other reason Rani might hide a relationship?" I said. "What if she were seeing someone of a different background or religion?"

"Shanda does feel strongly about marrying a Hindu. I don't know how adamant about it she is for Rani," Vina said.

"What if Rani's seeing a woman?" Lauren said.

Vina had started to reach for her teacup, and she knocked it over. Tea sloshed across the table. I grabbed a dishtowel from the kitchen counter and wiped it up.

"A woman?" Vina said. "That's something she would not want to tell her sister. Her family would never accept it."

"Are you sure Shanda wouldn't?" I said as I finished sopping the tea. I didn't know Shanda all that well, but over the years Carole had made her sound as if she were open-minded about political and social issues.

"It's one thing to believe, in general, that gay people should have the same civil rights as anyone else," Vina said. "It's another to find it morally acceptable. And even if Shanda would be okay with it, it would be a secret she would need to keep from their parents. Rani wouldn't want to place her in that position. She and Shanda disagree on many things, but Rani loves and respects her parents."

I rinsed and wrung the towel out in the sink, feeling my way in semi darkness. If Rani had met a woman, I didn't have any ideas on who that might be.

But it wouldn't surprise me that she would hesitate to confide in Shanda, or anyone who knew Shanda, if she had. I doubted my parents would be concerned about anyone I was seeing, as they rarely asked about my life. My Gram, on the other hand, was very much cut from the same cloth Vina described. She didn't think people who were gay should be discriminated against, but I suspected she'd be upset if she thought I were a lesbian. Ditto on dating a married man.

I draped the fragrant, spice-scented towel over the dish rack. "Do you see Shanda often?"

"No, but my aunt is one of her clients. I wouldn't tell my aunt anything about Rani's private life, but maybe she's wary of a connection."

"Was she worried about anything relating to staying in the country when she finished school?" I said as I returned to my chair.

It was the closest I wanted to get to saying Rani might no longer hold a valid visa. The more people who knew, the more chance it would get mentioned to the police whenever they finally arrived. Which might very well be the same reasoning Rani followed in keeping her new relationship, if there was one, secret.

Vina shook her head. "Not that she ever said."

~

December 13, 8:33 p.m.

Barry Jenkins leaned in his doorway, propping the door open with one arm. Lauren held her phone flashlight aimed at the wall next to him so we could see one another without anyone being blinded. Barry was mostly bald with a fringe of hair around the sides that might be brown or gray, I couldn't tell in the dim light. His nose sloped straight down and his chin thrust out, making me think of the phrase leading with your chin. About half a foot taller than me, he wore jeans and a long-sleeved T-shirt with faded lettering I couldn't read across its chest.

A narrow catwalk ran along all the apartments with a railing on the inside guarding against the wide open space in the center of the building above River Road. Barry's apartment was situated on the curve such that he had a view of Shanda's and Rani's door.

He didn't invite us in.

"Carole's a decent lady," Barry said. We'd mentioned her name to help convince him to talk to us. "She and her husband, I don't mind them. They started a business, they're working. They keep a beautiful home. They're quiet."

Barry's posture made me think he was in his fifties or maybe sixty, as he kept one hand against the small of his back as if it ached and held the door handle with the other as if to steady himself. Why I associated that with age, though, I don't know. Gram is in her late seventies, has no trouble with balance, and rarely shows her aches and pains.

"And some people who live in River City aren't?" I said, hoping if Barry got rolling on one topic he might simply keep talking.

"Damn straight. Between the students and these Indians it's impossible to get any peace and quiet. They got five or six people living in one-bedroom apartments, and they all leave their doors open so they can run between each other's places, probably because they have so little space of their own. Even Rani and Shanda. Two people in the tiny one bedroom. It's no wonder Rani ducks out every now and then."

"Ducks out?" I said.

"Sneaks out at night after Shanda comes home."

"How do you know?" Lauren said.

"I got trouble sleeping. Follow a routine at night. Brush my teeth, turn out the lights, come out on the walkway and look down at River Road for about ten minutes. Used be to a very nice road. Sad seeing it deteriorate."

I turned and shone my flashlight down. River Road, though ten floors below, was visible from here.

"How do you know she's sneaking?" I said.

I'd learned in my law practice to separate a witness's characterization of what someone does from the facts actually observed.

He pursed his lips and took a moment to answer. "She closes the door real soft. Hangs on to it so it doesn't slam. And creeps out, slow and quiet."

"Is she usually loud?" I said.

"She's not quiet. Lets the door slam shut on its own, clomps around in those big boots that are popular now. But not when she leaves at night."

I wished my neighbors would be as courteous as Rani at night. Late hours aren't my thing — another reason a life in theater hadn't quite suited me. Already tonight I felt worn out, and it wasn't nine o'clock yet. I had friends from my acting days I could never see before ten p.m. because they worked day jobs and were in rehearsal or on stage until nine or ten at night. And neighbors who, judging from slammed doors and loud voices at midnight, kept that same type of schedule.

"What time does she usually leave?" I said.

"Ten, ten-thirty."

"Where does Rani go?" Lauren said. "When she leaves at night?"

"You got me." He gestured south. "I see her head around the curve there. Toward the elevators."

"Does it seem like she's going outside?" I said.

His free hand rose to his hip. "How would I know?"

"Is she usually wearing a coat?" I said.

"A second ago I would have said no, but now that you ask...." Barry let go of the door handle for a moment to scratch his opposite arm. "Maybe."

"When's the last time you saw her leave at night like that?" I said.

"Could've been last night. Or the night before. Couldn't say."

"But this week," I said.

He agreed and said Rani's late-night exits had started about four or five months ago, timing that fit with her friend Vina saying she'd become busier and busier. She also went out late only five or six nights a month, which could fit with seeing someone married or who had limited availability, but could mean a lot of other things, too. The Harmoniums, the a cappella trio I'm in, sings about four times a month, a little more during the holiday season. For all I knew, Rani was going out to see a favorite band. Or to sing with one.

Barry had lived in the building for twenty-five years. I asked if he'd owned his apartment when it had been a condominium.

"Nope. Moved in as a rental, then my unit was bought by an investor. One of those who meant to flip it and got caught, so it went to shit. Finally did all the repairs myself. Maybe the building'll pay more attention to tenants now."

Barry knew Shanda mainly from seeing her pass by, though he'd spoken to Rani quite a few times. He didn't attend Tenants Association meetings, but he did belong to Save The Parks.

"You ought to talk to that Ty Hudson guy if you think something happened to Rani," he said.

I'd been leaning against the railing, but now I stood straighter. "Why's that?"

"He's a big-time developer. His company, brokerage, whatever they call it was first to talk about buying this building but it fell through. Rani hates him because he's so pro-development. She's all touchy-feely, save the whales. Never met a cause she didn't like."

Hate was a strong word, and a far cry from the friendly disagreement Ty portrayed. "I heard she clashed with him over development."

Barry eased one hand behind him to support the small of his back. "Screamed at him more like it."

"How well do you know Ty?" I said.

"Only from hearing him spout off in the laundry room about his company. Thinks he's sharp with those designer suits."

I felt grateful it was too dark to see Lauren's clothes well. She buys new T-shirts or tanks at Old Navy or H&M every season, but everything else she wears from boots to bras to jewelry is designer-made.

Barry said he'd never met Patryk Kaja or heard of Byerly-Kaja. The last time he and Rani had talked had been about her graduating college in June.

He shook his head and gripped the doorknob tighter. "Asked her what she's doing next, and she said more school. She applied for an MSW program. Go figure. Told her we got too many social workers already. She says she wants to work with immigrant populations. Says they need special help. I say they need help, let them get it from home. I got nothing against them, but our country's broke. Our state's broke. Our city's broke."

It was the first time I'd heard that Rani had applied to a graduate program. I wondered why Shanda hadn't mentioned it.

17

———————

December 13, 8:41 p.m.

Three wicks on a large dark cherry candle burned in the center of Shanda's coffee table, casting a circle of light around Shanda, Lauren, and me. The apartment faded gradually to black beyond it.

Carole and Aidan had been here earlier, but she'd volunteered to go look for her travel phone chargers and paper address book. She had numbers recorded in it for a lot of people in the building, including Jeff Chang.

I'd suggested Aidan go with Carole. Nothing about him made me think he had a hand in whatever had happened to Rani, but I couldn't ignore the possibility for anyone. Better to keep discussions about searching for Rani between Lauren, Carole, Shanda, and me.

And perhaps not even Shanda where I could help it.

"You didn't mention Rani volunteering at the Immigration Rights Center," I said to Shanda.

Lauren and I sat on the daybed. Shanda perched on the armchair across from us. She held her arms straight, her hands

101

flat on her knees. She'd pulled on thick black leggings under her skirt and wore quilted slippers.

"She does?" Shanda said.

"That's what we heard," I said. "Any idea why she wouldn't tell you?"

Shanda rubbed her forehead. "Who can say?"

I pulled a heavy maroon cardigan Shanda had loaned me around my shoulders. The draft from the windows made the living room area cold. "If you had to guess?"

"I often tell her she spreads herself too thin. Maybe she didn't want to tell me she'd taken on another project," Shanda said.

Lauren pushed another pillow behind her back. "How well do you know Jeff Chang?"

"He refers clients he thinks can benefit from my services. And I send people to the Center if they have legal issues and can't afford a lawyer."

"And outside of business?" I shifted on the daybed. It was too wide for comfortable sitting. Either I had to sit straight with nothing to prop behind my back or leave my feet dangling over the front, which made me feel like a little kid.

"We go to some of the same events and fundraisers," Shanda said. "That's about it."

"Did you know Rani applied to an MSW program?" I said.

"MSW? What? What does she'll think she'll do with that?"

"Be a social worker?" Lauren said.

Shanda shot her a look. "Well, of course. But it's barely better than the arts in terms of standard of living."

Lauren gestured at the small living space. "It doesn't seem like you're set on luxury living."

"I live simply by choice. I'm building my business and helping Rani get her start. Later I'll get a larger home and a new car if I need it. It's how many immigrants succeed in business where Americans fail. We don't spend on luxuries before we earn or even when we earn, but only once we're established."

"But you run a non-profit, too," I said. "So you're not against that type of work."

Shanda tucked her hair behind her ear. "It's important work. But I started my non-profit after I got on my own two feet and started saving for a home and retirement. To do it when you're not yet able to support yourself is irresponsible."

"But if it's what Rani loves — " Lauren said.

"We all have things we love," Shanda said. "But we can't always have them and we certainly can't always have them right away. My parents sent us here for the opportunities, not to earn less in real dollars than we would have done at home."

Lauren frowned. "Your parents ought to support whatever she wants to do."

From an emotional perspective I agreed. My Gram's encouragement throughout my life had kept me going when I'd struggled. But only people who'd never needed to worry about money had the luxury of ignoring the cost versus the benefit of their choices.

Shanda went to her kitchen to refill her water glass. I asked if she knew where Rani went at night. She didn't, and she hadn't known Rani had been going out late. But she didn't expect that Rani would tell her everywhere she went.

"Could Rani be seeing someone you or your parents might not approve of?" I said.

Shanda returned to her armchair. "Given how much else I'm learning I don't know about her? Possible. Also, she thinks I dislike everyone she dates."

"Do you?" Lauren said.

"I just look for different things. I see the need for stability — financial and emotional — in a mate. Rani looks for attraction. If her 'tummy flips,' that's how she puts it, she's all in without thought for anything else."

The snow outside the window blew sideways and, for a few

seconds, appeared to fly upward as the wind battered the glass. I belted the cardigan around my waist.

"What if you had a more serious reason for disapproving?" I said. "Let's say she's dating someone married. Or dating a woman."

Shanda drew in her breath. "You're telling me Rani is gay?"

"It's just an example of something she might not want to tell you," I said.

I drank some Pepsi, using it to wash down another Ibuprofen. My head had begun throbbing again on the walk from Barry's.

The soda was lukewarm, but the sugar and fizz made me feel more alert. I knew it wasn't possible for the caffeine to act that quickly, but I often used Pepsi or Coke for a jolt before going on stage.

The placebo effect can be your friend even when you understand what's happening.

"Good example. She'd never tell me that. I'd like to think she knows she could, that I love her no matter what, but it isn't something we've ever talked about."

The building creaked around us. Shanda's statement of loving Rani no matter what underscored for me how she viewed the possibility of Rani being gay. It would never occur to me that anyone might question whether I'd still love my sister, niece, nephew, or anyone else because of sexual orientation.

"Would your family disown her?" Lauren said.

"I wouldn't. Our parents, I can't say. But nothing Rani's ever said made me think she's gay."

"But she wouldn't say anything to suggest it, would she?" Lauren said. "Knowing how your family would feel?"

"Maybe not." Shanda crossed her arms over her chest.

"What about if she were seeing someone married?" I said.

Shanda sighed. "That's easier to believe. If she fell for someone and he said he was separated or planning to divorce she'd find a way to believe it would turn out okay."

"And would she tell you about that?" I said.

"I doubt it."

"Any chance she and Patryk Kaja were involved?" I said.

"Patryk?" Shanda froze with her water glass halfway to her mouth. "I — no, I can't imagine that." The glass clanked as she let it drop to the coffee table. "I saw them talking a few times at Tenants Association meetings but I never sensed any spark or connection there. With Patryk dead...is that why you're asking?"

"It could be a connection between them," I said.

Shanda's face looked ashen despite the warm candlelight. "No. No, I don't think so."

"Could she be seeing Jeff Chang?" I said.

"Jeff? Unlikely even if he were single. Too clean cut for her. Too professional."

"How about Ty Hudson?" Lauren said.

She frowned. "Ty? Same as Jeff. And he's not married, so why ask about him?"

"He's black," Lauren said. "Would that bother you?"

"Not at all. I'd be happy if she got involved with him. He's a real estate developer. Stable. Employed." Despite her words, Shanda shook her head almost imperceptibly as she spoke.

"Might Rani think your parents wouldn't like her seeing someone black?" I said.

I've found when asking about a sensitive subject, or something a person might not want to admit, it's better to frame it in what others might think. It's easier to say that someone else might harbor a bias.

"In our family there is a lot of pressure to marry someone Indian."

"Has she dated non-Indian men?" I said.

Shanda brushed a stray hair out of her eyes. "Yes. I'd never object to Ty for that reason. He'd be such an improvement over her usual."

Lauren poked some wax on the top edge of the three-wicked candle to reveal more of the flames. "What's her usual?"

"College boys with tattoos up and down their arms. Usually ones studying something completely unlikely to lead to gainful employment like theater or art or music. No offense," she said to me.

"None taken," I said. Her repeated comments about people in the arts were starting to get to me, but we needed to stay focused. "I heard Ty and Rani got into arguments at the Save The Parks meetings."

"I don't usually go to those."

"She never mentioned arguing with Ty?" Lauren said.

"As you've probably guessed, we don't talk that much."

Living in a glass house, I couldn't criticize either of them for that. But my sister Kendra and I don't work together, live together, or live in the same city. I hope if we did we'd know a little more about each other than Shanda and Rani seemed to.

Though we probably wouldn't.

~

December 13, 8:47 p.m.

Carole had found two travel chargers, but they'd been sitting in her closet so long they had no charge left. She and Aidan also brought flashlights and coats, Aidan staggering a bit under the weight of Lauren's shearling. She decided not to wear it, donning the cardigan I'd been wearing instead.

I pulled my zippered fleece over my blazer and tucked my thin knit gloves in a pocket. My parka, heavy mittens, scarves, and hat I left on Shanda's couch. River City was chilly near the windows but otherwise holding in heat pretty well.

Debbie had left a message on Carole's home landline that she and Ty had made it to Janelle's and that Janelle was insisting on coming to River City to see Patryk's body. Carole wanted to be in the lobby waiting for them, so she, Lauren, and I took the stairs down.

Aidan stayed with Shanda, who didn't want to leave the apartment.

"I know it's foolish," she said. "But I feel like if I leave, maybe Rani will come here and I'll miss her, especially now that a lot of cell phones may not be working."

Lauren led the way down the concrete stairwell on the south edge, shining one of the flashlights Carole had brought. The metal railing felt cool in my hand, and the stairwell smelled of concrete and dampness.

I filled Carole in on what we'd learned and asked what she thought of Jeff.

"I don't know him well, but I hear he puts everyone who comes into the Center at ease," Carole said.

"How?"

The backpack I'd filled with candles and candleholders and slung over my shoulder clunked as I started down another flight.

"No matter how backlogged they are," Carole said, "he greets each person who walks in the door. There is always coffee, hot water, and tea in the waiting room. It makes people feel welcome, rather than like a burden. Plus the ones who feel ashamed about not being able to pay, he tells them that things will get better and sometime in the future they will help someone else."

We paused on the sixth floor landing. I felt all right to keep going, but I'd noticed Carole gripping the railing more tightly and slowing her steps.

"Could Rani's connection with the Immigration Rights Center be an issue for someone in the building?" I said. "I got the impression some people don't like that a lot of recent immigrants live here."

Carole leaned against the concrete wall. "They don't mind certain immigrants. Frery and I, we are fine. We invite people over for wine and cheese and bake pastry. But people of color, as I believe you young people say, are not as welcome. Their culture is less familiar. Here, French food, French wine, it is gourmet for Americans. Haute-cuisine. Our artists fill your art museums. But Indian culture, food, some people appreciate it, but I'm sad to say people of my generation and older do not so much. I hear them say Indians are dirty, their food is smelly. Some want them excluded from the building, though they know it's illegal."

I asked about Barry specifically.

"*Ah, oui*, he is very vocal. He moved into his condo long before the 2010 flood, so it radically dropped in value and his landlord neglected it. I suspect that adds to his frustration." She stood straight. "I am ready to go on. I want to be here when Janelle arrives. I feel so bad for her. We must offer support."

Though I didn't know Janelle, I wanted to offer support too. But I had another motive. She was the most likely one to know if there was any connection between Patryk and Rani.

18

———

December 13, 9:02 p.m.

One by one Carole lit the tealights she'd set out on the security counter in small glass holders. She added two large cinnamon-scented colored pillar candles Shanda had given us. Together they lit the entire counter area.

There was no sign of Debbie, Ty, or Janelle. We tried calling Jeff Chang but got voicemail at his cell and office numbers. Carole left messages asking him to call her about Rani.

I took out my small yellow pad and pen.

"We must be missing something. Shanda says everyone liked Rani. The only person anyone mentioned her arguing with is Ty."

"And I'm pretty sure he was at the Tenants Association meeting the entire time I was there." Lauren leaned on the counter near the candles. "Which rules him out for Patryk's death. If we're assuming Patryk and Rani are connected."

"But did you have your eyes on him the whole time?" I said.

"Not every second. But I don't think he could've slipped out, killed Patryk, and scurried back before anyone noticed."

I felt less sure. The room hadn't been wall-to-wall people, but there had been enough that one person leaving for a while wouldn't be that noticeable, especially because visiting the restrooms meant leaving the party room. There'd be no reason to find it strange if someone left and returned.

"Ty's a maybe. Anyone else who might want to hurt Rani?" I said.

"Ty wouldn't want to hurt her. No one would." Carole sank onto a stool behind the security counter. "She's a lovely young woman."

"People who might be mad at her then. Or irritated with her," I said.

I rephrased often when questioning witnesses, including my own clients. Words matter, and which ones you use often determine the answers you get.

Carole propped her chin on her hand. "My mind goes blank. All I can recall is all the people who'll be devastated if something happened to her."

Lauren sat down on a third counter stool. She rolled back and forth along the curving counter. "We're assuming Shanda would be devastated, but you can tell the two didn't get along."

"Not getting along is not the same as being willing to harm Rani," Carole said.

"Let's hope," I said, but I added Shanda's name to my list. "I earn a lot from disputes over family businesses."

I'd majored in accounting in college and worked for a couple years at an accounting firm before starting law school, making me a natural choice as a lawyer when there were issues over how to split up a family business or partnership. The lawsuits could be as bitter as divorces, as they similarly involved money and family relationships. A lot of legal squabbles over inherited businesses were really about which child mom or dad loved more.

"But Rani is not 'in' Shanda's business," Carole said.

"But Shanda wants her to be," Lauren said.

I asked about the rest of Rani's family, and Carole told me her parents and two other sisters still lived in India. Only Shanda and Rani had come to the U.S. or wanted to.

"Is working for Shanda Rani's only job?" I said.

"As far as I know," Carole said.

"And Aidan's her only coworker," I said.

Shanda had told us she worked with a few independent contractors, including an offsite bookkeeping service, but Rani had no dealings with any of them. Her role was limited to photos and an occasional blurb or article for the newsletter. Aidan had been Shanda's assistant for over two years. Before that, she'd done everything herself.

"Do Rani and Aidan get along?" Lauren said.

"*Mais oui.* He is like an older brother to her."

Lauren glanced over my shoulder at my notepad. "You should think about what the police might ask about Rani and Patryk."

"What do you mean?" Carole said.

"The glove," I said. "The one found by the door. It matches the way Eliza Driscoll described the glove Rani was carrying around to give back to the homeless man."

In the aftermath of Marco's death, my view of police had improved. Slightly. I hadn't seen them trying to blame innocent people the way my parents said Edwardsville and Springfield law enforcement officials had done so long ago.

But they hadn't exactly done a stellar job. My efforts, and those of Lauren, Joe, and Danielle, had led to the truth about Marco, not theirs.

"Police could never believe Rani killed Patryk," Carole said. "*C'est ridicul.*"

"They can believe a lot of things," I said. "And to be fair, they have to if they want to do their jobs right."

In a different way, I faced similar issues as a lawyer. I couldn't do my job well if I didn't understand the opposing party's arguments. And that meant sometimes asking my clients questions they didn't want to answer or presenting them with what I expected the other side to say.

Carole rested her elbows on the counter. Her shoulder dropped. The candlelight softened the lines along her forehead, but she looked weary, and worried, all the same. "One more fear about what has happened or may happen to her."

The wind had died down. The turnaround drive came into focus through the falling snow beyond the glass wall.

"Why did Patryk speak at the Immigration Rights Center?" I said, my mind wandering back to the center as a possible connection.

"I assume because his parents came from Poland when he was very young. He speaks Polish. And he feels — felt — strongly about helping people do well in a new country."

After English and Spanish, Polish is the most common language in Chicago. A lawyer who sends business litigation cases to me built his entire practice on speaking Polish and his ties to that community. He writes simple wills and does real estate closings, and he refers out everything else, earning part of the fees because he stays on to serve as liaison and translator.

I was about to suggest Lauren and I go knock on Jeff Chang's door in person, as I didn't want to waste any more time. But the emergency door groaned and swung open, and three snow-covered figures entered.

19

December 13, 9:09 p.m.

A woman who must be Janelle staggered in, arms linked with Debbie and Ty. She wore a fuzzy gray hat and a long coat. She saw Carole and walked into her arms, her whole body crumpling.

Carole helped Janelle to one of the counter stools and brushed the snow from her blond hair, not flinching when ice crystals fell on her. "Janelle, *ma chere,* I am so very very sorry."

Janelle rocked forward and back. "How can it....I can't believe...tonight when he left...."

Carole eased Janelle's coat off her shoulders. I hung it over another chair to dry and Lauren shrugged off her cardigan so Carole could wrap it around Janelle's shoulders.

"We were getting worried about you," Lauren said to Ty and Debbie.

Ty shook the snow off his long wool coat. "We tried to convince her not to come out in the storm."

"I offered to stay with her." Debbie ran her fingers through her long, black hair, combing out tangles. "But she wants to see Patryk."

I nodded. I had stayed with Marco's body while waiting for the police, knowing he couldn't be aware of me there but unable to leave him by himself.

Carole kept her arm around Janelle's shoulders. "I will walk you downstairs if you like. Ty, you live on River Road, yes? Perhaps you and Quille could find something for Janelle to eat and drink and bring it here for when we come back."

River Road, though it was on the fifth floor, was the lowest residential level and so required climbing the fewest stairs.

"I couldn't eat," Janelle said.

"Some tea, then." Carole glanced at Ty and he nodded.

"I'll go with you," Debbie said.

"Actually," I said, "Lauren was just saying how she wanted to know more about which residents might be looking to buy condos, and I figured you might know."

Lauren came out from behind the counter. "It'd be a huge help to me," she said, though she hadn't said anything of the kind. But maybe she'd get some business out of it, and I'd get to talk to Ty about Janelle. I suspected he'd be more apt to fill in blanks without unnecessary drama. That could save me from firing questions at Janelle at such an awful time.

I remembered how that felt.

"Oh, I know all about that," Debbie said.

"This way," Ty said. "Good thing coffee's out. I've got no idea how to make it. Though I guess it wouldn't matter with the power out."

I took Lauren aside for a moment and borrowed her pepper spray, discretely slipping it into my front fleece pocket. It seemed unlikely even if Ty were a killer that he'd attack me when everyone knew we were heading to his place together, and Carole trusted him, but it paid to be careful. We headed down the hall and into the stairwell.

"You're not a coffee drinker either," I said. In a world filled with espressos, half-caf lattes, and cold brews, I always like finding a kindred spirit.

"Not ever." Ty used the flashlight on his phone to light our way. "Glad I'm not the only one. My first sales training course, the instructor's number one rule was everyone learn to drink coffee because most clients would be drinking it. I did not learn."

"Sounds like something the managing partner at my former law firm would have said," I said. "Or the accounting firm for that matter. We had a lot of runners there who swore by caffeine to get them started."

"Caffeine I'm all for. It's the coffee I can't stand."

"How was Janelle when you told her?" I said as we climbed the next flight.

"Stunned. Asked Debbie the same questions over and over again. Where we found him, how long he'd been gone from the meeting, how his face looked, whether anyone saw anything. We'd answer and she'd start all over again. Then it seemed to hit her out of nowhere as we reached River City and she just started sobbing."

I almost envied her being able to let go. It had taken me weeks to cry after Marco's death. I'd grown up hearing from my grandmother how important it was to pull yourself together during hard times and not withdraw from the world like my mother. Or my dad for that matter. It was Gram who pulled the family through crisis. Given a choice of whom to emulate, I had to go with her, but she wasn't much of a model for handling difficult feelings.

Ty swung open the door to the fifth floor and held it for me. "I didn't know what to say to her. You want to help, but there's nothing beyond 'I'm sorry'."

"Sometimes that's the best thing," I said.

Since Marco's death I'd learned the value of a simple "I'm sorry." Too often in the last eight months I'd struggled to stifle angry retorts to well-meaning comments about Marco's death being "meant to be" or part of God's plan. If some god had arranged for Marco's thirteen-year-old son to lose his father or for me to find the man I loved dead on the eve of us moving in together, I was a fan of a random and godless Universe.

River Road's wide-open space welcomed me after the dank stairwell, though I couldn't see much in the flashlight app's faint glow.

"A resident told me Rani screamed at you at a recent Save The Parks meeting," I said.

I would have liked to come up with a clever segue into the topic, but with the hours slipping away and the migraine still struggling to worm its way into my head I didn't feel I had the time or the mental sharpness for it. Better to just get to the point.

"Screamed?" Ty said. "She was mad at me, sure. But I've never heard Rani scream."

"He was pretty definite about it," I said.

We rounded a curve and for a second I thought I saw someone standing up ahead in our path. I stopped. "Who's there?"

Ty shone his flashlight and I saw it was the bronze sculpture of a woman.

"Spooks me all the time." Ty led me to a door across from it and unlocked it.

"Whoever told you that about Rani," Ty said, "might be one of those people who thinks any time a woman raises her voice it's a scream."

"How about yell then? Did she yell?" I said, in case "scream" was making him downplay the conflict.

"We argued, but we didn't yell."

Ty's apartment was a one bedroom with a wedge-shaped kitchen that opened onto a room that served as both living room and dining room. I followed him to the kitchen area. He had no table, just tall chairs at a counter that jutted from the wall and divided the kitchen area from the living room.

I ran my fingers over the counter. It felt like granite. I guessed it was black, though I couldn't see well enough to be sure.

"Tables seem optional here," I said.

My desire for at least a small dining or kitchen table had hampered my search for a condo. My Gram raised me to eat at the table whenever I was home because I ate so often on the fly when I was racing between school and theaters. She said it was healthy to respect dining time.

When I'd worked at the accounting firm and later during law school I'd eaten at my desk or the law school food court more often than at home. My schedule hadn't gotten better as a lawyer, especially during tax season when I practically slept at my office. I used my kitchen island when I drank tea, ate carry out, or worked, but I liked my dining table for when I cooked a meal. Home for me was where I could sit down comfortably and eat.

"I almost never eat at home," Ty said, "occupational hazard of being a developer."

"Working late?" I said.

He opened one of the cabinets over the microwave. In the blue light from the phone the glossy white doors looked ghostly. In normal light they probably set off the granite counter nicely.

"That or entertaining people." He grabbed a thermos. Ty was tall enough to reach inside the upper cabinets with a little bit of a stretch. I would have needed a step stool.

"Is that a big part of your job?"

"More or less. I'm on the marketing side." He spun and opened his refrigerator. "Not sure I have anything other than Diet Coke. It's all I drink."

"In the morning?" I said.

"All day," he said. "Sometimes I make hot chocolate. Not exactly gourmet, but I like it."

He shone the light on a bottle of Hershey's syrup in the refrigerator door.

It's hard for me not to like a guy who keeps Hershey's syrup on hand. I reminded myself that likable people could be criminals, too. Danielle had plenty of personable clients who'd nonetheless done what they were accused of.

"Could you hold this?" Ty handed me his phone and I shone the beam as he rummaged through a pantry cabinet near his fridge.

As he did, I asked him about the possible pairings of Patryk and Rani or Rani and Jeff. Ty said he'd never seen any chemistry between Patryk and Rani, though he didn't know them that well. He'd never met Jeff and hadn't known the name of the person who ran the Immigration Rights Center.

"Anything you can tell me about Rani or Patryk that I might not know?" I said.

"Something hit me as we were walking to Janelle's." Ty moved aside a couple cereal boxes on a middle shelf. Behind them was a bag of Doritos held closed by a binder clip. "But it's not about Patryk. Aidan came to me a couple months ago for advice. Said he was getting the feeling Rani had a crush on him, and for him it was a friendship."

"No one mentioned that. Including Aidan." Distracted, I let the flashlight beam slip too low. I lifted it. "Why'd he want your advice?"

If true, Aidan's concern raised so many questions, including whether he'd ever gotten involved with Rani and whether he'd thought Ty might be seeing Rani and was trying to confirm it.

Ty pulled out a stack of paper plates and some Styrofoam cups and set them on the counter. "Said he was worried if Rani told him how she felt and he rejected her, it would hurt her feelings."

"That seems like a lot of forethought for something that might never happen," I said.

"Yeah, that was my first thought too. But he said they were good friends and he didn't want things to get awkward."

"And he asked you because...?"

"He didn't want to ask Shanda. He said that might be awkward and hurt their working relationship."

A lot of worrying about awkwardness. If I were cast in the role of someone like Aidan in a play I'd construct a backstory for the character that included some time when innocent actions had been misconstrued and damaged a relationship.

Ty found a small covered wicker basket in the cabinet. "My girlfriend's tea. She's Starbucks' best customer for coffee, but she liked herbal tea at night." He put the basket on the counter and returned the plates and cups to the cabinet. "Ex-girlfriend. We broke up."

"But why ask you?" I said. "Aidan, I mean. Why not ask one of Rani's friends?"

"Maybe he doesn't know any of her friends."

As I lifted the cover from the basket, Ty's comment about his personal life hit me. Mentioning the ex and the break up when it had nothing to do with anything suggested he was still reeling from it. Or there was some reason he wanted to bring it to my attention. "Were you seeing each other long? You and your girlfriend?"

"Two years. I had no idea she was unhappy. Thought things were going great." His arms dropped to dangle at his sides and his shoulders drooped. "Kind of hard with Christmas coming."

"It must be," I said.

If Ty were hiding that he'd had a relationship with Rani, he was going to a lot of trouble to do it, inventing an ex who left her tea. But he might do that if he also had something to do with Rani's disappearance.

The wicker basket held a plastic bear full of honey and a cardboard Bigelow tea sampler box. Five tea bags were left, all peppermint. Apparently those had been the girlfriend's least favorite.

Ty dropped a teabag in the thermos, then stared down at it. "Oh. No way to heat it."

"We can steep it in cool water like iced tea," I said. "Not ideal, but it's something other than diet soda."

He filled the thermos from a plastic bottle of water from the fridge.

"Do you think Rani might have a crush on Aidan?" I said.

I didn't like the word "crush." It sounded like a grade-schooler's, not a young woman's, feelings, but I wanted to use his word. He and Aiden, both in their mid or late thirties, might see a college student's feelings that way, but it wasn't like Rani was twelve.

"Ah, not sure. They sit together at Save The Parks meetings if he happens to attend, which isn't very often, but that's all I've seen."

I dropped a second teabag into the thermos. "So what did you tell Aidan?"

"To talk to her. They'll be working together for a while, at least until Rani finishes school. Better to clear the air."

"Kind of a tough conversation," I said. "Do you say, by the way, I think you have a crush on me and I just want you to know I'm not interested?"

At the large law firm where I worked before opening my own practice, a male lawyer down the hall from me had exactly that happen. A newer woman lawyer he worked with sensed he might be interested and told him she didn't date people she worked with. Her preemptive rejection offended him, and he did his best to be sure she wasn't staffed on any case he handled after that. It was a big place and she got plenty of other work, so it didn't hurt her career and she didn't complain. But it caused me to rethink my view that it's always better to be upfront with people and confront situations head on.

"Yeah, there's no great way to phrase that. But if they're really friends, he ought to be able to find it." He turned back to the cabinet. "I feel like we ought to bring food. Cookies? I might have cookies."

"It couldn't hurt," I said. Carole's bringing me scones and hot cocoa at the café hadn't always registered during the first weeks after Marco's death, but being there was the one place I'd felt safe, and that had been part of it. "Do you know if Aidan ever said anything to Rani?"

Ty found an unopened bag of Pepperidge Farm Milano cookies and some cheese and cracker packets. "I asked. He just thanked me for the advice and said it had all worked out fine."

20

———

December 13, 9:25 p.m.

"How are you doing?" Ty shone his light on the floor in front of us, illuminating the worn tiles of River Road. "You seemed really shook when we found Patryk's body. Not that anyone wouldn't be."

"It was awful. I feel terrible for him. And Janelle," I said. "And it took me back. I found my boyfriend's dead body last spring. In his apartment."

The words came out easily though I rarely told strangers about Marco. Something about the dark, quiet indoor road made me feel more comfortable talking.

Ty's flashlight beam dropped, creating a small circle of light on the tile between us. We both stopped walking. "I'm sorry," he said. "And here I was talking about a bad breakup."

"You didn't know."

"Were you together long?" he said.

"Not long," I said. "But it felt like I'd known him forever. It felt like — we were about to move in together."

"And now it's the holidays," Ty said.

"Yes."

We started walking again.

"Do you have holiday plans?" Ty said. "Sorry. I shouldn't ask. Everyone asks me that, and it's driving me crazy, and I'm not dealing with nearly as difficult a time as you."

"I don't," I said. "Did you figure out what you're doing?"

We'd reached the stairwell. He opened the door. "We were supposed to go to Maui. The two of us. So I'm going anyway."

"Really?" I said. "Won't you feel sad going alone?"

"I'll feel sad here, too. I'd rather feel sad in the sunshine by the ocean."

As we exited the stairwell, the air grew colder, probably from the emergency door in the lobby opening and shutting.

"If you had to guess where Rani is what would you say?" I said.

"I've thought about it but really, no idea."

"But if you had to guess? No matter how out there it seems," I said.

It was a line I often used when interviewing employees of clients. It helped them feel safe saying something they felt intuitively but had no evidence for. Or that they suspected their employer wouldn't want them to say.

Ty stopped walking. A glow came from the windows of the management office ahead of us. Voices murmured behind the closed door, but I couldn't distinguish any words.

"Rani's got a big heart," Ty said. "You don't have to know her well to see that. Somehow, some way, I think that got her into trouble."

～

December 13, 9:36 p.m.

Janelle sat at the main desk in the management office. Candles burning around her lit the area. She wrapped her hands around the cold thermos of peppermint tea as if it could warm her, but she didn't drink any. "No one would want to hurt Patryk."

It's normal to believe no one would hurt someone you love. And most of the time, for most of us, it's true.

I sat kitty-corner from her on a rolling office chair. "But if someone did?"

"He always says people are what matters. That if you can't run your business without treating people well, you shouldn't be in business. He's such a good man. Was. I didn't deserve him."

"Why do you say that?" I said.

I'd learned the hard way from my first boyfriend that if someone says he doesn't deserve you, you should listen.

"It was probably random," Debbie said before Janelle could answer. She stood in the open doorway to a connected inner office. "That homeless man demanded money, Patryk said no, and they had a fight."

"We don't know that," I said.

Janelle banged the thermos down on the desk. "I should've insisted management deal with that man. Maybe Patryk would still be here."

"You contacted management about him?" I said.

"Yes. After I saw him, and I complained when I heard he was still around." The candlelight gave her skin, which was pale, a warm glow at odds with the way her lips twisted. "I crossed the parking lot to the back entrance and he came out of nowhere, yelling at me, demanding money. If he hadn't been shouting I would have given him something, but he made me nervous. No one else was around. So I ran inside and into the grocery store."

"Did he follow you?" Carole said. She'd pulled her chair next to Janelle. Ty stood near the door to the lobby. We'd shut it behind us to keep the wind out.

Janelle shook her head, her blond curls bouncing. "No."

"Have you talked to anyone else who saw him?" I said.

"One of the business security guards mentioned seeing him. The young black woman. I forgot her name."

"Novia?" Carole said.

"Yes. She said she'd seen him. Said the management was debating locking that back door earlier at night since he seemed to hang around there."

I made a note to call Novia. She might still be awake and could tell us more about the man.

"Can you describe him?" I said.

"I didn't get a good look. Tall. Jeans. Trench coat and a red scarf around his neck. Another around his face."

I flipped pages until I found Eliza's description of the man. On the margins I added what Janelle had said. "Gloves?"

"Probably. And a hat. The kind with ear flaps."

"What about his voice?"

"It was hoarse. Like he'd just gotten over a sore throat. Or was just getting one."

"Any idea about race or ethnicity?" I said.

She shook her head.

"Do you know Rani Singh?" I said. "She supposedly was trying to find him."

"I met her a couple times," Janelle said. "Probably she thinks she can help him."

I glanced up from the notepad. "Why do you say that?"

"Because I was thinking the same thing. Until now." She banged her hands on the desk. Her movement created a rush of air that blew out the pillar candle in the center of the desk. "Instead of running him off, I thought people ought to be giving him food or encouraging him to find shelter. But now — now all I can think is I wish someone had called the police and they locked him up."

"But you called the office to complain about him." I reached for the candle and relit it. The sharp scents of pine and sulfur mixed.

"I thought they should call one of the shelters to come get him."

I bit my lip, imagining Joe's reaction to that. He'd told me once that some people want you to collect homeless people like stray animals and cart them off somewhere out of the public eye. But I felt sure Janelle had only meant that she wished the management could find help for the man.

At least that's how she'd felt before Patryk's death. And however she felt now, I wasn't about to criticize her for it unless she were somehow involved in Rani's disappearance or Patryk's death.

"How often do you see Rani?" I said.

"Rani?" She ran her hand through the front of her hair, stopping when she hit a tangle. She yanked at the hair, wincing, and pulled her fingers all the way through to the ends. "I used to see her at Save The Parks meetings. Why?"

"Rani is missing," Carole said. "Quille's been helping us try to find her."

"Missing? I don't know how I could help." She stared at the flickering candle. "I stopped going to STP meetings five or six months ago. Patryk and I decided to split the organizations we were in together. Cover more ground separately. Maybe if I'd gone with him tonight — "

Her hand dropped on the desk again, nearly bumping the candle. I slid it further away. "Did Rani and Patryk know each other?"

"Maybe they met at the meetings." She slumped in the chair. "I don't know."

Ty rested a hand on Janelle's shoulder. "My apartment's not far. Do you want to rest there while you wait for the police?"

"All right." Her voice sounded flat, all the anger from moments before gone.

I set down my pen and pushed my notepad aside.

The day was almost over, and we had one person dead and no

idea where Rani was. I couldn't help feeling I was in over my head.

Whatever magic had happened, whatever combination of luck and skill and determination, that had made me able to find the truth about Marco didn't seem to be coming to anyone's rescue today.

21

———

December 13, 9:45 p.m.

"Did Janelle and Patryk have any marital problems?" I said.

"I don't know them that well," Carole said. She'd taken Janelle's place at the main desk.

Lauren and I sat opposite her, the long counter that held the office computers behind us. Debbie had sunk into a chair, her coat draped over the back of it, near the doorway to the inner office.

"Serious problems," she said.

"Such as?" I said.

Debbie spun her chair to face Lauren and me more directly. "She was considering leaving him. She'd been unhappy for a long time."

I turned to a new blank page. "When did she tell you that?"

"Mid-summer? Maybe. We were walking the path around the park and it was beautiful. Warm. Lots of kids running around."

The weather didn't narrow it down much. After our cold and rainy spring, the city hadn't grown warm until after July 4th. But it had stayed that way through early October.

"Had she met someone else?" I said.

Debbie leaned forward. The gold pendant she wore swung out from her chest. "Not that she said. But I thought she might've."

"Because?" I said.

"Just a feeling. Nothing concrete."

"And she didn't leave Patryk," Lauren said.

"No," Debbie said. "She told me later it would be too hard. They built their entire investment business together. Unwinding it would be almost impossible."

"Janelle said that?" I said.

"In so many words."

I wished I knew exactly what those words had been. Debbie might be reporting accurately or reading the tea leaves, but she'd never admit to the latter.

"Did she say anything else?" I said.

"That she came to the realization that Patryk was a good person, and she ought to focus on that and be grateful for what she had. I thought it was really strange. She did a complete 180 overnight."

The lawyer part of my brain, the part that proofreads everything twice and debates whether to use "allegedly" or "supposedly," appreciated that Debbie had referred to a 180 turn, not 360 as a lot of people say. If you turn 360 degrees, you end in the same spot you began.

But I had a feeling the 180 reference had drawn my attention away from something else, something that mattered.

"Did she seem happy after that?" I said.

"Not at all! She hardly smiled for weeks."

If she'd truly wanted to leave Patryk, or if she'd met someone else, that might be why Janelle had said she didn't deserve her husband. Or maybe she simply felt guilty. I'd had no reason to, but I'd felt guilty when Marco died. I still did. Some part of me believed I could've prevented it. If I'd asked more about what he was doing while I was holed up in my office juggling other people's taxes and lawsuits. Or spent more time with him in person during the week before he died.

All the same, however much sympathy I felt for Janelle, a woman who'd seriously considered getting a divorce and decided not to for financial reasons had a motive for murder. Just because the majority of violent crimes are committed by men doesn't mean that women never commit them. And Danielle always tells me that most crimes aren't that complicated. The obvious suspect is usually the one who did it, which put Janelle in the running.

Though I supposed the homeless man might also be obvious.

22

————

December 13, 9:51 p.m.

I felt relieved when Debbie said that Janelle might like a woman friend with her and scurried off to Ty's. If she hadn't, I'd have had to find some way to get rid of her for a while. I didn't know her well enough to trust her, and I wanted to talk again to Aidan. I asked Carole to think of a reason to get him to come to the lobby.

While I'd been at Ty's, Lauren had researched him, Ty, and Jeff Chang on her phone. She told us Ty and Jeff had work experience that fit their current positions. Ty had been an architect for five years, which Wikipedia said was an area of expertise many development firms want, before joining a large development firm in Milwaukee. He was now a principal in a smaller firm here in Chicago.

According to his LinkedIn profile and the Immigration Rights Center biography pages Jeff had majored in philosophy at Duke, then gone to Cornell for law school. He'd begun working in the non-profit world right away.

Both his and Ty's Facebook pages, as best I could see on Lauren's phone screen, looked carefully curated. Jeff's had

131

updates on immigration law issues and photos with his wife doing things like hiking, picnicking, or attending concerts in the park. Ty's were filled with striking shots of Chicago buildings and restaurants that served artistically-arranged plates of tiny bites of food garnished with everything from twigs to fog to sparkling lights.

The major development Rani had supposedly been against looked like it had failed for multiple reasons. Reading between the lines, those reasons included opposition from a major political donor whose real estate developer son had conflicting plans for the area. I couldn't tell how much neighbors' complaints had mattered, so I didn't know how likely it was that Ty would hold a grudge about them.

Aidan's background appeared to be more varied than that of the other two men. He had a B.S. from McGill, a prestigious university in Canada, with a major in physics. His time there probably accounted for why his pronunciation of "about" and similar words sounded slightly more like Joe's, who'd grown up in Minneapolis, than Lauren's, who'd lived in the northern suburbs of Chicago most of her life. He'd started an online travel agency about ten years ago. It catered to golfers and still existed, but he was no longer listed as a partner. For a couple years he'd run a pool and hot tub store in Florida, and then he'd moved to Chicago and started working for Shanda. On Facebook he posted now and then about his cat, a shaggy tabby named Chewbacca.

I called Shanda from the office with the door shut. Aidan had just left Shanda's apartment. I put the phone on speaker so Lauren and Carole could hear and asked if she thought he might be interested in Rani.

"I wish," Shanda said.

Lauren leaned toward the office phone. "So you'd be okay with that?"

"The age difference would bother me a little, but he'd be good for her. She's so flighty, and he's so focused and has a good work ethic."

Carole frowned. "I don't see this flightiness you keep speaking of. Rani is a lovely young woman, very responsible."

The difference in how Shanda and other people saw Rani might simply be about the difference between a critical older sister and friends. But it could also suggest Rani hid large parts of her life or personality from her friends or Shanda or both.

"Does Rani know you think Aidan would be good for her?" I said.

"I mentioned it once. She rolled her eyes at me."

So that wasn't the secret Rani was keeping from her sister, if there was one.

All the same, I'd ask Aidan about it.

December 13, 9:58 p.m.

Tapping my toe against the floor, I waited for Aidan at the security counter. Carole and Lauren were looking through the management office for employee contact information so we could call Novia and maybe other security guards to ask about the homeless man.

I'd lit enough candles on the counter so I'd be able to see well. When he arrived, Aidan held a paper bag of supplies I'd asked Carole to have him forage from Shanda's apartment and office. Looking at him head on, I realized I'd been remembering him wrong. I'd been thinking of Aidan as the grown-up high school athlete too aware of his good looks, but in doing so I'd edited his face, adding a strong chin that simply wasn't there.

He spread the contents of the bag on the counter to one side of the burning candles. He'd found more candles, matches, a lighter, batteries of various sizes, and two more flashlights.

"How long have you been working with Shanda?" I said.

I wanted to see if what he'd tell me would match what Lauren had learned. Though it occurred to me we'd relied mainly on his LinkedIn profile which he would have crafted himself, so he ought to say the same thing regardless whether it were true.

"A little over two years," Aidan said. "It's been amazing. I've learned so much."

"What did you do before that?" I said.

"I feel like I'm being interrogated." Aidan frowned and squared his shoulders.

"You are." I fitted a battery into a flashlight that had blinked out earlier. "Rani's missing, possibly hurt. It's important to ask anyone and everyone questions."

"You know her well?" he said. "Because I don't think she's mentioned you."

"Since when she first moved here," I said. "And Carole's like another mom to me. She's worried, so I'm worried."

More to the point, Carole was not like my mom, who struggled too much with her own mental health issues to have room to be concerned about me. It was something I'd finally understood through therapy during college, but that still disappointed me every time we talked. Or, more accurately, every time my mom talked and I listened and made appropriately supportive responses, an arrangement that was never reciprocal.

"Fine, I'll answer." Aidan's frown didn't fade. "Not sure how my work background matters, but I ran a travel company with my ex-wife."

Nothing online had indicated that Aidan had partnered with his wife at the time. Maybe she'd used her own name rather than adopting his when she'd gotten married, or at least used her own for business.

"Travel agencies are still a thing?" I said.

I hadn't gone on many trips other than long drives for singing jobs with The Harmoniums. It was hard to imagine using an agency if I did travel. Though I thought my Gram might use a travel agent.

He smiled at last, and it brightened his entire face. "Not the old school kind. But we aimed at a niche. Golfers, especially ones traveling alone. Helped them plan itineraries and choose restaurants and connected them with smaller group tours or individual tour guides. It worked."

"So why not stay in that business?"

"I wanted a new start. It's so much more exciting."

I wondered if the ex-wife had actually started the company and so had kept it. That often happened when law firms split. Everyone claimed to have been the one bringing in the business or who had gotten the big verdict or settlement though they'd been part of a larger team. It looked better on the resume or website bio.

I sat on one of the counter stools, both tired of standing and thinking Aidan might talk more if he didn't feel I was grilling him. "I'm a little surprised you got a job after having your own company. It'd be hard for me to go back to working for someone else."

When I'd been acting, I had basically been running a single-person business. I'd chosen accounting in college and later gone to law school because both professions lend themselves to working for yourself. I'd been a good employee when I'd been at other firms because I knew what I'd want when I hired people. But my long-term goal had always been to work for myself.

He nodded. "True, true, true. Working for someone else wasn't first on my list. I had another business in between, and I'd like to again, but I'm not yet sure what type. Working for Shanda I'm able to learn IT recruiting and finance and money management."

"But do you have credentials for those?" I said, as if I hadn't already researched him.

"I'm a quick study," he said.

"Ty Hudson mentioned that a while back you thought Rani might have feelings for you."

Aidan fiddled with one of the flashlights on the counter, but it didn't turn on. "Must be out of batteries. I did wonder that."

"And?" I opened a package of batteries and handed him one.

"I was wrong. When I mentioned it, she said she thought of me like a big brother." He shrugged. "Not usually what a guy loves to hear, but in this case it was good thing."

"Could she have said that to save face?" I said. "Guessing you weren't interested?"

"Anything's possible. But she seemed surprised I thought otherwise, so I don't think so."

"What made you think she might be interested?" I said.

"Rani's very demonstrative. Hugs everyone, puts her hand on your arm when you talk, that kind of thing. I didn't grow up that way."

Neither had I. I could understand how he might have misinterpreted.

My first boyfriend had come from a hugging family. His sister had hugged me the first time we met, and I'd found it strange. Later, it was the one thing from our relationship I was glad I took with me.

"How long ago did you talk to Rani about this?" I said.

Aidan glanced at the ceiling, as if looking for the answers there. "A while. Two months? Three months?"

Most people don't remember exact dates unless there's a significant reason for it, so his uncertainty weighed on the side of him telling the truth. At a trial or deposition, a witness who can immediately trot out names, dates, and places with no trouble is one who's spent a lot of time preparing those answers.

That's not unusual. All good attorneys prepare their witnesses, having them review documents and search their memories so they're ready to testify. But in day-to-day life most people don't sit down and review the facts of their lives in case anyone asks a question.

"So not recently enough for her be embarrassed or upset enough about it to take off?" I said.

"No, no, no, not at all."

"Did you know she volunteers at the Immigration Rights Center?" I said.

His eyebrows twitched upward. "Does she? I don't think she mentioned it."

"Shanda was surprised too."

"You've probably guessed Rani doesn't tell Shanda everything. I realize I'm being critical as I say this, but Shanda's very critical. It makes people hesitant to share about their lives."

Aidan didn't know Jeff Chang, and didn't remember Rani mentioning him or the supposedly homeless man.

"Do you think she might've talked to or tried to talk to him?" I said.

"Seems like something she would do. I hope nothing happened to her. At first I told myself Shanda was right and she just got distracted or lost track of time. But it's been so long now that I'm worried too."

23

____

December 13, 10:08 p.m.

I brought the extra candles into the office where Lauren and Carole worked with a single vanilla candle providing light. Normally that scent would help me relax. Now it barely registered.

Aidan followed behind me, as I hadn't thought of a good way to get rid of him.

"I think Lauren and I should go to Jeff Chang's apartment," I said.

"But I found Novia's number at last." Despite her success, Carole's shoulders sagged and her back hunched in the office desk chair. I had to remind myself she was nearly thirty years older than me. More to the point, she got up at four a.m. every day to open the café by five-thirty, as traders who lived in the neighborhood liked to stop by before they went to their offices. I didn't often think about it because she was so high energy whenever I saw her, but if I was tired Carole must be ready to drop from exhaustion.

"In your address book?" I said.

"No, I only had the number for the Office of the Building

listed for her. But she's in the white pages." Carole pushed a note with two phone numbers handwritten on it toward me. "Two Novia Joneses are. Both in Blue Island."

"White pages?" I glanced around, thinking of the old phone books that used to be kept under the checkout counter in the store where Gram works.

"Online," Carole said. "You must think like a middle-aged lady who remembers life before cell phones."

"Right." I ran my hand through my hair.

"Though I did nearly drain the battery power on my phone," Carole said.

Lauren pushed away from the counter. "Why don't Aidan and I go check on Janelle while you call Novia. I can use a break before we climb stairs to Jeff's."

It took me a second to realize this must be Lauren's way of distracting Aidan. With any luck and a little help from Lauren, who was good at maneuvering people, Aidan would stay at Ty's apartment or go somewhere, anywhere, else. I didn't want him shadowing us on the way to Jeff Chang's. In the meantime, we could try to learn more about the homeless man from Novia.

"Okay, but come back quickly," I said.

Lauren headed out, linking her arm with Aidan's and asking if he'd hold the flashlight.

I shut the door and dialed the office phone. My own phone battery was down to 10%.

A man answered at the first number, and he'd never heard of Novia Jones.

A woman answered at the second number.

"Novia?" I clicked the landline onto speaker so Carole could hear.

"She's not home. May I take a message?"

"My name's Quille Davis. I'm calling from River City," I said. I introduced Carole as a longtime building resident. "We're snowed in here, and I have a couple questions for Novia."

"River City?" The woman's voice squeaked on the "y" in city. "She isn't there?"

"No," I said. "She left early to get home before the storm got too bad."

"How early?"

"I'm not sure." I flipped pages on my notepad, trying to remember what time Lauren had arrived, as Novia had definitely been gone by then. "She was gone by about six or six-thirty."

A quick intake of breath came through the phone. "Hours ago."

"She didn't make it home?" Carole said.

"No."

"She could be stuck in traffic with a dead cell phone," Carole said, but she gripped my hand. Her fingers felt like ice.

"Or on the train," I said. "She mentioned taking the train home."

"I'll look for train alerts." Carole took out her phone.

The woman told us she was Novia's mother, Leslie Jones.

"I assumed she was coming home her usual time," Leslie said. "I was praying the roads would be clear by then."

"There were delays on the Rock Island line," Carole said.

The Rock Island Metra railroad line runs from downtown to the south suburbs.

"But over four hours?" Leslie said.

"The trains stopped running at four," Carole said.

The entrance to the LaSalle Street Metra station was only two blocks away, but it could be a treacherous walk. You need to climb a steep staircase, as the entryway is high above street level, or enter through the Chicago Board Options Exchange, which would have meant Novia crossing Congress Parkway. The six-lane street is divided by an island and leads into the city from the Eisenhower Expressway. Not the safest place to cross in the middle of a blizzard with low visibility.

"Let's figure out if she drove or tried the train first," I said. I glanced at Carole. "Do employees have assigned spots?"

If Novia had driven, that wasn't much better. If she'd left soon after Carole and I had talked to her she'd been on the road for nearly six hours. Surely if she'd pulled off somewhere for shelter she would've called home to let her mother know.

Carole shook her head. "No one does. But most employees park in the garage, not outside."

Leslie said Novia drove a five-year-old silver Dodge caravan. I searched for a photo online so I'd know what it looked like, though to me all SUVs look like other SUVs and all sedans like other sedans. I recognize Volvos because I drive Lauren's, but that's about it.

I promised to call Leslie back as soon as we knew anything.

"Novia's mother had a heart attack about six months ago," Carole told me after I hung up. "Novia was worried she might need to go into a nursing home, but she must have decided to move in with her and care for her."

Using the office phone again I called Shanda, who said she'd meet us at the garage, and then Lauren. Lauren said she, Aidan, and Debbie would join us to help search as well.

Janelle was asleep. Ty planned to stay with her while the rest of us looked for Novia.

~

December 13, 10:15 p.m.

Our footsteps sounded like a stampede in the otherwise silent stairwell. I led the way, shining a real flashlight in front of us. Lauren, at the rear, shone a flashlight as well. Between the two of us we had enough light for everyone to see.

We split up in teams so we could search more quickly. Only a couple people were still getting cell phone reception, so we agreed to meet in fifteen minutes at the indoor garage entrance after we checked our areas.

Aidan and I took the back section. We found two cars that might have been Novia's. One had a baby seat in the back, and Novia had no children. Another had a sticker for New Trier, a high school on Chicago's North Shore. Carole had told me Novia had lived in Blue Island all her life, so it seemed unlikely to be hers. All the same, we looked inside both vehicles and didn't see Novia or anything unusual.

We had just walked away from the second car when I heard muffled shouting.

We hurried toward the front of the garage.

"What's wrong?" Aidan called out.

Shanda answered, yelling that we should come to the east side.

After a moment to orient ourselves, we headed that way.

Novia lay on the ground, her braids sticking out, near the driver's door of a Dodge Caravan parked head in against a gray brick wall. The spaces next to it on either side were vacant.

I struggled to keep the flashlight beam steady as Lauren performed CPR. Unlike Patryk, there was no blood around Novia, but a red scarf hung loose around her neck.

Novia's face didn't look blue, but I didn't know if that was the way someone who'd been strangled would look.

Shanda half-sat, half-leaned against a black sedan. "It was around her neck. The scarf. Twice around her neck when we found her. She isn't — wasn't — breathing."

Aidan put his hand on her shoulder.

I stood on Aidan's other side, the backs of my thighs against the sedan. Time slowed in that way it does during emergencies and yet moved quickly at the same time. Lauren continued chest compressions. With the dim lighting, the wind screeching outside, and another dead body it was as if I'd plunged into one of my nightmares about finding Marco.

Lauren finally stopped. She sat back on her heels as Aidan took over.

Lauren's skin is fair anyway, and now her face looked almost alabaster in the glare of our flashlights. "It's no good. Her body was cool when we found her."

The garage normally was heated. While it was chilly with the power out, it wasn't freezing.

"This — this can't be an accident," Shanda said. "Not Patryk and Novia. Not both of them."

A door slammed behind us. I jumped.

"It's Carole." Lauren gripped my arm to steady me. "Coming from the stairwell.

Carole's steps clacked on the floor. "*Mon Dieu.*"

Debbie was right behind her.

"The police," she said.

"For all the good it will do. They still haven't come for Patryk." Lauren touched Aidan's back. "It's no use. She's not going to revive, and no one's coming to help."

Shanda rubbed her hands over her arms. "What if Rani's out there, lying somewhere? Like Novia. Like Patryk."

I straightened and took a deep breath. "We will find her. I promise you. We'll find her."

24

—————

December 13, 10:21 p.m.

I called the police from the office, sitting behind the main desk. Most of the cell phones were out of power, and none had reliable reception. Lauren's had the best, so we wanted to conserve the battery.

Shanda and Carole came into the office with me, and I put the office phone on speaker. Debbie, Ty, and Aidan had gone to Ty's to check on Janelle.

The dispatcher said it was still impossible to get through to River City.

"That's unacceptable," I said, bending over the speaker. "Two people have died and one is — two are dead. This is Chicago. You must have some way to get through. Snowmobiles, something. And personnel from other police stations."

"First responders are deployed throughout the Chicago area, ma'am. But downed power lines have created electrical hazards south and east of you." The dispatcher's words came out in a rush and sounded rote, as if she'd needed to repeat them many times tonight. "The Harrison Street Bridge cracked under the snow and ice, and there are multi-car pile ups and crashes on Lake Shore

Drive. If the river weren't frozen, we could approach by boat, but that's impossible."

"How long will it be?" Shanda said.

"Impossible to say."

"These deaths may not be accidents," I said. "Some people in the building have complained about a man, a stranger, lurking around who may be homeless. A glove like one he supposedly wore is on the floor near one of the bodies. And a red scarf is around the neck of Novia Jones, the woman we just found. The man wore a red scarf."

The dispatcher questioned us about how Novia looked. She didn't give an opinion on whether or not she'd likely been strangled.

"We'll do our best to get to you as quickly as possible. In the meantime, residents should shelter in place, keeping their doors locked."

Shanda had started typing on her phone toward the end of the conversation. After I hung up, she said, "News says it's a nightmare downtown and all over the South Loop. Whatever the city's been doing since 2011, it hasn't been preparing better for weather disasters. At least not enough."

"Once the police do get here," I said, "we'll have to tell them that Rani said she'd seen this homeless man, and she carried a glove that might have been his that looks like the one at the scene."

"And then they'll question her immigration status," Shanda said.

"It might also give them a good reason to find her. She's been gone so long I'm more worried about what's happened to her than her being deported. But the immigration issue is another reason to talk to Jeff Chang."

I rubbed the back of my neck. A wire of pain had shot up one side while I'd been talking to the dispatcher despite the Ibuprofen I'd taken earlier.

"But you're going to call Novia's mom?" Lauren said.

I nodded.

It was the police's job to tell her, but I'd promised to call her back. Also, as busy as they were, I couldn't leave it to a harried police person to do it. Especially when it sounded unlikely they'd get there in person.

25

———————

December 13, 10:30 p.m.

"What are you saying? What do you mean no one could revive her?" Leslie Jones said.

I paced the office, the phone cord trailing behind me as I spoke. I hadn't felt right calling about something so personal on speaker or with an audience, so Carole and Lauren had gone out to the security counter. Carole was writing a new email, using Lauren's phone, to let residents know about Novia's death and to avoid the indoor lot.

"I'm so sorry," I said for the second time. "We've called the police."

As if calling the police had made any difference.

"But what happened? How could this happen?" The pitch of her voice rose. "She was fine this afternoon. When she left for work."

"We don't know." I sank into a chair, my knees shaking, and it rolled sideways. I gripped the desk to stay stable.

"Where are the police?"

Though I explained twice about the weather hazards, Leslie

kept asking the same questions. I doubted she took in much of what I said.

I gave her the number of the First Precinct so she could call herself and had her repeat it to me to be sure she'd gotten it right. Something concrete to do seemed to help, as her breathing became less labored and less audible through the phone.

I took a breath. "There's another young woman missing from River City. It's part of why I came here, to try to help find her. I'm sorry to ask you questions at this awful time, but did Novia ever mention someone named Rani? Rani Singh."

Leslie cleared her throat. "Rani? I think Novia worked with her."

I let the chair roll forward and back an inch or so, finding the movement soothing. "Rani lives at River City, but she doesn't work here. She's a student."

"No, not as a security guard. At the Immigration Rights Center."

My feet flattened on the floor, stopping the chair. "The Immigration Rights Center? Novia worked there?"

"Volunteers. She did. Once a week."

Rani, Novia, Patryk. A connection between all three.

It seemed strange that Novia hadn't mentioned that, but Rani hadn't been missing very long when we'd talked to her. Maybe it hadn't seemed important.

I asked if Leslie knew what Novia did there. She said that Novia interviewed people who came to the Center so the lawyers could assess whether or not they could help.

"Did she talk about anyone else who worked there?" I said.

"The man who runs it. I forget his name."

"Jeff Chang?"

"Seems right."

"What did she say about him?" I wound long, heavy strands of my hair around my fingers.

"I don't know. She likes — liked — working with him. But

nothing else I can remember, not now." Her voice sounded squeezed, as if her whole throat had closed. "I can't think right now."

"I understand. I'm sorry." That word again, so meaningless yet I felt compelled to keep repeating it. "I'll try not to keep you too long, but does the name Patryk Kaja ring a bell?"

"No."

"Was Novia seeing anyone? Dating?"

"What's that got to do with anything? Why are you asking these things?"

I propped my elbows onto the desk and wrote notes with my right hand, keeping the phone crimped between my right ear and shoulder. My neck ached but I felt too tired to straighten my head. "I'm fishing. Struggling for some connection between her and Rani. Maybe they double-dated."

Or dated the same man, Patryk Kaja or Jeff Chang, but I couldn't say that to Novia's mother. Couldn't suggest her daughter might have been seeing a married man, especially when I had absolutely no evidence of that.

"Well, she wasn't. I wanted her to. She needed to get out. Not spend all her time working or volunteering or caring for an old lady. How was she ever going to get married again if she didn't? But she said no one interested her."

I underlined "married" on my notepad.

"Could she have been seeing someone and not told you?"

"I don't think so, no. I hounded her so much, too much probably, about finding someone, that I'm sure she would have said."

If Novia had been seeing a married man, I doubted she would have told her mother any more than Rani would have told Shanda. For that matter, they could have been seeing each other if you went with Lauren's idea. But for both of them it was a thin thread made up of a lot of guesswork.

I glanced at my notes in the flickering candlelight. "What happened to Novia's first husband?"

"They got married very young. Too young. She met him when I took her to Nigeria to visit family. He came here and they stayed together for four years, but it didn't work. Now he lives in California." Her voice choked up. "I must call him and tell him."

"I'm so sorry." The words had begun to sound like random nonsense syllables. I'd heard them so many times over the past year, and now I'd said them again and again. I felt more sympathy for people who'd had no idea what to say to me about Marco, even those who uttered the "God's will" claptrap that infuriated me. "Did Novia mention a homeless man around River City?"

"Homeless man? What? No. Is that who did this?"

"Some people, including the woman who's missing, saw a man around the building who they thought was homeless. There's no reason, though, to think he hurt Novia."

"But someone did. My daughter didn't simply drop dead."

I tended to agree, but it does happen that people have hidden heart defects or other issues.

"Did Novia have a red scarf?" I said.

"Red scarf? Maybe. She had a lot of scarves. Chicago's so cold."

"Did she go out much? Not necessarily on dates, but with friends or for fun?"

A sigh came through the line. "You really think all these questions may help you find the missing young woman?"

"Maybe. I hope so."

"All right. I don't want another mother to lose a daughter. But Novia rarely goes out. Now and then she leaves for work early to have lunch or coffee with someone."

Her voice cracked on the last word. I heard sobbing again through the phone line. I waited until she quieted. Another "I'm sorry" wouldn't help anything.

"The same person?" I said finally.

"I don't know. I don't think so. It's the only way she fits in any social life, I think. A home health worker comes here about five-thirty to spend most of the evening with me, so I'm not alone very long even if she leaves early. Once in a great while she goes somewhere on a Saturday evening."

"How often does she leave early?" I said.

"Once a week. Sometimes twice."

"And you don't know who she meets?"

"No. No idea. Different friends, I think."

Leslie said Novia went out with friends from high school on weekends the rare times she did.

I shut my eyes for a moment after we finished talking and put my throbbing head in my hands. Along with her loss, I wondered how Leslie would care for herself without her daughter. Whether she could pay for the health worker or had money for her own home. I realized I hadn't asked if she had other children or where Novia's father was.

Wind shook the building. I raised my head. Dwelling on the sadness wouldn't help find Rani. I needed to act.

I didn't need to review my notes to know whom to talk to next.

～

December 13, 10:36 p.m.

I've never hit a runner's high. Or so much as a runner's mid-point, from which I've concluded the human body was not meant to run long distances. The knee replacements two of my more active under-forty friends needed last year confirm that. But anywhere I go that's less than two miles away, I walk, assuming the temperature is at least fifteen degrees and the skies aren't pouring rain. It's my inexpensive, time-friendly way of fitting in exercise, and normally I welcome an excuse to climb stairs for the same reason.

Today, though, I'd already climbed over a dozen flights by flashlight, it was past the time I typically went to bed, and the day's events had left me on overload. The ache that had started at the base of my neck and crept up behind my eyes now threatened to morph into a thousand daggers eager to plunge into my brain.

Aidan and Lauren had returned from Ty's. Janelle had been asleep, Aidan said, so they'd let her be. He offered to climb again with me to go see Jeff Chang.

"I'd rather you stay here with Carole," I said. "Lauren can come with me."

Lauren opened and shut her mouth, clearly not thrilled with a twelve-flight climb in her high-heeled boots, but, I hoped, reading my mind that I didn't want anyone who might be involved in Rani's disappearance to be with me.

Carole, seeing where I was going, rested her hand on Aidan's arm. "I would so appreciate if you would stay with me. With Frery gone, I feel quite vulnerable."

I didn't believe this for a second. The lighting was too dim to read on Aidan's face whether he did, but he didn't object.

This time as we stepped into the stairwell, we paused and listened carefully, alert for any sign that anyone else might be inside.

Not hearing anything, we started up. Lauren led the way, holding one of the larger, clunkier flashlights from the stash on the security desk.

"Thanks a lot," Lauren said. "I did thirty minutes on the stair machine already this morning, I don't need this."

"It's good for our hearts," I said.

Our footsteps rang in the stairwell. The bouncing flashlight beam created flickering shadows that made me flinch.

We paused at the ninth floor landing and leaned against the concrete wall. I wasn't completely winded, but I welcomed a few minutes to catch my breath. Aside from our breathing, I didn't hear any signs anyone else was nearby.

"Did you decide about Christmas?" she said.

"Dinner with Marco's family before they head to Alaska. After that, I don't know."

Marco's brother lived there, and his ex-wife thought it would be good for their son and Marco's mother to do something completely different for Christmas.

"I thought you decided you ought to let those connections go," Lauren said.

"You suggested that," I said. We'd talked about it the last time Lauren had invited me over for dinner. "I want to stay in touch."

"You can't live in the past," Lauren said.

"Eric's not the past." Marco's son and I had become close while I'd been seeing Marco and more so after, as he was the one who'd convinced me to look into Marco's death. He was a great kid, just starting high school and struggling with the loss of his dad. I hoped we'd always stay friends.

"Just tell me you're not going to spend every holiday with Marco's family."

"It's enough to think about this one," I said.

"But you're not. Thinking about it. You've been telling me 'maybe' about Park City for a month. My mom's travel agent can probably still get you a ticket, but you've got to let her know. Like, as soon as we have power again."

I'm not a skier, but in another year I'd go. Sit by the fire, read a book, and sip hot cocoa or Earl Grey tea and enjoy the overflow of men who hover around Lauren.

"Let's keep going." I started up the next flight of stairs.

On the twelfth floor Lauren shone her flashlight on the numbers on each door as we followed the curve around the building.

We found 1240 and banged on the door. Three times.

"A minute," a voice from inside said.

26

December 13, 10:55 p.m.

"Who's there?" said what sounded like a man's tenor voice but could be a woman's alto.

Lauren angled the flashlight so it would illuminate our faces and we could be seen through the eyehole.

"Quille Davis," I said. "And this is Lauren Hughes. We're friends of Shanda Singh and Carole Ports. Carole tried to call earlier. I'm sorry for the late hour, but it's really important we talk with Jeff."

"Hold on."

I heard the voice saying something to someone else, though I couldn't make out the words.

A moment later Jeff Chang stepped out in his stocking feet, holding the door open a crack behind him. I clicked on my flashlight, too, to get a better look at him. He looked younger than in his photos, late thirties if that. He wore dark, narrow-legged sweat pants and a long-sleeved T-shirt. His kept his black hair short, almost in a crew cut. A tattoo of a series of vines wound up the back of his left hand and disappeared under his sleeve. The right, holding the door, had a tattoo of the scales of justice on the back just above the wrist.

"My cell phone's been out of juice for hours," he said.

"Did you get Carole's email before the power went out?" I said.

"Once I leave the office, I'm done. My wife and I ate dinner and watched the storm after the power went out."

It sounded like last Christmas Eve. Marco and I had made hot cocoa in the kitchen, turned off all the lights except the ones on the Christmas tree, and watched snow fall out the window. Not snow like today's, but beautiful, big flakes that drifted to the ground as if they had all the time in the world.

I studied Jeff as Lauren told him about Patryk's and Novia's deaths. His shoulders pulled back at the news and his spine straightened. In the dim light of the flashlight, though, I couldn't see his face well enough to tell if his expression, too, looked surprised.

"Patryk? Novia? Both?" he said.

"Yes, I'm sorry," I said. "Did you know them well?"

He put his hand against the wall. "But how? Why?"

We told him what little we knew.

"I can't believe it," he said.

"Do you know them both?" I said. He hadn't answered me the first time.

"Novia volunteers at the clinic. Once a week. Patryk gives — gave — talks every other month or so. Not sales. Information." He shook his head. "No one knows how it happened? What about the police?"

After we'd explained about the delays, I told him we'd like to look around the Immigration Rights Center.

"Now? Why? You can't think we're related to Novia's death. Or Patryk's."

"Rani Singh is missing," I said.

His head jerked back. "Rani...that's — she also volunteers at the clinic. Or she did."

"So you see why we think there might be some connection," I said.

"I don't know what it could be. But yes, let's go look."

"You said she did volunteer," I said. "She stopped?"

"Last week. Said she had too much on her plate. That school was really busy, and she was worried about finals."

"Are you and Rani close?" I said.

"Close? She's a great volunteer."

"But do you have a personal relationship?" I said.

"Personal?" His laugh echoed in the hallway, then cut off abruptly. "Sorry. Nothing's funny with people dead. But if you're suggesting an affair, something like that, no."

"Why is it funny?"

"It's not. It's just, me, in my stocking feet in the dark with strangers asking me about Rani. A college kid."

I wondered if he protested too much. It wasn't as if a man being interested in a younger woman who worked for him would be a novel event. "She can't be that much younger than you."

"I'm forty-five."

"Really," Lauren said.

"Curse of my genes. I've always looked ten years younger than I am."

"Most people would be happy about that," Lauren said.

"Not most lawyers. Not men anyway. When I started practicing I looked like I was twelve. Not easy to get taken seriously, believe me."

I wasn't sure why he thought it'd be easier for women who looked young. I guessed he'd never been called "sweetheart" by an older male lawyer or judge. On the other hand, law is still a pretty heavily white profession. Asian men probably also struggled with the entrenched stereotype of the old white guy lawyer being the one most experienced and knowledgeable and who was therefore the "safe" choice for a tough case.

"Still," I said. "An age difference doesn't prove you and Rani weren't involved."

"We weren't," he said. "I don't know that I can prove a negative, but we weren't. How long has she been missing?"

"Last anyone saw her was about six-thirty this morning," I said. "Shanda was already worried, but with Novia and Patryk dead it's hard not to think the worst."

"Let me get my keys."

He waved us in. We stood near the mirrored closet. Five or six candles were lit, all placed near a recliner by the window. A book sat on the end table next to it. Jeff's wife was nowhere to be seen, but the door across from the bathroom was part of the way shut, so I guessed she'd gone to bed.

After finding his keys, Jeff put on gym shoes and followed us out.

"Do you think it's strange Rani would miss an appointment with Carole?" Lauren asked as we headed down the stairs again by the light of her flashlight. I'd clicked mine off to save batteries.

"Very," Jeff said.

I overshot a stair and almost tumbled into Lauren. I grabbed the metal railing for support. It felt cold under my palm. "So she's reliable?"

"No question. She never misses a session or fails to follow up."

"And she's been volunteering how long?" I said.

"Over two years."

The difference between the views of everyone else we talked to about Rani and Shanda was becoming more and more striking.

"The Center wasn't open today when Carole and I passed by," I said as Lauren's flashlight started to flicker. "Did anyone come in?"

"We have three employees, and they all live outside the city. I didn't want any of them making the trek in, so I covered the morning, then closed early."

The flashlight went out as we reached the third floor, known as the Upper Level, and exited the stairwell. My flashlight cast a dim circle on the floor. The offices along the curving outer wall, the same ones Carole and I had checked out in the late afternoon, faded into the darkness.

Every ten or twelve steps Jeff flicked on his phone flashlight app to check a suite number.

"Any chance Rani might have gone to the Center despite it being closed?" I said.

"She still has a key. I don't remember if I collected it from her."

"Why wouldn't you?" Lauren said.

Jeff stopped in front of the glass door to the Immigration Rights Center. "I was hoping she'd change her mind. Come back. She's good with the clients."

"Is there anything dangerous in the Center?" Lauren said. "Where she could get hurt?"

"It's just an office." My flashlight beam flickered, casting his face in alternating light and dark. "But it'd be horrible if she's there and needs help and couldn't reach out for some reason."

~

December 13, 11:02 p.m.

The jingle of Jeff's keys filled the empty hallway. After opening the door he automatically reached around to flip the light switches. Nothing happened.

He gave a half laugh. "Habit."

My flashlight faded out. Lauren fished out a slender birthday candle and matches from her cardigan pocket.

The flickering light showed two offices with glass-paneled

walls to the right of the entrance. Each held two plain wood and metal desks much like the ones in Shanda's outer office. On first look there were few personal items in the offices. No computers or laptops, but the credenzas on the long walls between the desks held a LaserJet printer each. Each desk had a banker's lamp with a green shade.

"No laptops?" I said.

"These offices are for volunteers to do intakes or lawyers to have initial meetings," Jeff said. "They all bring their own laptops and hook into our system."

"And that's what Novia did here?" I said. 'Intakes?"

"Mostly. She also sometimes helped us with administrative things. Rani too."

Lauren drifted further down the hall and I followed.

"Did they ever work together?" I said.

"Our volunteer days are Tuesdays and Thursdays. They both worked Tuesdays, Rani noon to two and Novia one to three."

He told us there were two other non-lawyer volunteers who worked on Thursdays. Novia had been volunteering three years. So for at least two years, Rani and Novia had seen each other at least an hour a week when their shifts overlapped.

Beyond the two offices was a workroom. All four of us entered.

Lauren lit a second slim candle off hers and handed it to me. Two long tables filled the room. Papers and files, sometimes stacked two feet high, covered them. A small dishwasher, sink, microwave, and dorm-sized refrigerator lined the far wall.

Gripping one of the tables, I crouched down into the shadows. My candle wobbled. For a moment I was back in Marco's living room, about to step around the couch to look for him.

I tilted my head to peer under the table, expecting to find Rani dead on the floor.

____

27

December 13, 11:08 p.m.

I saw only cardboard boxes filled with more files and office supplies.

"Nothing." I let my breath out and pulled myself to my feet.

Jeff led us toward the reception area. Its glass walls faced the outdoor walkway above Wells Street that Carole and I had walked earlier.

Couches upholstered in durable dark fabric sat along and across from the windows. Jeff told us it served both as a waiting area and seating for when Patryk or other guest speakers spoke. The reception counter had room for three people to sit.

"That's my space." Jeff pointed to a half-enclosed cubicle beyond the reception counter. "I like to work in the middle of things, unless I'm meeting with a client, so I know what's going on and how people who come in are treated."

"Do you have lawyer volunteers, too?" I said.

"Yes. The community volunteers take basic information about what people need, and what a lawyer might need to know about their backgrounds. I meet people who've been screened already on Mondays and Wednesdays, a volunteer lawyer also comes in on Mondays and another on Fridays. Both are semi-retired. They mostly work from their own offices after the initial client meetings, but they can use our space if it's available."

Lauren and I stood near the reception counter, our candles casting a circle of light around it.

"Was Novia upset about anything lately that you noticed?" I said.

Jeff ran his hand over his hair as if to smooth it, though it was so short that it couldn't possibly get messy. "Not that I can think of. But we're so busy each day I don't spend a lot of time chatting. Every few months I buy donuts and coffee for everyone and we hang out, but last time I did that was months ago. There's so much need for our services these days."

"How long has Patryk been speaking here?" Lauren said as she headed for the closet behind the counter and peered inside. I couldn't see what she was doing, but rustling and clinking suggested she was pushing coats around to be sure no one had been hidden inside.

"Since we opened. So about ten years. He's always helpful. Gives great basic financial info. No sales pitch. Most of our clients aren't in — weren't in — his and Janelle's pool of potential clients."

"Which was what?" I said.

Joe works in the financial services industry and his clients usually have five to twenty million dollars in assets. A few at the bottom end are entrepreneurs or professionals who started with nothing and experienced great success. The others all come from well-to-do families that pass on and maintain their wealth generation after generation.

Jeff scratched his nose. "Last time I asked, I think he said around five hundred thousand to two million in investable assets. I'm guessing the under one million are mostly people with personal connections to him, sort of a favor."

I aspired to be in that range one day, and Shanda might very well already fall into it. I'd never be one of Joe's clients short of winning the lottery. Which I don't play.

Jeff said he'd never heard anyone, including Novia or Rani, mention the homeless man. He'd never seen anyone he thought might be homeless in River City or in the parking area or anywhere right nearby.

"Is Rani your client?" I said. "Or has she ever been?"

In normal circumstances, an attorney can't reveal what a client said. I wanted to be sure Rani wasn't a client before asking Jeff anything. That way if he had something to hide he couldn't claim out of nowhere that he'd been her lawyer to protect himself.

Jeff rested his elbows on the counter. "Rani? No. Why?"

"Then you can tell me if she ever said anything about problems with her student visa."

"No, nothing. Is there a problem?"

"If there is, is that something you'd do? Answer questions for staff or volunteers?"

The windows rattled and a cold draft hit me. I zipped my fleece to my neck and pulled the sleeves down over my hands, careful to keep the candle away from the fabric.

"If it's immigration, sure," Jeff said. "If it's complicated I might refer them somewhere if they can pay because we have limited resources. But a few questions or a basic matter, I'd definitely help. I can't pay the volunteers, obviously, but I do my best to do what I can for them. I wouldn't think Rani would go anywhere else, at least not without asking me first."

Lauren's back was to us. She'd moved in front of the window near the exit, watching the snow plummet toward the patio. "She might if she were embarrassed that she messed up."

"Maybe," Jeff said. "But I hope I never gave anyone the impression that I'd look down on them for making a mistake."

Lauren turned toward us. "What if she were afraid Shanda would hear about it?"

His head drew back. "I'd never tell Shanda — or anyone — if Rani asked me about something. If she were my client, that is."

"But you're telling us about whether or not she asked you about immigration status," Lauren said. "Why wouldn't you tell Shanda?"

"I don't have to keep confidential what someone doesn't say," he said. "But what's this about? Did Rani have a visa issue?"

"It's why Shanda and Carole are afraid of police involvement," I said. "Do you mind if I look through the desk Rani used?"

~

December 13, 11:13 p.m.

Jeff agreed I could search both offices, except for any cabinets with client files, which were confidential. I pulled on rubber gloves from the kitchen area.

Lauren and Jeff stayed in the reception area and called the other volunteers to ask if they'd heard anything from Rani or had ideas about where she might be.

My temples throbbed. I was skating on thin ice looking through desks Novia might have used. They would likely be part of a police investigation.

But Rani might have used them, too, and I couldn't wait for the police. Maybe if we'd found Novia sooner, we could have saved her. I wasn't about to make the same mistake with Rani.

In the back of the middle drawer in the desk Jeff had said Rani used most often I found a heavy brown envelope filled with ticket stubs, purchase confirmations, and paper programs. The earliest date was February of this year and the latest was from a few weeks ago. If the envelope was Rani's, I didn't know why she hadn't taken it when she'd quit, but maybe she'd forgotten about it.

I didn't want to take anything from the office, so I took the items out one-by-one, laying them out in order. Shining my phone flashlight app so they'd be visible, I took photos with Lauren's phone. I returned the items in the same order to the envelope and put it back in the desk.

A framed photo of Novia and her mother I hadn't noticed before stood on the credenza. The background showed trees with thick trunks and wide leaves along a river or canal. Novia and Leslie had their arms around one another's shoulders next to two heavy-framed mountain bikes. It must have been nice for both of them to have an activity they shared and to get along so well.

Gray threaded Leslie's black hair and eyebrows but, like Novia, she wore long bike shorts and a dark T-shirt, both with neon green stripes, and riding gloves. She'd been an active woman before her heart attack.

I found no other personal items. Jeff said he hadn't seen the envelope before and didn't know whose it was.

"What could cause Rani to lose her student visa?" I asked Jeff as we exited the Center.

A loud clank filled the dark hallway as Jeff flipped the key that shot the deadlock. "I don't buy this idea of Rani overstaying her visa. Student visa requirements are basic. Stay in school full time, don't work unless it's approved, on campus, and in your field, and you're good."

"Maybe she switched to part time," Lauren said.

"I don't know why she would. She knows that would invalidate her visa."

"Did she know?" I said. "Shanda makes it sound like Rani's a bit flighty."

Jeff pocketed his keys. "Rani told me she had a rough time her first year here. Didn't understand how to handle her money. Ironic given Shanda's non-profit to help immigrants with financial issues. But she got on track. And she knew what she had to do to keep the visa current."

We headed toward the front of the building, our candles

bobbing. Lauren's had burned down so that it had barely an inch left.

I ran my hand along the wall to my right as we walked. "Could Rani's volunteering have caused a problem with her visa?"

"We didn't pay her. It wasn't a job."

"So it wouldn't affect the visa?" I said.

"It wouldn't," Jeff said.

"Could she work for pay for her sister?" Lauren said.

"A job's a job so no."

I'd have to ask Shanda if she paid Rani for the newsletter photos. There'd be more irony if Shanda had invalidated Rani's visa while blaming her sister for being irresponsible. But she'd been working on the newsletter for years. I didn't know why it would pose a problem now. Politics had raised scrutiny of people's immigration status, but that had been the case for the last couple years. Nothing had changed in the last few months.

Escalators led from the Upper Level to the Lobby Level. We walked down single file, Jeff between Lauren and me. I held my candle out to the side so I didn't accidentally catch the back of his T-shirt on fire.

"Tell me again what Rani said when she quit," I said.

"That she had too much on her plate, and she'd come to the realization that to get everything done she had to drop something. I thought maybe she was getting behind in school or Shanda was giving her more work."

I paused, one hand still on the railing. "Are those the words she used? She came to the realization?"

When I was a kid, the two main reasons I was cast in a lot of roles had nothing to do with acting talent. First, I could and would follow directions. Second, I could memorize my lines. I was lucky in that it came to me fairly easily. Also running lines was one of the only activities other than singing that my mother summoned the energy to do with me, though I could do it alone in my head, too.

As a result, I'd developed a good ear for dialogue and, in real life, often remembered the exact words people used. It helps me in my law practice. I notice more easily than other lawyers when a witness's word choice changes. I can also remember what clients told me on one day and contradicted the next, making it easier to sort out the facts.

Exhaustion and stress must be messing with my mind, though, for while I felt sure I'd heard this phrase or something similar two or three times today I couldn't remember which people had said it.

"I'm pretty sure," Jeff said.

I filed it away in my mind, hoping my unconscious would provide an answer.

We started down again.

"Did anything happen at the clinic that might have caused Rani to leave?" I said.

"I want to say no," Jeff said. "But now that I think about it, I walked in on her and Novia the week before and there was this silence. Not like a natural lull in conversation but silence with a capital S. They were in the file room collating pages and not talking."

"Could they have just been focused on the work?" Lauren said as her candle fizzled out. I slowed, unnerved by the steps below Lauren fading into the shadows.

Jeff shook his head. "It was pretty mindless work. Another volunteer had run copies of manuals we hand out to clients but hadn't collated them. So they were putting them in order. The kind of thing that's sort of a mental break, where you usually take some time to chat."

We'd reached the Lobby Level and paused at the base of the escalator.

"Did you ask her about that when she quit?" I said.

"No, I didn't think about it then. But now that Novia's dead and Rani's missing I wish I had."

~

December 13, 11:34 p.m.

Lauren and I stood near the mailboxes to talk. She pulled her cardigan sleeves down over her hands. Carole had left tealight candles, which I'd lit from my birthday candle, in holders on the ledge people used for opening their packages.

The area was deserted, and at least in the candlelight the floor looked clear. No tracks of snow or ice to suggest anyone had come into the building recently.

After we'd assured him we'd be fine on our own, Jeff had left us to return to his apartment, saying we should knock on the door if we needed anything else no matter how late it was. Voices murmured inside the management office. Through its window, which overlooked the mailbox area, I saw Shanda and Carole sitting across from one another at the main desk. Shanda was on the phone. They had shut the door, probably to try to keep what heat remained inside.

"You think Rani and Novia really had a fight or disagreement?" Lauren said. "Jeff was going totally based on atmosphere."

"If he's telling the truth, those gut readings of a room or people are usually accurate," I said. A costume designer I know makes a solid side living as a psychic, and the only power she uses is paying attention to her instincts about people. "If he's telling the truth."

"Maybe Rani and Novia actually were seeing each other and they broke up," Lauren said.

"Maybe." I tapped my fingers on the ledge. It felt smooth and cold. "Or could be they were both seeing Jeff and figured it out."

"He is married," Lauren said. "And totally hot. If you don't mind skinny and bookish."

"But Patryk doesn't fit in either scenario. Not to mention we've got no evidence for any of it."

"If they were both seeing Patryk and figured it out that could definitely cause a fight," Lauren said. "Though they should be mad at him, not each other."

"It would tie the three of them together."

I rubbed my jaw on both sides. Part of the fun of the pre-migraine stage is my whole face hurts. I did my best to ignore the pain and focus. "Except there's no more support for that idea than that Rani and Novia were seeing each other. Jeff might have just walked in during a quiet moment. It's all speculation."

In a trial, you can't ask a witness to speculate or guess. Witnesses are required to testify to facts or educated opinions based on facts.

But story matters, too. Drawing connections between facts or highlighting them in a way that tells your client's story is often what wins the day. I felt I could fashion any number of stories putting together what we'd learned so far. I wasn't looking for something to convince a jury or an audience, though. I was looking for truth.

That's much harder.

28

December 13, 11:41 p.m.

While Lauren and I had been tracking down Jeff, Shanda and Carole had called as many of Rani's acquaintances, friends, and neighbors as possible from the office landlines, most for the second time that day.

"No answers?" I said.

Carole stood and stretched her arms over her head. "Answers, *oui*, to say they have not seen or heard from Rani today and have no idea where she might be. We also were scolded for calling so late. Though everyone understood when we explained why."

She asked Lauren to walk with her to the Women's Room.

I took Carole's seat across from Shanda, filled her in on our visit to the Immigration Rights Center, and told her about the envelope filled with mementos of events. I spoke fast, aware of the time slipping away.

The only one Shanda felt sure about was that Rani had gone to Ravinia, an outdoor music venue north of downtown Chicago. She didn't recall which concert, though.

The expensive seats at Ravinia are in a pavilion with a roof overhead. You can see and hear the performers even from the back row. But far more people buy lawn tickets. You listen through speakers and don't see the performers, but on a warm night it's perfect for a picnic. Some people bring blankets, soda, and chips. Others make it into an outdoor dinner party, setting up folding chairs and low tables, lighting candles, pouring wine into fancy glasses, and serving entire pre-cooked meals.

"She won tickets in a contest at school or something," Shanda said. "I asked because I was worried about her spending so much."

She didn't know who Rani had gone with. She assumed a friend from school.

I asked if Rani got paid for her work on the non-profit's newsletter. Shanda said no.

I also asked whether it was done in exchange for room and board or tuition. As part of my practice, I handle taxes for artists and actors. Under IRS rules on barter, if I paint a portrait for you and you fix my plumbing in exchange, that's taxable income to both of us though no dollars change hands. If it were the same for immigration rules and someone found out, maybe that had been the issue.

But Shanda said the work had nothing to do with tuition or Rani living with her. It started because Rani loved taking photos for fun and suggested Shanda could use some for the newsletter.

"Are you thinking the newsletter work caused the visa issue?" Shanda gripped her bottle of water so tight its center squeezed together and water started spurting from the top. She let go.

"Jeff said volunteer work should be fine," I said. "But what did Rani say about why she'd lost the visa?"

Shanda slumped in her chair. "She never told me. Carole did. Rani often confides in her what she won't tell me. Says a lot for me as a sister, doesn't it?"

～

December 13, 11:49 p.m.

My head pounded.

I needed peace and quiet if I hoped to stave off a migraine or sort through anything. Having learned from watching too many horror movies as a kid, rather than wander off alone, when Lauren and Carole returned I asked Carole to help me find somewhere quiet but not too far away to sit. I borrowed Lauren's phone because hers had the best reception. If I took Lauren herself, though, she'd want to help in the process and talk it through, and that isn't how my brain works. She understood and stayed in the office with Shanda.

Carole and I lit two small candles, each in a glass bowl holder, and walked up the frozen escalator, returning to the same level as the Immigration Rights Center. We sat on a set of three wide steps that led into a conference room. To my right the floor-to-ceiling glass wall showed the walkway above Wells Street. Snow piled several feet against the glass, making it feel as if we were in a half-built igloo.

Chill from the tiled stair I sat on seeped through my jeans into my thighs. I pulled out my thin knit gloves and put them on. They kept my fingers warm enough but allowed flexibility so I could still write on my notepad.

I'd brought a lukewarm can of Coke from the office refrigerator. I downed three more Ibuprofen — Vina had been nice enough to give me extras to take with me — and ate some vanilla wafers I'd found in a drawer. Carole sat in silence, her back resting against the closed conference room door, wrapped in her puffy down coat, which she'd been wise enough to bring with her. Her fuzzy round hat was pulled down over her ears.

The only sound was the wind rattling the glass. Outside snow flew sideways in a white blur. When the wind shifted, for a second it appeared to fly upward, then plummeted straight down.

I shut my eyes, imagined my head being pulled up from

above as if by an invisible string, and breathed in and out slowly and fully, picturing the Ibuprofen as cool blue gel coursing through my body to my brain. It was an exercise I'd learned from a chiropractor the year before.

When I opened my eyes again the pain in my head had dimmed to an ache.

"I wish we had talked with Novia longer this afternoon," Carole said. "*Peut-etre* she knew something more. And if she had gone to the parking lot earlier or later, she might still be alive."

I groped for reassuring words and could think of none. With two people dead and Rani missing, there simply weren't any. "Maybe. Maybe not." I wound my hair between my gloved fingers. "But we can't change it now. Better to focus on what we can do."

I tapped the photo icon on Lauren's phone and found the first of the ticket stubs, then handed the phone to Carole. "We found these in an envelope in a desk Rani used. Did Rani mention going to any of these places?"

The phone flashed a 20% battery warning.

Carole flipped quickly through the photos. "The Sox game perhaps."

"She's a baseball fan?"

"No, but she likes the one dollar hot dog nights. And tickets were plentiful this summer with the way they were playing."

"A cheap night out," I said.

"Yes."

"Do you know if Patryk was a baseball fan?" I said.

"Is there a man who is not?" Carole said.

Marco hadn't been. It was one of the things we'd bonded over.

"But you don't know for sure?" I said.

"I do not. You persist in thinking Rani was seeing Patryk?"

"I'm not persisting. I'm keeping it in mind as a possibility." I rubbed my hands together. The thin gloves weren't quite enough, but I'd left my mittens in Carole's apartment.

Carole shook her head. "I simply cannot see Rani and Patryk together. From my perspective he was a nice looking man, but to someone Rani's age *je suis sur* he would look quite old."

I didn't disagree. Some women I knew — including Lauren — were attracted to much older men, but Shanda had said Rani's boyfriends were mostly right around her age or younger.

Also, people tend to gossip and exaggerate if they sense a little spark between people. It doesn't take much for rumors of affairs to start. That no one jumped on the bandwagon any time I floated the idea suggested there had been no chemistry between Rani and Patryk.

Which brought me back to why there seemed to be so many connections between them.

"Anything else ring a bell?" I said. "In the photos?"

Carole scrolled to a Museum of Science and Industry ticket. "This exhibit. She mentioned liking that it included engineering schematics. And Ravinia—"

"What about Ravinia?" a woman said from behind us.

I twisted around, my pulse racing. The voice had sounded familiar, but I didn't recognize it, and it was impossible to see anything beyond our circle of candlelight.

Debbie Stillwell emerged from the shadows. She must have come from the interior hallway.

"You scared me," I said.

It was too dim to see Debbie's shoes, but they must have had soft soles or she'd been stepping very carefully.

"Sorry. I've been checking with neighbors for portable chargers, and I got two," Debbie said. "The first one ran out after charging my phone halfway. I'm convinced people are hoarding them. Chargers, not phones."

"You knocked on doors alone?" Carole said.

"Ty went with me after a neighbor came to sit with Janelle for a while. We also asked if anyone had seen Rani today. No luck. So what about Ravinia?"

"Carole and I were just talking about places Rani might have gone recently. I found some ticket stubs and other items that might have belonged to her," I said.

Lightning flickered outside, followed a couple seconds later by rolling thunder.

Debbie held out her hand. "Let's see."

Her lurking in the shadows made me uneasy. I was tempted to put the phone away, but she'd already overheard us talking. I handed it over.

Debbie sat next to me and flicked her thumb over the screen. "She definitely mentioned this Ravinia concert. I was surprised because I didn't know she liked classical music."

"Did she say who she went with?" I said.

"Herself," Debbie said. "She wanted to go, and she got a student rate on pavilion seats. She told me she was trying to take better advantage of everything Chicago had to offer. She felt like she'd been so immersed in school she'd been missing out."

"Weird that she saved them." Saving ticket stubs and programs made me think the events were dates or had some other sentimental meaning. I peered at the screen, squinting. "And this is for a lawn seat."

A line formed between Debbie's eyebrows. "Really? I'm sure she said pavilion, but maybe I'm wrong."

Or maybe the tickets weren't Rani's after all, but I didn't voice that to Debbie.

Debbie had no other information to share, and she said she'd come looking for us to tell us about the chargers. She'd left both at the office.

There was no reason she shouldn't have sought us out. Still I felt as if she'd snuck up on us and purposely eavesdropped. It made me uneasy.

29

———

December 14, 12:03 a.m.

Debbie walked with us back toward the office. She'd left her phone there charging. I asked her to add Lauren's and mine to the charger while Carole and I finished talking near the security counter.

"What did Rani tell you about her visa issue?" I said. It had been the next question on my mental list after showing Carole the ticket stubs, and I hadn't wanted to ask in front of Debbie.

Carole sank onto a counter stool. "Nothing."

"What?" I gritted my teeth. I'd done what, as an attorney, I was trained never to do. I'd assumed Rani had told Carole or Shanda or both, but no one had said that.

"Rani never spoke to me about the visa problem." Carole took off her hat and lay it on the counter, then fluffed her hair.

"How did you find out?"

"Shanda told me."

"She says you told her," I said.

"*Mais non.* We were speaking this morning when Rani missed her appointment. I said if it was too long we'd call the police, and she said there might be an immigration issue."

I pressed my lips together. A perfect way to delay police investigation into Rani's disappearance was to manufacture a visa issue. I'd more or less assumed — there was that word again — that Shanda wanted her sister found. But maybe she didn't. Or maybe someone else didn't and had so subtly planted the idea in Shanda's mind that she'd come to believe it.

While Carole went to get Shanda, I lit four more candles and spread them across the counter. In addition to the two in glass bowls and one flashlight beam, I made sure I'd be able to see everyone's faces.

Carole stood with her hands on her hips opposite Shanda, whose back was to the outside wall.

"You said Carole told you about Rani's visa issue," I said. "When did she do that?"

"This morning." Shanda's arms dangled at her sides and her chin drooped toward her chest. "Why?"

Carole opened her mouth, but I raised a hand to gesture her to hold off. "What did she say? Exactly?"

"That maybe we shouldn't call the police because there was a visa issue," Shanda said.

"*Non*," Carole said. "I said we should not call the police *if* there were any visa issue."

Shanda's chin lifted, and she crossed her arms. "You said because. I'm sure of it."

"If."

I pivoted toward Shanda. "Let's say Carole said 'because.' Why didn't you ask what she meant rather than assuming there was an issue Rani hadn't mentioned?"

"Oh. Because I saw a search on my laptop about visa problems. She used mine sometimes at night after I left the office or before I got in. Mine's newer. And faster."

In my exhausted state, I was more concerned than ever that I'd missed something. I ran through the standard questions I use for a deposition, borrowed from journalism: Who, What, When, Where, Why.

"What did you see on the screen?"

"A page of a forum for students on visas. She'd opened it to FAQs about what if you lost your student visa."

"When did you see that?" I said.

"About a week ago."

"Why didn't you ask Rani about it?"

"I didn't think much of it at the time. I figured she was helping a friend or something or researching for a paper. But when Carole said that about immigration...." Shanda shrugged.

"Does anyone else have access to your laptop?" I said. "Like Aidan?"

"He does, but he doesn't have my personal password. And I had a temp in that day to help organize my tax files for year end. But why would either search about student visas?"

I drummed my fingers on my thigh. "The temp, maybe for personal reasons. Aidan, maybe to make you think Rani had a visa problem."

"To make me think...because he knew something would happen to her? Because he'd do something to her?" Shanda unwound her hair from its bun and ran her hands through it. "That's crazy."

"We need to consider it," I said. "Where is he now?"

"He's down in the office. I asked him to stay there in case Rani calls."

I turned to Carole. "Assuming you said *if*, what made you raise the topic at all?"

"I heard Rani on her phone at the café saying something about not wanting to risk her student visa. I did not ask her about it, not wanting her to feel I was hovering or eavesdropping. But when we talked about her being missing, it crossed my mind that I ought to see if there were a problem. Shanda confirmed, or seemed to, that there was."

"How long ago was this phone call?" I said.

"A week or two ago perhaps," Carole said. "I meant to ask the next time I saw her if everything was all right, but she rushed in and out of the café, hurrying off to a study date."

The lobby area had grown colder. The tips of my fingers, despite the gloves, felt chilled. I put my hands in my jeans pockets. "If Rani is seeing someone she doesn't want to tell either of you about, is there a chance it could be Jeff Chang?"

"I do not see it," Carole said immediately.

Shanda rubbed her hands over her arms. "I can't believe Rani is seeing a married man."

"But if she were?"

She sighed. "Rani admired his work, he's attractive, and he certainly looks younger than Patryk. But I'm telling you, she wasn't having an affair."

~

December 14, 12:12 a.m.

I knocked on Eliza Driscoll's office door. When I'd last talked to her, both Patryk and Novia had been alive. If she'd stayed in the building as she'd mentioned she'd might, I wanted to know if she had anything to tell me about either of them. And I wanted to know where she'd been all evening. After all, she was the last to see Rani. And she was the only person who'd said Rani had met a man who appeared homeless or been carrying a striped glove.

After a second knock, I heard footsteps. Eliza asked who it was. After I identified myself her security system beeped and the door opened.

Instead of her blazer and skirt Eliza wore sweat pants and a long pullover sweatshirt that draped past her hips, probably items she kept in the office for when she worked late. A dark wool coat lay on her office couch as if it had been thrown over her while she'd been sleeping.

I apologized for disturbing her.

She gestured me toward her office. "Come in, come in. Have you learned something about little Rani?"

"She hasn't turned up," I said. "But could I ask a few more questions?"

"Of course. I want to help."

She lit two candles on her desk and offered me water from the cooler in the waiting area. It was room temperature, which now meant chilled. It tasted good. All I'd drunk over the last couple hours were a few swallows of Coke.

"Were Rani and Novia good friends?" I said.

"You woke me at one a.m. to ask that?"

"You didn't see the last email from Carole?"

"No. My phone ran out of power around eleven." She brushed wisps of hair away from her glasses. "Something else happened?"

"It's Novia."

"Novia? Something happened to little Novia?"

I drank more water. The remnants of aching behind my eyes began to fade. "I tried calling her, and her mother told me Novia never made it home. We looked in the garage for her car. She was lying outside it. Not breathing."

Eliza pressed her hand to her stomach. "You revived her, right? Tell me someone revived her."

"I'm sorry. It was too late."

"No. Oh, no." Eliza took off her glasses and rubbed the skin above her eyes and under her brows. "She's such a lovely person. So pleasant with everyone. How can this be happening?"

"I wish I knew," I said. "When the police get here—"

She whipped her glasses back on. "They're not here? We pay all these ridiculous Chicago taxes and they're not here?"

I explained what the dispatcher had told us and answered

Eliza's questions about the situation as best I could. When she became calmer, I asked again about Rani and Novia.

"I suppose they were friends. When the weather was nice sometimes I saw them in the park or sitting near the marina eating lunch together."

So Rani might be the person Novia left for work early to meet. That by itself didn't tell me much. It could be two friends spending time together, or it could fit Lauren's theory that the two were involved.

"Any chance they were seeing each other? Romantically?" I said.

"Romantically?" Eliza's forehead lowered. "I never saw any sign of that. Why would you think that?"

"A friend of Rani's suggested she had a secret relationship," I said.

"A lesbian one? She was divorced for heaven's sake. From a man."

I wasn't sure why Eliza thought having had a heterosexual relationship ruled out a same-sex one, but it didn't matter. Either way, she didn't think the two had been involved, which might or might not be because she had a blind spot about it.

"Did Novia ever mention the homeless man to you?" I said.

"Novia?" She removed her glasses again and cleaned the lenses on the hem of her sweatshirt. "Not that I can think of."

"You mentioned Rani and Shanda had some trouble getting along. I think you said normal sister-type things. Can you tell me more about that?"

Sometimes skipping around topics is a way to throw a witness off balance. The surprise of it can elicit the truth, or at least more of it than the witness means to share. But now it wasn't strategy on my part. I was just tired.

"This is crazy," Eliza said. "First you think Rani's a lesbian, now you think Shanda hurt her?"

"No, no." I put my hands up in a surrender gesture. "Remember, I don't know anyone here well except Carole. I'm asking questions other people raised. There's no sign of where Rani is or why no one's heard from her. I'm trying to imagine reasons why she might not contact Shanda."

Eliza rested her head in her hand for a moment. "I'm sorry. I didn't mean to bite your head off. But I don't see why you're involved."

"Carole's my friend," I said. "And I met Rani when she first came here, tried to help her get settled. And sometimes a stranger can see what others can't."

My reasons sounded inadequate to my own ears. The police ought to be investigating. Or a real private detective, the kind I hired when I couldn't locate a defendant or a witness or — in a pro bono case I got through Joe — my own client. But if the police couldn't reach us, neither could anyone else. I needed to do whatever I could to help.

"It's all so frightening," Eliza said.

"It is," I said. "Shanda and Rani?"

"The usual things."

"Give me some examples?" I said, not having much of a frame of reference.

Kendra and I had far from a usual relationship. Our age difference and the death of our middle sister before I'd been born hung over us. Kendra had never been mean to me when we were kids, but she hadn't exactly embraced me. She hadn't been the type of sister who taught me to draw or tie my shoes or who gave me advice about sex or college.

"Rani thinks Shanda's too anal about that newsletter," Eliza said. "Here little Rani is volunteering her time and taking these lovely photos, and the newsletter never even had photos before. But Shanda would look at them and say no, she didn't want so many views of the building taken from the marina or she wanted more aerial shots of the river or she wanted more with people in them. That's a big one. She always wants people shots, but Rani likes architecture and art and buildings."

I didn't think that was terribly unreasonable. Shanda's newsletter went to recent immigrants and she wanted to connect with them personally. While I liked photos of buildings and street scenes, lots of people preferred seeing shots of other people.

"Anything else?" I said. "However minor?"

"Well, Shanda went to bed so early Rani felt like she had to sneak around her own apartment. That's all."

"Did Rani ever say anything to you about overstaying her student visa?"

Too much time had passed to keep dancing around the topic. I had to hope Eliza would never raise the issue with anyone if we found Rani safe.

"What? No. She'd never let that happen. It was so important to her to stay here."

Eliza thought the idea of Rani being involved with Patryk or Ty unlikely. She said no to both. She couldn't think of any reason Rani wouldn't have told her about Ty in particular. And while she conceded that sometimes people got involved with a married person and didn't tell anyone, she said she couldn't see Rani with Patryk even had he been single. She cited not only the age difference but that the two had no particular chemistry.

"And you know those forbidden relationships," Eliza said. "Always a huge spark because both people are trying to suppress it. It adds to the excitement. I'm sure I would've sensed something."

It was a good point. "When did you see them together?"

"Every now and then when I went to Tenants Association meetings. Also, when Rani mentioned Patryk she never seemed particularly excited. Her eyes didn't light up. She didn't talk about him a lot."

"What about Jeff?" I said. I'd saved him for last because he was the only one Shanda admitted might be a possibility.

"Jeff Chang?" Eliza said. "From the Immigration Rights Center?"

I found it interesting that her mind went there immediately. Jeff's a common name.

"Yes."

Eliza frowned. "I don't think there was anything going on there."

"But you're not sure?" I said.

"No. No 'but.' He's too clean cut for Rani."

My hands dropped onto the chair arms. So far everyone agreed Jeff was too clean cut, but that applied to every man I'd met tonight. Patryk, Ty, Aidan. Maybe I was spinning my wheels looking for a romantic relationship, straining too hard to be fair to this homeless man, and doing it at Rani's expense.

Yet Eliza had hesitated.

"You said you don't 'think' there's anything going on. When I asked earlier about Aidan and about Patryk and Ty you rejected the ideas right away. What's different about Jeff?"

Eliza sighed. "She does talk about how much she admires him. The work he does. But there's no reason to think she's *interested* in him."

30

———

December 14, 12:25 a.m.

After Eliza confirmed she had nothing else to share about the glove or the supposedly homeless man, I tried to persuade her to go to Carole's apartment rather than staying in her office alone. She insisted she felt better there. I understood, or at least thought I did. Since Marco's death, I'd felt more comfortable in my office than at home. At the office, I felt like I had some control over what happened. In the rest of the world, I clearly didn't.

But this situation was different. There might be real physical danger in River City. Eliza was adamant, though.

I asked to use the phone in her spare office and called the number for Danielle's friend who did immigration law. It rang multiple times before she answered. I started by apologizing for calling so late.

On that point she wasn't too upset. Unlike me, she was a late night person and told me she often worked until midnight.

I told her what I knew and asked what would happen if Rani was no longer complying with the terms of her visa and whether her school would notify the authorities.

"You'd have to check the University policy, but my guess is they'd stay out of it. There's no incentive to get rid of paying students."

I leaned sideways, propping my head up with my right arm. "And when she finished school? Could she retroactively fix her visa status?"

"It'd be tough. Sometimes you can get a waiver if someone messed up accidentally, but these days you're more apt to be denied. And it takes twice as long. Plus she could be prosecuted for fraud."

"A pretty good reason for Rani to keep it to herself."

"Well, keeping it to herself makes it less likely ICE would hear about it. Like if some do-gooder reported her. But she'd still run into trouble when she graduated and tried to get work. And if she wants to work for the government, forget it."

I sank lower and rested my head on my arms, facing the phone. "Unless she worked for her sister."

"That's a big risk. Her sister could end up getting deported too if she did that."

"Could there be a situation where ICE thinks a person is working and she's a volunteer?"

"Like how?"

I explained about Rani taking photographs for Shanda's newsletter.

"I don't see it," Julie said. "If the sister's not paying her, either as a W2 employee or on a 1099, there's nothing to prompt an inquiry. And if she takes photos all the time anyway as a hobby and doesn't get paid for it, I don't see it raising any suspicions."

"Probably right," I said.

"Not my business," Julie said, "but shouldn't everyone be more concerned about finding her than her visa? You can't come back into the country if you're dead."

"You're right. But I'm wondering if — or maybe hoping — Rani took off to keep her sister from getting in trouble."

"If she overstayed the visa that doesn't hurt her sister as long as she hasn't hired her."

I asked Julie if she knew Jeff Chang. She'd sent some clients who couldn't afford to pay to the Center. I pushed, but she had nothing but good things to say about him.

~

December 14, 12:31 a.m.

After putting my thin knit gloves on again to warm my hands, I flipped through my notepad again. No sounds came from the office next to me. I guessed Eliza had fallen asleep.

The more I thought about it, the more I held out hope that Rani was alive and in hiding.

If the same person had killed Patryk and Novia, that person wasn't going to great lengths to hide the deaths. Patryk had been where we'd expected him to be, outside the ATM. And Novia lay next to her SUV. Whether Rani knew about the deaths or not, if she suspected someone was after her maybe she'd made the sensible choice to get away from the building.

That still didn't explain why she hadn't contacted Shanda, though. Or, if Shanda were part of the problem, at least Carole.

I drew one eye after another on a blank notepad page. I'd doodled eyes often in college when I'd felt trapped in dull, lengthy lectures after so many years of independent study in high school. In my mind I went over today's earliest conversations about Rani. Two things everyone agreed on were that she had a big heart and she loved taking photographs. One of those two things, or both, could hold the key to where she'd gone or what had happened to her.

When I'd first talked to Carole, her biggest worry had been Rani getting hurt taking pictures. I dialed the management office.

Carole picked up and put the phone on speaker. Shanda and Lauren were with her.

"Does Rani take photos for any organization other than the newsletter?" I said.

"Sometimes her photos appear on the Tenants Association site," Shanda said. "They love her photos of River City."

"How about Save The Parks?" I said.

"I don't belong," Shanda said. "Carole?"

"I also do not belong," Carole said. "The attitude there, it is a bit too anti-business for me."

The entire building creaked as a gust of wind hit it.

"I'd like to look at the websites for both. Look at photos Rani posted since we can't get into her iCloud site."

"My phone's got power and a signal," Lauren said. "You could use it to check. Not as good a view as a monitor or laptop, but the wireless is still out."

"Couldn't you create a hot spot?" Shanda said.

"I hate to use up Lauren's battery," I said. "We don't know how much juice that charger has left."

"I never switched to wireless at home," Carole said. "DSL should work."

"Let's try," I said, though the thought of climbing fifteen flights — again — held no appeal.

31

December 14, 12:41 a.m.

Lauren's boots, unlike Nancy Sinatra's, were not made for walking let alone stair climbing. She, Carole, and Shanda met me at Eliza's office, and Lauren decided to stay there. It made me feel better about Eliza's safety.

On the eighth floor landing Carole placed a hand against the wall and bent forward, breathing heavily. Once she caught her breath, she said, "This reminds me. Much as I intend to live quite long and so feel I'm barely in middle age, sixty-three is not thirty-three. I may stay in the apartment the rest of the night."

My own knees and upper thighs burned.

At least the climb paid off. The laptop computer in Carole's home office was connected to a separate keyboard. The screen showed two hours of battery power left, and her DSL line was fully functional.

"Now I find middle age a good thing. Low tech," she said.

"I have to agree," I said. "DSL plus your paper address book. Very helpful."

Carole found a pair of old tennis shoes that might fit Lauren, then dropped into the armchair next to the antique roll top desk and shut her eyes. Shanda drew a wooden chair near me so she could watch the screen over my shoulder. We'd lit a series of tealights and set them along the top of the desk. Their caramel scent was soothing. I struggled to keep my eyelids from drooping.

The Tenants Association website included photos from inside and outside River City. On the Community Concerns page, we found a photo that matched the way people had described the homeless man. A note underneath said he'd been seen around the building and asked residents to please give him information about local shelters and soup kitchens.

Shanda drew in her breath when she saw that his gloves had yellow stripes around the palms.

"You told me, but I didn't quite believe it," she said.

I nodded.

The man wore two scarves — one red and one dark gray — and a trench coat. Between them and the low brim of his hat, it was impossible to see his face. The photo looked like it had been taken from forty or fifty feet away and was slightly cockeyed. Also, the man had turned sideways as if he'd been trying to flee the photographer.

"Is it the same scarf?" Shanda said.

I zoomed in on the photo. The ends of the red scarf around Novia's neck had been fringed. The edges of this man's red scarf had been tucked under his coat. It was also hard to tell if that scarf was bright red like the one around Novia's neck or a duller shade.

Shanda ran her fingers through her hair, which still hung loose around her shoulders. "I feel almost relieved at more evidence this homeless man killed Novia and Patryk, which is terrible to say, but — "

Carole raised her head. "Better than believing someone we know did it?"

Shanda wrapped her arms around herself and shuddered. "Except if Rani crossed his path."

Despite that the glove could point to Rani, I didn't think so. We hadn't uncovered anything that looked remotely like a reason Rani would kill Patryk or so much as have a fight with him. Plus the scarf didn't connect to Rani.

"What are these for?" I pointed to a row of lockers stacked double-high behind the man. He stood slightly taller than them. I remembered the lockers from when Carole and I had toured the Marina Level, but I hadn't thought much about them.

"The drycleaner down the street picks up and drops off," Shanda said. "You get a code and leave your clothes in a locker. They're returned there after being cleaned."

I peered again at the man's clothing.

It made him appear bulky, but dark green cuffs peeped out from the trench coat arms, so he wore at least one layer under it. His shoulders looked broad, but that, too, could be the result of layers. And as anyone who's been horrified by a candid shot knows, photos can be deceiving. You can look svelte or double-chinned on the same day depending on the angle of the camera and the photographer's skill in posing you.

The lighting didn't seem bright enough for daytime, though there wouldn't be much in the way of outside light in that corridor. The lockers ran along an interior wall twenty or thirty yards from the health club on the Marina Level. No other people appeared in the photo. The offices beyond the lockers were dark. It made me think it had been taken late at night or early in the morning. Otherwise, I would have expected to see construction workers from the health club remodeling or people heading to the grocery store.

Unless it had been taken this morning, when everything had already started to shut down due to the blizzard warnings.

The Save The Parks website included photos of River Road, the marina, and the park in spring or summer with kids riding tricycles along the path. Rani had a credit at the bottom of that site. Some aerial photographs of the neighborhood looked like they'd been taken from the roof. A couple of those showed snow.

None of the captions included dates, but a few showed the Alta, the glass luxury high rise on the south side of Polk Street with a landscaped park behind it. "This wasn't finished until a year ago, so the photo's recent."

"Unless it's from a stock photo site on the Internet," Shanda said. "Before Rani moved here I sometimes used those, so maybe STP did too."

"I don't think so. These show the Alta in construction." I pointed to a photo series that started with a truck with what looked like a giant corkscrew winding into dirt. Later shots showed steel beams rising, workers adding drywall, and windows being hoisted on cranes and fitted into frames. "It would take a lot of time to hunt down stock photos of each phase of development."

"What difference does it make?" Shanda said.

In her chair, Carole's head drooped forward. I lowered my voice. "I'm trying to figure out where she takes them from. Maybe there's somewhere we haven't looked for her yet." I enlarged a photo of the elevated park behind the movie theater that anchored the Roosevelt Collection. I hovered the cursor near the bottom corner. "This one must have been taken through a window. There's a streak from cleaning."

I found several more photos where streaks, water droplets, or a faint reflection showed they'd been taken from a window.

"Could she have taken them from here?" Shanda said.

"She would have gone onto one of the balconies, I'd think," I said. Carole's and Frery's apartment featured a two-tier balcony that could be reached from the fifteenth or sixteenth floor connected by an outdoor spiral staircase. I stood and looked out the windows. "Anyway, Carole's view is due west over the river."

The office was the room that was the farthest south, so given the building's curve there was no way Rani could have taken photos of the Alta. It stood directly east of River City.

"It can't be from our apartment," Shanda said. "We look north. The view that new complex blocks."

"Did Rani have other friends with apartments on upper floors looking east?" I said.

"No one I can think of," Shanda said.

I thought back to the other homes I'd visited. "Doesn't Jeff Chang's apartment face east?"

32

December 14, 12:45 a.m.

Jeff hadn't mentioned Rani taking photos from his apartment, but I wasn't about to assume that meant it hadn't happened. He answered the door more quickly this time and let us in. I asked if Shanda and I could look at the views from all his windows to compare to the photos. Carole had roused herself to help us use her color printer so we could take the most important ones with. Then she'd said goodnight, though only after I encouraged her to. Her pale face and drooping eyelids made me concerned for her health if she pushed herself too much. She still needed to fly to Paris next week to be with Frery.

We set her security system before leaving. Carole gave me the codes and her spare key in case we needed to return to use her computer equipment.

With the snow still blowing outside and the neighborhood lights out we couldn't see anything from Jeff's living room. From how he described his view, though, it would be possible to see the Alta. But with the angle and the Paper Place lofts in the way it would take a contortionist to get the shots that Rani had.

I'd need to check with Lauren. Back when the building had

been condos, she might have shown apartments in the same position as Jeff's, and she could tell us whether she agreed with his assessment.

I asked Jeff if we could see the bedroom view as well, despite that we couldn't expect to actually "see" anything. I promised to be quiet so as not to disturb his wife.

Not in any way slow-witted, Jeff said, "You want to be sure I don't have Rani hidden somewhere in here."

"Better to rule it out," I said.

It was why Shanda and I had come together. I didn't want either of us knocking on doors alone.

"Fine." Jeff's tone was flat, but he opened each door, including the bathroom and closets, and showed us the bedroom.

His wife was half-awake. He told her he'd explain later why two women were traipsing through their home.

We didn't find Rani.

❧

December 14, 12:55 a.m.

Shanda, still hoping Rani might appear at home, wanted to return there. Jeff sighed, put on his gym shoes, and offered to help us out for the rest of the night. He said as long as we'd awakened him again he might as well. I thought that was very kind of him. And gracious considering we suspected him.

Either that or he wanted to keep tabs on our efforts.

After Jeff and I dropped Shanda off, we headed downstairs to Eliza Driscoll's office. I wanted to ask Lauren about places in the building from which Rani might have taken the photos. As a realtor, she'd probably looked out the windows and evaluated the views of more apartments than anyone who lived here.

I also needed to talk to Janelle. I hated disturbing someone absorbing such a terrible loss. But if Patryk, Novia, and Rani were linked in some way that related to the deaths, Janelle was the one person most likely to know it. Plus she'd seen the homeless man.

Lauren came to the door right away in her stocking feet, carrying her boots. Eliza still refused to come with us, but she promised to reengage her security system.

I handed Lauren the plain white tennis shoes with thick soles that Carole had found for her.

Her eyebrows rose and her lips twisted. "Seriously?" But she sat on the floor and put them on. "Almost fit. But you are forbidden from taking any photograph of me."

"No problem," I said. "No power."

"Mine's almost completely out too. We should stop at the office, see if there's anything left in that charger."

I handed her the printed photos. "Can you look while we walk?"

"Because?" Lauren said.

Jeff shone a flashlight on the pages as the three of us headed for the stairwell to walk up two flights to River Road.

"I'm trying to figure out which apartment they were taken from." My flashlight beam was weak and only illuminated a couple feet ahead of us, requiring all three of us to take the stairs slowly.

"Rani took them?" Lauren said. "Could be a lot of apartments. I'm guessing eleventh or twelfth floor at the lowest. East side obviously but toward the north. Also there are a couple conference rooms that look that way on Fifteen."

"Maybe you and Jeff could check those while I talk to Janelle."

It made me a little uneasy to suggest Lauren go somewhere alone with Jeff since we didn't know if he was involved in any of the incidents. But Lauren had proven the previous summer she could handle herself, plus I'd know he'd be with her, so I couldn't see him trying anything.

"Wish you'd known about those when we were at my apartment," Jeff said. "But what the hell. I can use more exercise."

"May as well use these lovely tennis shoes," Lauren said.

They walked me to Ty's apartment first.

I slipped the pepper spray into Lauren's hand before we said good-bye.

~

December 14, 1:06 a.m.

I stood in the doorway of Ty's bedroom, a wide pillar candle in my hand, scenting the air with cinnamon and apple. The spicy scent clogged my nose, and I set it on the dresser near the bed after moving some stacked papers aside. It threw a faint glow around the room, leaving the corners and far side of the room dark.

Janelle had curled in a ball under a comforter, clutching a pillow, her fists near her mouth. I watched for a moment, rolling my shoulders forward and back to release some muscle tension.

I wished I didn't need to wake her. I awoke most mornings in a similar position. At least lately I couldn't remember the dreams that made me feel the need to curl around myself as if to protect from some outside threat.

Janelle extended her legs and rolled onto her back. "What? Who's there?"

"Quille," I said. "Sorry to wake you."

She sat. "Is there news?"

"No, I'm sorry."

"Stupid." She sagged against the headboard. "What news could there be?"

"Can I get you anything? Water?"

For the first time I understood why people kept advising me how to handle the holidays or prodding me to do things like eat more. Offering even useless things feels better than doing nothing.

"No. I'm fine." She laughed, a high-pitched almost-shriek that trailed away. "Fine."

I sank onto a straight-backed wooden chair next to the dresser. "I'm so sorry to disturb you, and I wouldn't if it weren't important. Rani Singh is still missing. Since this morning."

Janelle rubbed her hands over her face as if washing it. "Rani? Did you ask about her before?"

"Yes. She was supposed to meet Carole Ports yesterday morning and didn't show. No one's heard from her since."

She looked at me. "You think it relates to Patryk's death."

"I hope not," I said. "But it might."

"Did she kill him?" Janelle said.

"What? No." My hands clutched my thighs right above the knees. "I don't think so. But maybe the same person was after them both. And Novia."

"Novia?"

It hadn't occurred to me that she might not know about Novia, but she'd been here asleep. There was no reason Ty would awaken her to tell her about another tragedy.

"The security guard. You didn't know? She was found dead outside her car. In the parking garage. Late last night."

"Novia....I thought Patryk, I thought it was some kind of accident. Or a fight with that homeless man."

"Can you think of any connection between Patryk, Novia, and Rani?"

"Connection?" She shook her head, sending her curls in all directions. In the dark, they looked like springs sticking out of her head.

"Did Patryk know Novia?"

"He chatted with everyone and anyone, and she was at the door, so he must have."

"Did he ever mention her?"

She wrapped her arms around her knees. "I don't think so."

"Or Rani?"

"I'm sure he did. We both knew her from Save The Parks and the Tenants Association."

"But do you remember anything particular he said about her?"

"No."

"Were you and Rani friends?"

"Acquaintances." She rubbed her eyes. "We nodded hello."

"Did you not like each other?" A kink had formed in the muscles between my shoulder and neck on the right, and I reached with my left hand to massage it. It didn't help much.

"Everyone likes Rani. Just like everyone liked Patryk."

I wondered if, by implication, she was saying everyone didn't like her. Or if she were linking the two, unconsciously if not consciously.

"What do you mean?"

"About Rani? You can't not like her. She's so enthused about everything she does. Shanda's non-profit. Photography. Save the Parks. The Tenants Association. I remember feeling that way when I was her age."

"And that changed?"

"How could it not? Nothing feels as new or exciting as when you're twenty."

At thirty-three, I wasn't sure I could comment much on aging yet. Gram, though, had a lot of things she got excited about despite how much loss and pain she'd had in her life. But maybe she'd been twice as enthusiastic in her youth.

Or maybe Janelle was talking about her marriage. Maybe Janelle, not Patryk, had found someone new. If that were so, it might fit with Patryk's death, but I didn't see how it fit with Novia's or with Rani being missing.

"And Patryk? Everyone liked him?" I said.

"Maybe I'm exaggerating." She rocked a little forward and back. "But he's so outgoing. A natural extrovert. Loves talking with people. Loved."

The way she said it made it sound like she envied him that. "And you're not?"

"No. I don't know if you can understand. Being a lawyer. But for some of us all the connecting, it gets exhausting. I can do it, sometimes enjoy it, for a while. Then I run out and I need quiet. Patryk worked the room. Not to acquire a client, but because he really liked seeing and talking with a lot of people."

"You're more one-on-one."

"Yes."

I understood better than she thought. A lot of lawyers and performers are introverts. It doesn't mean that we can't or won't get up and speak or act or sing on stage. Or enjoy it. As long as I've prepared, and prepared well, I love doing all those things. But I hit a point where it wears me out, just as Janelle described. It's part of why I keep my tax preparation practice. It's not about being in court or arguing or interacting. It's figures and numbers and papers. It's time alone calculating and reasoning and sorting. All of which I find calming.

Also, numbers are predictable.

I wanted to ask Janelle about the homeless man, but I needed to cover everything about Rani first. "I know you said you don't know her that well, but I'm asking everyone. Do you know if there's anything Rani's been worried about lately?"

"Well, I'm sure that visa problem weighed on her."

33

———————

December 14, 1:11 a.m.

My mouth dropped open. "Visa problem?"

I'd become convinced Rani hadn't had one. And now Janelle knew about a visa issue where no one else did.

Janelle unbent her body and sat straight. Behind her, out the windows, snow pelted down. "Maybe I shouldn't have said. She overstayed her student visa and she's worried she might get deported. Or cause Shanda trouble over it."

"Rani told you that?"

Janelle toyed with the edge of the comforter. I wished there was enough light to clearly see her expression. "I think so. Or I overheard her telling someone."

"It doesn't seem like something she'd blurt out in the middle of a meeting," I said.

"Not in the middle. Probably before or after. When people chat."

I stood and paced at the side of the bed, staying within the small area of candlelight. The floorboards creaked under my feet. "But you don't specifically remember talking with her about it?"

The comforter rustled as Janelle drew it to her chest. "No. She might have told me or maybe someone else did."

I didn't quite buy that Rani was so worried she told random people but not anyone with whom she had a closer relationship. Or that Janelle didn't remember the conversation.

"Who do you think told you?"

"Maybe Shanda. If I see her at a meeting, I usually talk with her."

I paused mid-step. "How long have you known about the visa issue?"

Her hands, gripping the comforter already, tightened into fists. "No idea."

"More than a month ago?" I said. It's an old lawyer's trick. When people say they don't know when something happened, usually they mean they don't know an exact date. But they almost always know roughly when it happened if you ask the right questions.

"Not that long."

"More than a week?"

Her hands relaxed a bit. "Definitely."

"More than two weeks?" I said.

"Probably. Two or three weeks."

It likely hadn't been Shanda then. Assuming she was telling the truth, she'd only learned about a possible visa issue a week ago.

"Could it have been Patryk who told you?" I asked.

If it had been, it would suggest Rani and Patryk were so close she confided something she'd told no one else.

"Patryk? Why would he know?"

"Same way you say you might have. Overhearing at a meeting. Or talking to her."

"It wasn't Patryk. I can't remember ever talking with him about Rani."

That fit with what she'd said earlier, but I still needed to ask outright about whether Patryk might have been having an affair with Rani or anyone else. I squared my shoulders. "I understand you and Patryk were having some problems."

She looked down. "Every couple has problems."

Not exactly a denial.

"But not all serious enough to contemplate divorce," I said.

Her chin jutted out. "Who told you?"

Her answer suggested she'd told someone in addition to Debbie or she would have known who'd betrayed her confidence.

"I'd rather not say." I had no particular loyalty to Debbie, but if you want people to tell you things it's good to keep everyone's confidences. "I'm only asking in case Patryk's death is connected to Rani being missing."

"I don't see how it could be."

"What if Patryk and Rani were involved?" I said.

"Patryk and Rani?"

Janelle laughed again, that disturbing half-shriek. If she hadn't just suffered a loss I would have found it strange, but everyone reacts differently to grief. I'm sure the detective who interviewed me after I found Marco thought I was far too controlled and reserved for someone who'd suffered such a shock. That had been my way of dealing with it.

"Sounds like you think that's wrong," I said.

She wiped her eyes. "It is wrong. Patryk wasn't having an affair. And if he'd ever had one, it wouldn't have been with someone three decades younger. He felt too old for me, and we're only ten years apart."

"But you don't think he had an affair at all."

"He didn't." Her voice had grown quiet. "You're right. We talked about divorce. We decided to stay together. There was no affair — not him, not me — we'd just gotten into a rut. Couples go through it. They get past it. Except now we won't."

I wondered why she'd denied she'd had an affair when I hadn't asked. She might have guessed it would be my next question, but it might be on her mind because she had gotten involved with someone.

"Any thoughts on anyone who would want to hurt Patryk?" I said.

She rolled the edge of the comforter between her fingers. "I've been lying here thinking about that. All I can think is he confronted that homeless man. I told Patryk he made me nervous. I wish I'd never said anything. Maybe he confronted the man because of me."

"When you saw the man yourself, did you notice if the red scarf he wore had fringe on it?"

"Fringe?" Her fingers stilled as she thought. "No. I didn't see. He was in my face and I backed off as fast I could, ran into the building."

"There's a photo on the Tenants Association site that matches the description of the homeless man," I said. "Have you seen it?"

"Yes, I showed it to Patryk."

So the photo had been there for a while. "Any chance you know who took it?"

"Rani did," Ty Hudson said. "She took all the photos for the site."

I twisted around and saw him in the doorway, though it was so dark I wouldn't have recognized him without having heard his voice. It struck me again how tall he was. I tried to imagine him with a couple layers of clothing on. He could easily be the homeless man if he dressed that way.

Maybe we weren't looking for a homeless man at all.

34

December 14, 1:17 a.m.

When I'd been trying to find out what happened to Marco, I'd disguised myself a few times, using wigs and make up and varying my clothes. I'd also used my skills from my stage acting days to vary my mannerisms and my overall look. Someone dressing as a homeless man wouldn't need to go that far. In the photos, the scarves and hat obscured the man's face and layers of clothes hid his frame. I hadn't been able to see his facial features or skin tone.

Carole had said the lockers were about three feet tall each, and they were stacked two high. Ty was the only man I'd met in the last twenty-four hours that tall, though Jeff might be close.

But if the "homeless man" was Ty, I couldn't see why.

If his clashes with Rani over Save The Parks had been the screaming fights the neighbor described, Ty might have lashed out at Rani in anger and hurt or killed her. He seemed calm, polite, and personable, but that didn't rule out being abusive or having a bad temper. But that scenario didn't answer anything about Patryk or Novia.

I shifted the candle toward the middle of the dresser so I

could see him better and turned to Ty. "How do you know Rani took the photos?"

Ty folded his arms over his chest and leaned against the door-jamb. He wore a rumpled T-shirt that showed off his arm muscles and flannel pajama pants. "She mentioned it at a meeting a month or two back."

"Why?"

"I'd just been checking on the site and was telling Debbie Stillwell that the photos of the neighborhood were stunning. I asked if they'd been taken from our building. Rani heard us and said that she was the photographer for all the pictures on the site."

"Do you know where she took the aerial photos from?" I said.

"No idea," Ty said.

"She had a friend in management who let her take photos from a vacant upper floor apartment," Janelle said.

If true, Novia could have been the friend who let her take photos. She wasn't technically in management, but I guessed security guards had access to a key to each apartment in case a tenant lost theirs. In my condo building, the guards had access to spare keys for each unit.

Which would also give Debbie access if those keys were kept in the management office. While in theory no one in the office should let her take another tenant's keys, Debbie struck me as someone who could get what she wanted.

I swung back toward Janelle. "Rani told you that?"

"No." Janelle shifted position, stretching her legs under the comforter. "I heard her talking with someone else about the photographs and she said that."

"Talking with who?"

"I don't remember."

It seemed like something a person wouldn't want to advertise, as I was sure whoever had let Rani use a vacant apartment wasn't supposed to do that. The building management wouldn't want the liability. It also was something else Janelle knew about Rani while claiming to be barely acquainted with her.

I asked Janelle if she'd ever seen Novia and Rani together or the two of them with Patryk. She hadn't. She also told me she hadn't come to the holiday party the night before because Patryk usually went to the Tenants Association meetings and other River City and South Loop events. She went to events in the West Loop and River North.

She claimed she had stayed home and watched TV alone rather than go to the meeting.

The only theory I could think of that made Janelle responsible for Rani's disappearance and both deaths was that Patryk had been having affairs with both Novia and Rani, Janelle had found out, and she'd attacked all three. In that scenario, the homeless man had nothing to do with any of it other than perhaps Janelle had attempted to frame him.

It struck me as preposterous.

I doubted Patryk could have had two affairs without anyone I'd spoken to suspecting. Also, life might be stranger than fiction, but it generally wasn't a soap opera.

My only other theory didn't strike me as very likely either — that each incident was unrelated.

I perched on the straight back chair by the dresser again.

"Did the man who approached you seem familiar?" I asked, conscious of Ty hovering in the doorway.

Janelle propped a pillow behind her and shifted to face me. "I couldn't see his face."

"Could you tell if he was white? Black? Indian? Asian? Latino?"

She shook her head. "No."

"Are you sure it was a man?"

Eliza Driscoll was tall enough, and she had broad shoulders. Nothing said the disguise couldn't be hiding gender.

"Oh, yes, a man."

"How do you know?" I said.

She drew her legs toward her chest and wrapped her arms around her knees. "He sounded like a man. And the way he walked, it seemed like a man."

I pushed, but she couldn't expand on what she meant by that.

"Was the way he moved familiar? Or his voice?"

Janelle not seeing the man's face didn't mean she couldn't figure out who it was if she knew the person. I'd learned in Evidence class that most people have poor memories for faces. It's one of the reasons eyewitness identifications aren't that reliable despite how persuasive a lot of juries find them. I'd discovered the same thing as an actress. My facial expressions mattered. But body language, posture, clothes, hair, and mannerisms all mattered as much or more in building a character the audience believed.

"No, I — you know, actually, yes, he was a little familiar," Janelle said. "Now that I think of it, it's part of why I feel sure it was a man. But I can't say why. Maybe I'm imagining that he seemed familiar."

I wasn't so sure.

Someone planning a murder could do worse than to dress as a homeless person, make some appearances around the building, and then leave clues, like a distinctive glove and a red scarf, to tie the deaths to that person.

~

Decumber 14, 1:22 a.m.

"Where were you today before the Tenants Association party?" I asked Ty. We'd left Janelle in the bedroom so she could try to rest. Jeff and Lauren hadn't returned for me yet.

Ty sat in the leather armchair across from me, his feet on an ottoman. I sat on the sofa, back straight, hands on my knees. The pillar candle burned on the coffee table between us, making the living room smell like apple pie with a too sweet aftertaste.

"You're wondering if I killed Novia? Then snuck out of the party, followed Patryk, killed him and got back in time for people to see me?"

"It's possible."

I sipped Coke from the can he'd given me. I wished I drank coffee for the stronger caffeine buzz, though Ty wouldn't have any anyway, and I'd need to drink it cold, which turned my stomach. Hot coffee I at least understood for the warmth. Cold brew left me puzzled.

"No, it's not," he said. "But I can't blame you for asking. I just got back from a long weekend in Milwaukee."

He told me he'd taken an Amtrak train. It had arrived at 5:10 p.m. the day before rather than 1:30 because the blizzard had caused railroad switches to fail. His walk home had taken him about thirty minutes. Union Station, where his train would have gotten in, is a little over a mile from River City. I'm a fast walker and would usually make it in less than twenty minutes. But with the wind and snowdrifts it wouldn't surprise me that it would take half an hour.

He'd changed clothes and gone to the Tenants Association holiday party at about ten to six. While chatting with other early birds he'd helped set up the last of the tables. He'd also helped take them down and rearrange for the Save The Parks Meeting, which had started at seven.

"There's no way for me to check on whether you were on Amtrak." Almost against my will I leaned into the sofa's arm, resting my elbow on it.

"But the police can. You can tell them what I told you. They'll check to see if it matches."

If he was telling the truth, it pretty much ruled him out for Rani and Patryk.

"How many security guards work here?" I said.

Ty tapped one finger after another on his leg as he spoke. "Usually there are two on duty for each shift, and there must be at least three shifts. So two, four, six, eight? Maybe ten?"

That was a lot of people to have access to keys. I supposed it wouldn't help to have tenants' keys if the guards couldn't get them. I'd look around the office and see if I could figure out where the keys were and if any were missing.

I felt a stir of hope. Maybe Rani was in the building in an apartment. We could figure out which apartments were vacant and search them.

I tried not to think about why she wouldn't have gotten in touch if that were the case. First things first.

35

December 14, 1:37 a.m.

"I can't believe someone was letting Rani into vacant apartments." Lauren rubbed her hands together and breathed on her fingers before she returned to typing on her phone. She stood in the doorway between the main building office and the smaller windowless one connected to it. She was searching for apartments for rent in River City. "That's totally against any management company policy I've ever heard of."

"I'm sure it is," I said.

"So you think you can rule Ty out?" she said. "Because I think he's totally into you. And he seems nice, not shady like some developers."

I shone a flashlight along the counter against the back wall. Above it a large, flat metal box was bolted to the wall. It was padlocked shut. I hoped it held the tenants' spare keys.

"I get the impression he's his firm's wine-and-dine guy at least some of the time," I said. "That makes it his job to seem personable, not shady."

I fumbled with Debbie's key ring, grateful she'd never asked me for it back. She wasn't answering her cell phone, and her apartment was on the ninth floor.

My fingers felt stiff, as the entire building was getting cold. I found a couple small keys. The second one fit in the padlock. The small metal door swung open.

"That doesn't mean he doesn't really like you. Here's the numbers."

Lauren thrust a written list of apartments from the tenth floor up that she thought most likely to be vacant.

I took the list. "No, but he's a professional salesperson. Gram always told me if I find someone charming, ask myself why he's trying to charm me."

It was one of many warnings I got growing up. No one knew the details of how my middle sister had been taken, but police suggested the killer had managed to appear friendly and helpful and lured her out of the restaurant where she'd been at a birthday party.

I started collecting the keys for the nineteen apartments on the list from their labeled spots.

"Sounds like something your Gram would say," Lauren said. "But you admit you find him charming."

"I was quoting Gram."

No keys were missing, which almost disappointed me. I supposed Novia or Rani could have had copies made.

"But would you go out with him if he asked?" Lauren said.

"He's a suspect until the police rule him out." I put the last set of keys in my front jeans pocket.

"But if he weren't?"

I shut the cabinet door with a bang. "Let's just focus on Rani."

She drew back. "I'm focused, Ms. Cranky. It's after one in the morning. I've hiked up and down fifteen floors three times already and I'm about to do it again. What more do you want me to do?"

"Sorry," I said.

She touched my arm. "I'm just trying to help. You say you don't want to become like your mom, all withdrawn. Going out with someone new, being social, those are good things."

"We can talk about it later," I said.

Jeff and Ty waited for us at the security counter. Ty had asked a neighbor to stay with Janelle so he could help us. He'd changed into jeans and a turtleneck and put on a heavy leather jacket. Jeff had added a zippered sweatshirt over his long-sleeved T.

"Ready to climb?" Jeff said.

～

December 14, 1:53 a.m.

It would have been quicker to split up the apartments, but I didn't feel sure enough about Jeff or Ty. If one or the other were behind any of the deaths, they could be looking for Rani to harm her, not help her.

"We'll knock on doors of any that might be vacant and let ourselves in if there's no answer," I said as we reached the tenth floor.

"And if someone does answer?" Ty said.

"They'll probably be really mad we woke them up," Lauren said.

"We'll explain that Rani's missing and ask if they've seen her," I said.

Twenty minutes later we stood at the door to 1425, the last of the vacant apartments on that floor. All the apartments we'd checked so far had been empty, and we'd placed a red Post It note on each door so we'd know we'd checked.

We got no answer to our knock.

A door slammed from somewhere down the hall. I jumped.

"Who's there?" Lauren called out.

No one answered.

In the faint yellowish light from the flashlight Jeff held I found the right key and unlocked 1425.

When the door swung open a gust of icy air hit my face as Lauren and I entered. Jeff stepped around us and shone the flashlight beam around the room, stopping on the glass balcony door. It stood open a crack. Snow had blown in. A thin line of sparkling white trailed into slush and then to water.

Lauren and I grabbed each other's hands. Something on the floor near the door glinted in the faint light.

"Cell phone," Lauren said.

"Anyone know if Rani's is silver?" I said.

"I think yes," Jeff said. "But maybe only because I'm afraid it's hers."

"Thousands of phones are silver," Lauren said. "Hundreds of thousands."

"We need to see if she's out there," Ty said.

"I'll go," I said, though if she were the odds of her being alive were slight.

Jeff and Ty argued with me, but I convinced them I was the best one. From all my years on stage I was used to picking my way around microphone and electrical cords and staying on a defined path, which made me the one who'd be best able to check while disturbing as little as possible for when the police came.

Lauren gave me her phone so I could use it as a flashlight or if I needed to take photos.

Ty loaned me his leather jacket. It hung heavy on my shoulders. I pulled my hair back in my ponytail holder and tucked the ends under the coat collar, hoping that would keep it from whipping into my eyes.

I put on my knit gloves and stepped onto the balcony. Icy flakes hit my face and neck. I edged along the building's concrete wall. It was unlikely anyone would walk so close to it so I hoped I was less apt to trample evidence. Only a foot or so of snow piled at the balcony's north edge, a result of the wind blowing from the northeast. Snowdrifts reached the top bar of the balcony railing at the south side and sparkled whitish-blue in the phone's light.

At first I thought what I saw near the south edge might be shadows. I stepped closer, struggling to propel my legs through the heavy snow, and aimed the light at the far balcony corner.

What looked like dark sticks and twigs poked up through the snow.

36

December 14, 2:18 a.m.

My boots were nearly knee-high. Snow and ice got into them anyway as I plowed toward the large drift.

What had looked like twigs were thick, dark strands of hair stuck together. My leg muscles strained against the dense snow. My eyes blurred and my face stung as snow and ice hit me. Hair came loose and whipped into my cheeks.

When I reached the mound I brushed the snow aside as fast as I could.

A woman's face peered up at me, muscles frozen in place, eyes staring. I grabbed the railing, barely feeling the snow through my thin gloves as the balcony and the park below seemed to revolve. I squeezed my eyes shut and drew in a deep breath. Bitter air made my throat ache. When I opened my eyes again I forced myself to keep pushing snow aside. I couldn't help whoever this was, but we all needed to understand what was happening.

Death had robbed her face of color, so that her skin looked far paler than Rani's meant nothing. The black, straight hair was like Rani's but the face was wider at the cheekbones and the eyes larger and topped by perfectly arched and shaped dark eyebrows.

Debbie Stillwell.

A long gray scarf wound around her neck. It looked like one end had caught on the railing, but I couldn't push snow out of the way fast enough to tell before more blew over it. A story my Gram had told me flashed through my mind. Something about a famous dancer or actress whose long silk scarf caught in the rear wheel well of a convertible she was driving. The scarf tightened around her neck and she was dragged from the car into the street where she died.

There was a remote chance the wind had caught Debbie's scarf, wound it around the railing, and tightened it around her neck. But the odds of that series of freak events had to be close to zero. Far more likely someone had strangled her.

She wore no coat, suggesting she hadn't expected to be out on the balcony. I felt an urge to give her Ty's leather jacket, as if that could help her now.

With stiff, frozen fingers I yanked off one glove and worked Lauren's phone out of the jacket pocket with stiff, frozen fingers that ached from the cold. Afraid the photos I took would all be blurred because I was shaking, I took shot after shot, the snow flying in my face and ice crusting my eyelashes and lids.

At last I inched back toward the door, fanning out my legs and moving sideways and back so I'd hit anyone or anything else buried under the snow. My jeans and boots with their fleece liners kept my legs warm, though my toes had gone numb. The wind died down for a moment and the whole city fell silent, as if I were all alone in the world.

Fresh snow covered my tracks within seconds.

The others waited near the open door to the common area hallway.

I stumbled in, hugging the wall, and plunged toward them, almost falling as I reached the apartment's exit.

Lauren caught me in her arms.

"Not Rani," I said.

My knees no longer wanted to hold me up. I slid down against the wall and sat on the carpet. Not Rani, but Debbie. That she was gone and her friends and loved ones would suffer rather than Rani's didn't make it better.

Lauren and Ty brushed the snow and ice off me. Lauren helped me out of the jacket and into her cardigan, which felt warm and soft. I couldn't unbend my fingers. Jeff took off his zippered sweatshirt and wrapped it around my hands.

"I've got to get downstairs," he said. "Check on my wife. I can't believe I left her alone."

"Try calling her." Lauren held out her phone. "I've still got service."

"Won't help. Her phone died."

He took off at a half-run toward the stairwell.

"I don't think this was an attack by the homeless man," Ty said. "Or any kind of random attack. No one climbs fourteen flights and happens into a locked apartment."

I hadn't mentioned to him or Jeff the idea that someone might be posing as homeless. Otherwise, I agreed with him. An encounter with Patryk that got out of hand could have involved someone begging for money or trying to get into the building. If we stretched it perhaps the man, or woman, hid in the parking garage afterwards. Novia surprised him, he got scared or angry, and attacked her. But the idea that he'd climbed fourteen floors for no particular reason and happened on a vacant apartment where Debbie happened to be — it was too much.

Lauren, Ty, and I agreed we ought to check the phone that lay inside the apartment given how unlikely it was the police would arrive soon. Lauren donned my wet knit gloves, turned over the phone, and pressed different buttons. But it was out of power, and the screen had a diagonal crack across it.

We left it on the floor. There was nothing to be learned there about why Debbie had come to this apartment.

We huddled in the nearest elevator bank, blocked from the

atrium and far from any windows. Ty turned on a flashlight so we could see one another. Lauren kept one arm around my shoulders. I wished we had her heavy blue coat.

"Was the scarf like the gray one in the photo of the homeless man?" Lauren asked.

I rubbed my hands over my arms as I tried to envision the colors of the two scarves the man had wrapped around his face and neck. "It was light gray and long."

"Like scarves probably a million people are wearing all over the city," Ty said.

Given Chicago's nearly 2.75 million residents, I agreed.

"The dropped phone definitely means something," Lauren said. "Maybe Debbie was chased out there and dropped it."

"Or it slipped out of her pocket." I wound my hands deeper under the sweatshirt, closing them into fists to try to warm my chilled fingers. "With the noise from the wind she might not notice."

Ty rubbed the side of his chin. "If Debbie had no coat, she didn't go there planning to go outside on the balcony."

I nodded. "Maybe she figured out who the killer is and knew the person would be there."

"So she wanted to confront him?" Lauren said. "Totally not smart to do it alone."

"But it seems like something Debbie might do." I stamped my feet, hoping to get more feeling back in my toes. Also, now that my initial shock had passed, I felt like I couldn't stand still.

Ty frowned and shook his head. "I don't think so. She liked knowing everything that was going on, but she wasn't foolish enough to confront a possible killer just to get an inside scoop. More likely she asked too many questions when she was trying to help find Rani, and someone convinced her Rani might be here and ambushed her."

It made sense. Once here, Debbie might have gone out on the

balcony voluntarily thinking, as we had, that Rani might be out there. Especially if she arrived and found the balcony door open.

"And Debbie was there when Rani talked about taking pictures from vacant apartments," Ty said. "Which fits with her thinking this would be a good place to look for Rani."

"But how would she know which apartment?" Lauren said.

"Same way we did," I said. I turned toward Ty. "But if she knew Rani took photos from a vacant apartment why didn't she mention it to us?"

"She forgot?" Ty said. "I forgot until you were asking Janelle questions and it triggered the memory."

"But how did she get in?" Lauren said. "No keys were missing from the lockbox downstairs."

"She looks a little like Rani from the back," Ty said. "If she came here all on her own, maybe the killer mistook her for Rani."

Despite Debbie's tendency to get involved, it seemed unlikely she'd made copies of all the tenants' keys. Rani might have told her about the apartment and given her a key to it, but Debbie hardly would have forgotten that when Rani went missing. And her death likely ruled her out as the killer of anyone else. The odds of two killers had to be astronomical.

All of which made me feel sure the killer had lured her to the apartment. The killer had the key. And could be the man standing across from me or the one who'd just taken off to check on his wife.

"Mistaken identity?" Lauren said.

"If it is, it might mean Rani is still alive," Ty said. "But it also means someone's looking for her."

December 14, 2:35 a.m.

Lauren called 911 from her cell phone. The dispatcher sounded more alarmed at three deaths, but also more harried. Additional power lines had blown down, and a newly-built section of a bridge over Wells Street had collapsed, cutting off another route here from our police precinct.

While Lauren argued with the dispatcher, we knocked on doors of neighbors. Those few people who answered were ones who recognized Ty through the peephole. In addition to being angry and scared at being awakened after two a.m., they hadn't seen or heard anything. I wasn't surprised. Even if Debbie's death had happened earlier, with the power out and Carole's emails about the deaths I wouldn't expect anyone to be wandering the halls in the dark.

Ty walked us upstairs to Carole's door, then insisted he needed to go check on Janelle. We didn't want him to walk downstairs alone.

"I can take care of myself," he said. "There's no sign any weapons were used, and I was on the wrestling team in high school and college. I'll watch my back."

I wasn't convinced wrestling would help, though it did seem like each of these killings had involved the attacker getting very close to the victim. And short of blocking Ty's path, there was nothing we could do to stop him.

Inside, I hurried upstairs to Carole's bedroom. She lay asleep, breathing evenly. I watched for a few moments, the flashlight beam trained on the foot of the bed so as not to wake her. Relieved she was all right, I joined Lauren in Carole's office.

Lauren wanted to look at the photo of the homeless man again. Carole's laptop still had power, but it was down to fifty-eight minutes.

Wrapped in one of Carole's afghans but still shivering, I

watched as Lauren scrolled until she found the photo. She enlarged it. "Something doesn't seem right."

"I'm not sure he's homeless," I said.

"Oh, please. Look at the way he's dressed. He totally is."

We'd both been awake far too long and seen too much trauma for me to debate her about judging people by their appearance. "So what bothers you?"

"Can't put my finger on it. But something's off." She shook her head, her blond hair reflecting the light from the screen. "With what he's wearing."

That it had to do with clothes didn't surprise me. Lauren is my personal fashion maven, always pushing me to wear something other than my uniform of jeans, tank tops or T-shirts, and blazers. I alternate jeans with suits for court and a few dresses for going out, but mostly I stick with the program. After years of working in theater and constantly constructing my on stage and off stage image, I like being able to dress easily and quickly the same way that men do. Lauren ensures that at least my clothes are good quality and flatter my figure, and that when I do deviate from my norm I choose something stellar.

Mostly, though, she makes clear she finds my approach to dressing too boring for words.

"So you think he looks homeless, yet the clothes don't seem right for someone homeless?"

"No," she said. "I can't think who else would wear such a worn trench coat with layers under it when it's this cold out. And the double scarves."

I thrust my head forward to study the photo. "Can you tell his skin color?"

Huge sunglasses hid the man's eyes, and the lowered hat brim and earflaps hid the forehead and the sides of his face down to the scarves.

Lauren peered at the screen, leaning so close it almost touched her eyelashes. "No."

"I'm a little surprised he's that far inside the building," I said. "I'd think he'd be afraid a resident would call the police."

"He could just run off again," Lauren said. "It looks like that's what he's about to do."

She was right. He was turned partway, as if about to pivot and run away from the photographer.

I reached for the touchpad and manipulated the photo. Much as I tried, I couldn't see anything about his scarves that would tell us if they matched the ones around Novia's and Debbie's necks.

"He's wearing both scarves and his coat's buttoned all the way. He must have walked in to get warm and planned to leave again right away," Lauren said.

"I'm surprised he let Rani get that close. Unless he didn't see her."

"Yeah, even if she zoomed in Rani had to be nearby. Maybe she took him by surprise," Lauren said. She enlarged the photo again.

"Anything?" I said.

She shook her head. "It'll come to me."

37

December 14, 2:56 a.m.

Shanda unearthed a small, clunky black cylinder that looked like a cross between a thermos and a kettle from Carole's under-the-sink cabinet. It seemed more suited to camping than to Carole's elegant kitchen, but it was battery powered which was all that mattered.

We'd gone down the hall to get Shanda, persuading her that if Rani did return home and didn't find Shanda at their apartment, she'd try Carole's next.

Not that any of us really expected Rani to simply appear.

"I knew she had one of these." Shanda's hands shook as she ran water into the kettle. "And if ever I needed tea, it's now."

I retrieved the green glass canister set from the baker's rack alongside the stove, my own hands still unsteady.

Lauren had shut the blinds beyond the dining table to try to keep the room warmer. Its centerpiece had artificial daisies around a wide white candle with three wicks. It lit the entire table area. A row of tealight candles burned in a row above the sink.

While I poured four heaping teaspoons of Earl Grey tea into a diffuser, Lauren and I answered Shanda's questions about Debbie. Judging from the rattling glass and the periodic banging sounds from outside, the wind hadn't died down at all. All the same, we kept our voices low so as not to disturb Carole.

"Who saw Debbie last?" Shanda said.

Lauren opened a bottle of Dang! gourmet root beer and sat across from Shanda at the marble island between the kitchen and dining area.

"Probably me," Lauren said. "Other than whoever killed her. She came to the office to drop off two travel chargers she got from neighbors, then went to find Quille and Carole. Maybe five or ten minutes later she popped her head into the office, gave me my phone and Quille's to charge, and took off."

"She didn't say where she was going?" Shanda said.

"Something about checking on Janelle," Lauren said.

"But Ty swears she never got to his place," I said. "If Ty's telling the truth we think she detoured and started asking other people questions."

The kettle's lever popped, and I poured boiling water into a china teapot. Lavender and vanilla-scented steam rose, heating my face as I told Shanda how Debbie had surprised Carole and me by creeping out of the shadows.

"Too bad we don't know who she talked to next," Lauren said.

I flattened my hands on the counter. "What I told Debbie about the ticket stubs might have raised the questions that got her killed."

Lauren squeezed my hand. "You didn't tell her to go investigating. If she thought she had a clue to where Rani was, she ought to have told us."

I stared at the teapot, waiting for the water to steep long enough to bring out the flavor and, more important, the caffeine. "Debbie thought Rani had pavilion seats at Ravinia this summer, not lawn seats." I turned toward Shanda. "Do you remember which?"

"Pavilion," Shanda said. "I'm sure. I was worried about her spending so much, and she kept saying don't worry, she won the ticket and it was a great seat. Seventh row. Or maybe second."

I poured Shanda a cup of tea, then poured one for myself and joined them at the island. "Which suggests the lawn ticket was Novia's, not Rani's. So they didn't go together."

"Maybe someone was double-teaming," Lauren said.

"What?" Shanda said.

The tea had steeped too long, making it bitter. I hoped that meant the caffeine would head straight to my brain. I reached for the sugar.

"My last semester in college I was seeing two guys," Lauren said. I'd heard the story before over too many glasses of wine after the law school final that had caused Lauren to end her brief law school career. "Neither was serious. I knew I was moving to Chicago for law school in the fall. To keep it simple, I went the same places and saw the same movies with both. So I never had to worry about saying something like, 'oh, when we watched Field of Dreams last week' and have it be the wrong guy."

"But it doesn't fit if we're assuming they were seeing a married man." I added extra sugar to my tea. "How much time can one guy have?"

"Jeff's wife is a partner at Kirkland and Ellis," Shanda said, naming one of the largest law firms in Chicago.

One of the lawyers I'd worked with at my old firm had interviewed there when he'd still been in law school. He'd told me the new associates had raved about the on-site chef for the dinner program and how much they liked their coworkers, saying that was good because they were together from eight in the morning until ten at night.

If Jeff's wife worked there and he finished by six most nights, he probably had lots of free time. It didn't mean he'd been having an affair, but it didn't rule him out.

"If they were seeing the same man it could explain the

tension between them. Rani finds Novia's envelope, recognizes the events, and figures it out," I said.

"And Debbie guesses all of that from just the ticket stubs and starts asking questions?" Lauren said. "I guess it's possible."

"If she wanted to know more about Novia, she probably called Novia's mom," I said. "And Jeff."

Shanda turned her teaspoon over and over. It clinked on the marble counter.

"Whoever she talked to," Lauren said, "if it included someone who used to meet Rani in the apartment he'd have keys to it. He could tell Debbie some story about why they should go there."

I rubbed my forehead. "But what's the connection between Rani, Patryk, and Novia if Patryk's not the one seeing them both? Though Janelle says there's no way Patryk was having an affair."

Lauren drained the last of her root beer. The bottle clanked as she set it on the counter. "What else would Janelle say? It's not like when your husband dies you're going to say you totally suspected he was having an affair. It's like putting a flashing sign over your head that you're the one who killed him. Not to mention — denial."

"We don't know Rani was seeing anyone," Shanda said.

"They're all connected through the Immigration Rights Center," I said. "Which points to Jeff again."

"It could be Ty," Lauren said. "I've been thinking you might be right. It's his job to be smooth. Maybe he's hiding something."

Shanda pushed away from the counter. "None of this makes sense. What motive could Ty have to hurt Rani?"

"The property development issues?" I said. It seemed weak to me, too, but it had more basis in fact than our other ideas.

"Ty must have more difficult foes on that front than Rani," Shanda said.

I was sure she was right. But I couldn't put aside that image of Ty looming in the doorway.

~

December 14, 3:10 a.m.

We returned to Carole's office because I thought of a password and user name combination I hadn't tried before. Each of Rani's passwords had used a particular number and symbol combination but with different words. I tried the combination with Ravinia as the base word on iCloud.

It worked.

I felt a flush of excitement. Not only did we have access to all her photos, it confirmed the importance of the Ravinia date.

But the photos were mainly variations on the ones we'd already seen of the neighborhood.

"Go back to the Tenants Association site," Lauren said. "I want to look at that homeless man photo again."

The icon in the laptop screen's bottom corner said we had only thirty-nine minutes of power though we'd put it in sleep mode when we'd finished using it before. I navigated as quickly as I could with my stiff fingers.

We studied the photo together. I pointed to the tile floor. "There's a trail of slush behind him," I said. "It must have snowed recently or still been snowing when this was taken."

Shanda sat on a loveseat against the wall behind us, her head propped on one elbow.

"Zoom in more," Lauren said. "There. The toes on the boots."

I enlarged until the boots filled the screen.

"Those are women's boots," Lauren said.

"How can you tell? Wait, are those heels?" Shadows over the back of the boots made it hard to tell.

"Could be. But some men's boots have an inch or more of a heel. Or a platform. It's the toes. They're too rounded. Men's boots aren't made that way."

"You're sure?" I said.

"I know my shoes."

Behind us, Shanda snored softly. I lowered my voice. "So maybe instead of a tall homeless man we're looking for a tall woman dressed as a homeless man."

"Or a short woman," Lauren said. "Depending how high those heels are and whether there's a platform."

"You're saying it could be Rani." I spoke in a whisper. It would mean Rani'd had someone else take the picture for her or set her camera app on a timer, but it could be done. Though I didn't see why she'd want to risk revealing herself by posting the photograph on the Tenants Association site.

"It could be anyone," Lauren said, speaking quietly as well. "Including Rani."

"So we can't find Rani because she's not dressed as Rani?" I said. "Except so far as we know she'd have no reason to do that."

"We haven't found a reason anyone would do it. She's no more or less likely than anyone else," Lauren said.

I drummed my fingers on the desk near the keyboard. "A person in disguise makes more sense than a random homeless person climbing to the fourteenth floor and happening upon Debbie in a vacant apartment."

"Unless a homeless person has a vendetta against certain people in River City," Lauren said. "But that's ridiculously farfetched."

"Could women's boots fit a man comfortably?"

"They fit some men well," Lauren said. "Just like some women feel more comfortable in men's shoes, some men's feet are shaped so women's shoes suit them."

I studied the boots, tapping my foot on the floor. The boots were russet brown and looked like leather, but could be imitation. They had no scuff marks. "If this person is homeless, being choosy about shoes probably isn't an option. If someone donated this new pair of women's boots to a homeless shelter and they fit, a man would probably take them." I scrolled sideways. "Wish we could see the heels better. We could at least tell how much height they add."

Lauren leaned back in her chair. "Basically, it could be anybody, any height. Rani. Janelle. Maybe she found out Patryk was seeing both Rani and Novia and went after them and Patryk. We've only her word that she was home alone when Patryk was killed."

"And who knows if Ty or his neighbor have been watching her like a hawk." I drained the last of my tea, which had gone cold. I felt more energized but had trouble sorting my thoughts. "For it to be Janelle, Debbie would have had to contact her somehow. So we should see if she stopped by Ty's. And what if Janelle was the one having the affair, not Patryk? She wants her husband out of the way, wants to inherit rather than split everything in a divorce."

"But what about Rani and Novia?" Lauren said.

"Maybe they figured out what happened."

"Or Janelle's lover is three-timing her and he's a psychopathic killer. Though it seems pretty far-fetched. It all does." Lauren pushed away from the desk, rolling her chair a few feet away and rocking it back and forth with her feet.

I stared at the photo without really seeing it. "It has to come back to Janelle. She knew about Rani's supposed visa issue but she can't — or won't — explain why. There's something she's not telling us, some connection to Rani."

The problem was, people lie for all sorts of reasons. I'd had clients lie to me directly because they were embarrassed about the truth and convinced themselves it made no difference to their lawsuits. Danielle had a list a mile long of things she'd discovered during a preliminary hearing or trial that her clients hadn't mentioned.

Lauren tapped the screen. "If Rani's being hunted, there's a reason. What could Rani know that threatens someone? I'm betting it's the identity of this so-called homeless man."

"Because?"

"Rani's the one who took a photo of him."

"Good point. But she disappeared before anyone died," I said. "So it's not a worry about Rani revealing the true identity of a murderer."

"Except if the deaths were planned," Lauren said.

"So we're back to who would kill Patryk, since he was first," I said.

"Couldn't Novia have been killed before him?" Lauren said.

Images of Patryk's and Novia's bodies flashed through my mind. I gripped the edge of the desk. "It was pretty cold in the garage. Novia's body could have been there longer than Patryk's. But we've got no one so far who'd want to kill Novia."

"But we do have people who knew all three victims plus Rani," Lauren said.

"Janelle, Jeff, Aidan, Ty." I ticked each off on my fingers. "Eliza Driscoll. The only person who claims Rani was looking for the supposedly homeless man."

"So those five," Lauren said, "and probably about five hundred other people who live here."

I stood and paced in front of the desk. "But those are the names that come up with all three victims. If the attacks aren't random, it has to be someone connected with all three. The only others are Debbie, who's dead, and Shanda and Carole, and one of us was with at least one of them for almost all the time. Unless Shanda and Carole are in a conspiracy, which I doubt."

Shanda stirred on the loveseat, stretching her arms. "Thanks for ruling me out in my own sister's disappearance."

I didn't say it, but she wasn't exactly ruled out for that.

No one was, since we didn't know what had happened to Rani.

38

———

December 14, 3:15 a.m.

Lauren refilled the thermos-like kettle and rinsed out my cup. I called Novia's mother from Carole's downstairs phone. I sat near the wall at the kitchen island. Shanda had stayed upstairs to rest in Carole's guest room at my and Lauren's urging. I didn't seriously think she was involved, but it was better to be careful.

Leslie Jones sounded groggy when she answered. The news that Debbie had been found dead shocked her awake.

"Debbie Stillwell? I just spoke to her. Maybe an hour ago," she said.

It's strange how we feel as if death can't come to someone we've just talked to.

I asked Leslie if she'd tell me what Debbie had called about in case it might help find Rani.

"She wanted to know if Novia kept a diary. A paper one, the old-fashioned kind."

"And?" I said.

It seemed an anachronism in the time of social media and

podcasts and blogs. But if you wanted to keep something truly private it wasn't a bad idea so long as you kept it locked away. The odds of a stranger reading a diary were a lot greater for one typed on a laptop than one written on paper and secured in a drawer.

"I said I didn't think so. Then she said something about Novia showing her a ticket from a play or an exhibit and asked if Novia saved things like that."

Which meant the envelope of mementos had prompted Debbie to call.

"And did she?" I said.

The kettle hissed. Lauren, not a tea drinker, found a box of teabags in the back of a cabinet.

"After I talked to Debbie I looked through her bedroom," Leslie said. "I never snooped, not when she was a little girl, not when she moved back in. And I know she's gone. It shouldn't matter. But it felt wrong. I kept catching myself thinking she might come home and get mad. But she's not coming home."

"Did you find anything?"

"Nothing. Novia's not a hoarder. Not now. When she was a child, she had tons of toys and stuffed animals all over the place. Now her room's bare. Like she doesn't really....like she doesn't...."

Her words trailed off, and I understood. Novia hadn't felt she lived there because she'd made a temporary move to take care of her mom. But now she really didn't live there.

Lauren set a steaming cup that smelled like Chai in front of me and opened another root beer for herself.

I asked Leslie if she remembered if Novia ever went to Ravinia and saw the Juilliard String Quartet.

"She did. Took an evening off, put together a picnic basket and wine, and went with a friend."

"Do you know who?"

"She didn't say. She didn't tell me a lot. I think it helped her feel she still had some privacy though she had to be here."

"I'm sure she wanted to be there," I said.

"She was a good girl." Her voice sounded choked.

I held my teacup tight with my free hand, wishing I could give her time to process. But we needed answers. "Do you remember if she had lawn seats? Or pavilion?"

"She didn't say, but she brought a blanket to sit on, so it must've been lawn."

Leslie also identified a movie and two White Sox games Novia had gone to that matched the ticket stubs.

"Why does this matter?" she said.

"It might not," I said. "I promise I'll explain later if it comes to anything. Again, I'm so sorry to disturb you."

"I'm getting no sleep tonight," she said. "I may never sleep again."

~

December 14, 3:23 a.m.

With Lauren's point about the boots, Eliza had moved higher on my list as someone who could disguise herself as the homeless man. On the way down to her office, we stopped at Jeff Chang's apartment.

I figured if I were Debbie, after talking to Leslie I'd try to reach him because the envelope had been found at the Immigration Rights Center.

Jeff answered the door on the first knock. He said he hadn't heard from Debbie, that he would have told us that right away. But he used Lauren's phone to call the Immigration Rights Center voicemail on speaker.

There was a message from Debbie. Her voice sounded hurried, but all she said was that she'd tried his cell and gotten no answer and she needed to talk to him. The call had come in about thirty minutes after she'd talked to Carole and me.

~

December 14, 3:31 a.m.

Already looking pale and drawn when she answered her office door, Eliza's face blanched further when Lauren and I told her the news. We stood in the small waiting area near the water cooler.

"Unbelievable." Eliza put one hand against the wall as if to prop herself up. "How can this be happening? Poor little Debbie."

An image of Little Debbie snack cakes flashed through my mind. It was the brand Gram always bought because Hostess was too expensive. A laugh threatened to bubble out of me. I put my hand over my mouth. The more I thought about how inappropriate laughing was the harder it was to hold back.

"It is," Lauren said.

"Have you told Aidan yet?" Eliza said. "Or Ty? I thought I heard him talking to Debbie in the hall when I was trying to get back to sleep after talking to Quille."

That sobered me. "Which do you think it was? Aidan or Ty?"

"Ty. But I couldn't swear to it. It was as I was falling asleep, or trying to."

I dropped onto the chair nearest the water cooler. "Could it have been Jeff?"

Eliza sat next to me. There were only two chairs. Lauren stood by the outer door, angling the flashlight at the floor between all three of us. I stared at the bright circle its light made on the carpet.

"Jeff?" Eliza said. "I don't think so. Doesn't he have a sort of higher voice?"

"Yes," I said. "This man had a bass voice?"

"I don't know about bass. But not high."

That could describe Ty or Aidan or any number of men, though I didn't think that many were out walking around after midnight.

234

"We have to tell Aidan about Debbie," Eliza said.

"He knew her?" I said.

"She stopped at Shanda's office a lot to visit with Rani. He'll be devastated."

39

———

December 14, 3:41 a.m.

Eliza insisted on going with us to tell Aidan. We found him in Shanda's office, slumped in one of the armless chairs with the other turned to face him so he could rest his feet on it.

He didn't wake up when I said his name. Lauren grasped his arm and jiggled it.

He sat straight, nearly toppling the chair. "Rani?" He blinked and looked from Lauren to me, gripping the chair seat with both hands. "News on Rani?"

"No, I'm sorry," I said. I told him about Debbie Stillwell.

"But I just spoke to her," Aidan said, echoing Leslie's words.

"When?" I said.

He glanced at his phone, then must have realized it was out of power.

Lauren shone the flashlight on her watch, a Bulgari with an emerald green band her mom had gotten her for Christmas last year. "It's about 3:40 now."

"About three hours ago then. She called here to see if we learned anything about Rani."

Eliza leaned in the doorway between Shanda's office and the

reception area, her frame nearly filling it. "Did she say anything else?"

"Something about Novia and Rani," Aidan said. "That they might have been seeing each other in secret. She asked if either had said anything to me."

"And?" I said. "Did they?" It didn't surprise me the thought had occurred to Debbie.

Aidan pushed the chair he'd been resting his feet on against the wall and stretched his legs in front of him, first one and then the other. "No."

The flashlight beam had dimmed. Lauren pulled candles from her cardigan pockets, set them along the counter to Aidan's right, and took out matches.

"What about Novia seeing someone other than Rani?" I said as Lauren lit the candles and took a seat in Shanda's chair.

"Novia? I've no idea. I didn't know her very well," Aidan said.

I half-sat, half-leaned on the counter that held Shanda's computer, facing Aidan. The candlelight made it easier to see him than the flashlight had, but his left side faded into darkness. His expression was serious, his mouth in a straight line, and he looked exhausted. His whole face sagged downward toward his almost-absent chin.

"You never spent time together?" I said.

He ran his hand through his thick, black hair. "Sure, sure, sure. We did sometimes. Had a cup of coffee in the park now and then before she started work."

Lauren spun her chair toward Aidan. "How'd you first get to know each other?"

"Her mom used to work in the travel business way back. One day at the front desk she mentioned it, and we started talking travel. Places we'd like to go. So I suggested we get some coffee if she ever got to work early, and a couple times she did."

Coffee with Rani in the morning and with Novia in the afternoon.

It raised a red flag, or at least an orange one. Still, within a six-block radius of my home I had my choice of Starbucks, Peet's Coffee, and Hero's coffee. There was a Dollop across from River City and a new Starbucks opening down the street. Obviously a lot of people got coffee every day.

"How often did you meet Novia for coffee?" I said.

"Once a month. If that."

Not quite often enough to match Leslie Jones' information that Novia left early once a week. But Leslie had said Novia might be meeting different people. And Aidan might be minimizing the meetings because he was guilty or because he thought it would make him look guilty.

"Did Debbie say if she planned to do anything about her idea that Novia might be seeing Rani?" I said.

"Do anything?" Aidan said.

"Talk to anyone," Lauren said. "Investigate."

"She said she might try to call the Immigration Rights Center. Talk to Joe? Jeff? But she didn't say why."

That suggested Debbie had actually talked to Aidan or he'd have no way to know about her trying to call Jeff.

While I had no reason to think he'd invent a conversation with Debbie, some people will say anything to get attention. My first boyfriend had fallen into that category, and it had taken me forever to realize that was what was happening.

I asked Aidan what he'd been doing since Debbie had called. He said he'd been walking the Marina and Lobby Levels and River Road periodically hoping for inspiration or some clue about Rani. He denied passing by Eliza's office or going anywhere with Debbie.

He rubbed his hands back and forth over his thighs. "Rather pointless, I know, walking the area. But it felt better than doing nothing. I can't believe Debbie was found in a vacant apartment. Any idea why she was there?"

"None," I said, which was strictly true.

"How did you know to check that apartment?" Aidan said.

"We didn't," I said before Lauren could answer, though I felt sure she shared my feelings about the need to be cautious around everyone. "We were going door-to-door looking for Rani. The door was open, so we went in."

I watched both him and Eliza as carefully as I could in the dim lighting for a reaction. Whoever had killed Debbie would know the apartment hadn't been left unlocked. I saw no shifting of their bodies, no drawing back or involuntary gestures of surprise.

"It's horrible," Aidan said. "Truly. Is there anything else we can do? Has someone told Janelle?"

"Ty might be telling her," I said, "unless she's asleep. How well do you know her?"

"Enough to say hello."

"Ever have coffee with her?" I said, careful to keep my tone even.

He looked up and met my eyes. "No. This must be a nightmare for her."

40

———

December 14, 3:47 a.m.

Ty answered the door at our first knock, but he didn't invite us in. Instead he slipped out into River Road. We stood near one of the large cylindrical storage lockers. In daylight it had looked traffic cone orange, but in the dim flashlight beam it looked closer to red.

"I don't want to wake Janelle," Ty said. "She just got back to sleep."

Aidan had remained in Shanda's office still hoping Rani might call or turn up. Eliza decided to stay with him, as she was feeling less and less safe alone. Leaving her alone with Aidan made me uneasy, but given the possibility that the "homeless man" was a woman and that Eliza stood a head taller than Aidan and outweighed him significantly it hit me that perhaps I ought to worry about him.

"You told her about Debbie?" I said.

Ty crossed his arms and leaned against the wall next to his door. "I didn't plan to. But she was awake, and she sensed something wrong. I couldn't find the words to hide it."

"How'd she take it?" Lauren said.

"Lost it. Sobbing. It's so much to take in."

"Did she know Debbie well?" I said.

"I'm not sure. But everyone knew Debbie. From the Tenants Association and, before that, the condo board."

"Debbie went in person to tell Janelle about Patryk. She wanted to check on Janelle after we found Novia," I said. "Makes it seem like she knew her pretty well."

Ty looked at the floor for a moment. "How do I say this? Debbie was...she liked drama. She might only have wanted to be on the front lines. But for all I know she was particular friends with Janelle."

"How long did Debbie stay at your place?" Lauren said.

"Fifteen minutes? Twenty tops."

"Did she say where she was going after that?" I said.

"To knock on doors," Ty said. "Ask people for information and see whether anyone had travel chargers. She'd already been doing that. She said she'd checked in with all of you, too."

"She did," I said.

I didn't add that it might have been what killed her.

Lauren shifted the flashlight so it shone a little higher, casting more light on Ty. "Where did you and Debbie go later when you took a walk together?"

He tilted his head to one side. "When we went to get Janelle?"

"No. Later," I said.

"Is this a trick question? Debbie and I didn't go anywhere together. I've been here at the apartment except when I was with you."

"Someone heard you and Debbie talking in the hall," I said.

He spread his hands wide. "Wasn't me."

"You don't want to know what hall?" I said.

"Don't need to."

December 14, 3:58 a.m.

"Maybe Eliza was dreaming," Lauren said as we retraced our steps down the damp-smelling stairwell. We were walking in the dark to conserve the flashlight batteries. "When she thought she heard Ty and Debbie talking in the hall."

"Or Ty was lying." My toe bumped the back of Lauren's calf and I slowed down. "Sorry."

"Yeah, careful there," she said. "I'm not keen on tumbling downstairs when emergency help is seriously absent. You really think that? About Ty?"

I gripped the railing with one hand and unzipped my fleece with the other. I was finally feeling recovered from the icy wind out on the balcony, and the stairwell was well insulated. "No. I don't know."

"He seemed sincere in wanting to help find Rani," Lauren said. "And feeling bad about Debbie."

"You can fake sincerity."

It was something my best friend growing up had said often, and he hadn't been talking about acting, though he aspired to be an actor. He'd meant in dealing with his parents. But I wondered later how much he might have been faking when talking to me.

"So what about Aidan?" Lauren said. "If anyone could fake sincerity, I'd bet on him."

"Why?" I said. "Not that I necessarily disagree."

Neither of us could face climbing again, so we'd decided to closet ourselves in the management office to figure out the next steps. I kept feeling I'd missed something about Debbie's death or about Rani's photos or both, but I couldn't figure out what.

"He's too calm." We'd reached the Lobby Level, and she pushed open the door to the hallway. "And no one's that uniformly polite. At least Jeff got a little pissed when you questioned him. Ty too. Aidan just rolls with it."

The colder hallway temperatures chilled my sweat and made me feel clammy.

"He got a little irked when I questioned him earlier." I kept my hand against the wall as we made our way in the dark toward the management office. I lowered my voice. "I'd been sort of ruling him out of the homeless man because he's short. But if those are heeled boots — "

"Though why would he volunteer that Debbie called him?" Lauren said. "If he's involved, he ought to have kept completely quiet."

"To seem open about it? In case we'd been able to check her phone."

We'd reached the office. Lauren shone the flashlight over my hands so I could find the key and open the door.

Lauren locked the office door behind us once we were inside. We moved to the windowless back room. No one passing by would guess we were in here.

I set the three candles on the edge of a desk but didn't light them yet. We knew what the office looked like, so no reason to waste them.

I peeled off my knit gloves and lay them on the desk. They still felt damp.

"So what kind of thing do you think you missed?" Lauren said.

"Something about the apartment she was in." I wiped my hands on my jeans and put them in my pockets to warm them, then shut my eyes and, heart pounding, imagined myself in the apartment again. It was something I used to do alone before the first night of previews to feel calmer and more like my character, more as if she really lived in the world of the play. I'd see myself on stage moving through each scene as if the finished set and props were all around me.

"It was deserted. Empty other than Debbie," I said.

Lauren stayed silent, sensing that I was talking mainly to myself.

I pictured the phone on the floor and the partly open balcony door. The snow outside and Debbie against the balcony railing. Beyond that, the expanse of Wells Street to the north and — from the far balcony corner — the frozen river and the river bank on the other side.

My eyes opened. "That's it."

41

———

December 14, 4:07 a.m.

"Where are Rani's photos of the river?" I said.

"What do you mean?" Lauren said.

"We went looking for vacant apartments because we saw photos of the Alta being built. We thought if Rani took photos from Carole's, it would have been from the balcony. It faces the river, not the Alta." As I grew more excited, I felt less tired and I sat straighter. My mind sorted through the conversations. "Eliza said Shanda complained that Rani took so many photos of the neighborhood *and the river*, not people. So where are they?"

"On her phone. Which we don't have," Lauren said.

"Except we looked at her iCloud site. No river photos there. And why didn't we find that photo of the homeless man on it?"

"She's got another phone?" Lauren said. "That would go with the secret boyfriend idea."

"Or a camera," I said.

It was something I couldn't believe I hadn't thought about before. My only excuses were how long I'd gone without sleep and that I'd never used anything but a phone to take photos.

"Oh," Lauren said. "Like an actual digital camera?"

"Right," I said. "She loved photography. Wouldn't she have an actual camera?"

"My dad has one. But he's fifty-five," Lauren said.

"I have a friend who does wedding photography. She's got three real cameras. You can do a lot more with them."

"You didn't find one in Shanda's apartment, did you?" Lauren said.

"No. Maybe she has it with her."

"Maybe that's the threat she poses," Lauren said. "She has photos someone doesn't want her to have. But wouldn't all the photos she took with it be backed up on iCloud along with those for her phone? So we'd have seen them all?"

"Each device might go to a different place. And her iCloud storage was maxed out," I said. "If we can find those photos maybe it'll tell us where Rani is."

Lauren scooted her chair next to mine and we searched backup sites for the photographs on Rani's phone. On each one I tried out Rani's email address and her iCloud password. I mentally crossed my fingers that Rani, like so many of us, used the same password across all her storage sites. On my fourth try, I found her photos.

There were thousands.

Lauren huffed out a sigh. "We can't flip through all these on the phone. And if we're hiking up to Carole's again, I totally need a minute. Or fifty. I mean, I'll do it—"

"She had almost no power left." My own leg muscles burned from thighs to calves. "And maybe there's an alternative."

I shone the flashlight around the office. It had one laptop that, when I opened it, still had fifty percent power. The blue light from its screen made the small interior office look like a scene in an old black and white movie. Lauren's phone had forty percent battery power and still had coverage.

"Try creating a hotspot," I said. "There's no one here you can call anyway."

Once we were online, I sorted the photos by date. Recent ones showed River Road but provided no clue to where Rani might be now. I sorted by folder instead.

Still nothing helpful. Some photos had probably been taken from the vacant apartment where we'd found Debbie and included glimpses of the river, but we already knew about that apartment. Rani also had taken quite a few of construction sites in the neighborhood, including the one next door.

There were several photos of the homeless man. One showed a side view. I zoomed in on the right boot. The hem of the jeans made it hard to tell, but from the heel's steep slant Lauren guessed it at least two inches if not three. The heel rested on a platform that looked at least another inch high.

Another folder included photos of different indoor work on River City. One showed the inside of one of the shiny new offices I'd seen during my tour with Carole. Other photos showed what looked like the back room at the grocery store, its shelves filled with cans and boxes. Another picture featured a larger space with tools, boards, and tarps on a concrete floor near an excavation.

Likewise, there were photos of the marina and the walkway in front of it. They showed a shed marked Garbage, another marked Electrical, and the locked marina gate. Some had been taken after the boats had been winterized and before snow fell. The shrink wrap placed around the boats to protect them from the elements looked a lot like construction tarp. I remembered the tiny piece of blue tarp I'd found on Rani's clothes in Shanda's hamper.

I zoomed in on a few photos, comparing them. And felt certain I knew where Rani was.

42

———————

December 14, 4:17 a.m.

Lauren thought we should get some help to check out my theory.

"We can't wait," I said as I hunted through the office for a first aid kit. "If Rani's where I think she is, the only reason she hasn't come out is she's hurt and needs help. And we still don't know who the killer is."

If Rani had been trapped or hiding, she'd been there nearly twenty-four hours already. The snow drifts against the glass walls were as high as my chest. I didn't think we could count on the police coming to the rescue any time soon.

Also, whoever the killer was had to be looking for Rani just as we were, hoping to finish the job.

"Who do you feel more sure about? Jeff or Ty?" Lauren said.

"Ty," I said. "If I had to pick. It would've been hard for him to get away to kill Patryk, and if everything's connected, that rules him out. But I'm not willing to bet on it."

I found a first aid kit in a bottom drawer of the security counter. It was stocked with the usual — bandages, anti-bacterial ointment, alcohol wipes. Nothing that would help a serious injury but better to have it than not. It had a strap, and I put it over my shoulder.

"I trust Ty more too." Lauren pulled her pepper spray from her pocket. "I'll go to Ty's first, you take the first aid kit and go find Rani. We'll meet you."

"That's crazy," I said. "We can't split up. Patryk, Novia, Debbie, each one was alone when they got killed."

Lauren had proven she could more than take care of herself when we'd resolved Marco's death, and I hadn't done too badly myself. But that didn't make us invincible.

"Probably because they trusted whoever it is. At least, that's true for Novia and Debbie. I know not to trust anyone, and so do you. And we know to watch for the homeless man, or someone dressed as him."

"We don't know how powerful this person is. We need to look for Rani together. Then we'll both go get Ty if we need him."

Lauren finally agreed.

We tried calling Carole's home phone from the security desk to tell her and Shanda our plans but got no answer. It was another worry, but I told myself both of them were sound asleep. I left a message.

I clicked on one of the three flashlights left on the counter. I chose one with a pretty strong beam that was heavy enough that it might double as a weapon. It was something to have with us along with Lauren's pepper spray. Lauren took a smaller one.

We left the door unlocked in case we needed to run back and barricade ourselves inside it.

"What if we're wrong and Rani's the killer?" Lauren said as we exited the office.

"Then she won't be where I'm expecting," I said. "She'll have found a much better hiding spot."

Debbie's keys jangled in my pocket as we hurried across the lobby and down the frozen escalator to the Marina Level. I clutched the railing in one hand, wary of the uneven steps, and the flashlight in the other. As we reached the bottom a figure emerged from the hall that led to Shanda's office.

I clicked on my flashlight at the same time Lauren turned on hers.

It was Aidan. I imagined him in boots with a one inch platform and a two inch heel. He'd be nearly six feet.

"Aidan," I said. "Where's Eliza?"

"We split apart for a few minutes." He approached us, hands in his jacket pockets. "We have an idea about where Rani might be."

I shifted my grip on the flashlight so I could more easily swing it around if needed. Rather than stepping back, though, I moved toward Aidan. I didn't want him to know I suspected him. Judging by Lauren's grip on her keychain and her moving in tandem, she'd followed my thought processes exactly.

"Really?" I said. "Where?"

"The back of the grocery store in the stocking area. Eliza ran down the hall to the restroom first, though."

That seemed unlikely given her concern about being alone.

"But you seem to be in a hurry," Aidan said. "Have you thought of something as well?"

"Yes," I said. "What made you think of the grocery store?"

"I've been thinking about all the places we looked, and I came to the realization that she could have tripped and fallen and we wouldn't have seen her when we did a look around," Aidan said.

My scalp tingled and the hair on my arms stood.

That phrase. It was the one I'd been trying to think of that different people kept saying with slight variations. I heard the voices in my head. Niu in the grocery store that Aidan and Rani frequented. Novia talking about traffic. Debbie quoting Janelle about her marriage. Jeff quoting Rani when she'd quit.

If Aidan were seeing Rani, Novia, and Janelle, each could have unconsciously picked up the phrase from him.

At the same instant, a recollection of Shanda's outer office flooded my mind. The Zappos shoeboxes against the wall. I'd assumed they were Rani's. But they could easily belong to Aidan. And have included a pair of women's platform boots.

I edged closer to Lauren.

"Why don't we check together," Aidan said. "Safer than any of us being alone what with a killer in the complex."

There was no way Lauren and I were going into the deserted grocery store with Aidan. It was two on one, but if he'd killed all three people today, he was a lot stronger than he looked.

"No," I said.

His body stiffened and one hand dug further into his pocket.

"I know where she is, and it's not the grocery store," I said. "I found some photographs she took. Come with us."

I headed straight toward him as if certain he would follow. Lauren followed my lead. I brushed his arm as I passed to show that I wasn't afraid of being near him. If ever I had done an acting job, this was it.

"Where?" He turned and fell in step between Lauren and me, matching our rushed pace.

I headed for the hallway that led to the parking lot exit, but skidded to a stop when I remembered Patryk's body lay directly in our path. "We can't go this way."

"Ugh," Lauren said. "You're right. I wasn't thinking. I just wanted to get to Rani."

I felt grateful she'd jumped in. It made it look less like I was making up a destination on the fly.

"You think she's in the parking lot?" Aidan said.

"No, at the marina," Lauren said. "She goes out into the harbor to take pictures."

I spun and headed back toward the escalators.

Aidan trailed after us but said, "Didn't you check there before?"

"Carole and I walked along the dock, but we didn't open the

sheds. There's some near the garbage bins. Boaters keep supplies there."

When we finally exited onto the concrete steps above the marina, wind smacked my face, stinging my cheeks. I'd grabbed my parka when we'd last been at Carole's. I wore it now with my knit gloves. My mittens still lay on her couch, though. But it wasn't a long walk to the dock, and I had a plan to immobilize Aidan. If he wasn't guilty, it would make him angry and confused, but he had a coat. And I'd make sure someone ran out there to bring him in as soon as we checked on Rani.

The shed next to the garbage bin had a board and bolt across it to keep vermin out. The whole area smelled of trash despite the wind.

"Why would she be there?" Aidan said.

"I think she came here looking for the homeless man," I said. "She must have suspected he was sleeping here. And then she fell or slipped on something and got locked in by mistake. Maybe by maintenance."

It was a weak story but all I'd been able to think of.

"You don't think someone killed her?" Aidan said.

Lauren slid the board back, but couldn't maneuver the bolt because she'd put her bunny fur mittens on. "We hope not. Though if she found that man and he is homicidal it's totally possible he did."

If Aidan had been disguising himself as the homeless man, I hoped he'd think we'd bought his ruse.

I undid the bolt as Lauren shone her flashlight beam on it. My fingers felt stiff but finally it came undone and I pulled the door open.

As I did, from the corner of my eye I saw Aidan swing his flashlight at the back of Lauren's head.

We hadn't been playing Aidan, he'd been playing us.

43

December 14, 4:22 a.m.

Lauren's foot slipped on the ice in the same instant Aidan swung, propelling her forward. He connected with her upper back rather than her head. Her wail rose over the wind's shriek as she fell face forward to the ground.

I lunged at Aidan, hitting his torso with my shoulder. We landed on the concrete. The First Aid kit and my flashlight skidded into the river.

Aidan shoved me off him and kicked me. My whole body flew sideways toward the water. My butt hit something hard like metal. Pain shot down my legs. I scrabbled at the ice and snow, fanning my arms. My right hand hit a metal handgrip near the concrete's edge. My right foot plunged into the water just as my left hand found its own grip.

My foot and lower leg seared as if burning. The bubbler that kept the harbor water from turning to ice must barely keep it above freezing. But I hung on to the metal handgrips and hauled myself back onto the dock.

Aidan's flashlight, still lit, lay a few feet away. It pointed toward him, leaving me in the dark, and the wind covered the sounds of my movements. He kicked Lauren, who'd gotten to her feet and had her back to him, disoriented. Her knees buckled and she hit the ground.

Leg and foot still burning, I forced myself to my hands and knees and crawled forward. Long ago Danielle had told me women's greatest strength is in their legs, so it's often better to stay on the ground.

I angled sideways and swung my good leg out, aiming for the back of Aidan's knees. I connected well enough that he lost his balance and fell flat on his back.

Lauren rolled away from him and staggered to her feet.

In concert, we shoved him into the open shed.

I slammed the door shut and threw the bolt.

Lauren collapsed.

❦

December 14, 4:28 a.m.

I had no idea how long the shed would hold Aidan. Lauren was barely conscious. She answered to her name and could move her arms and legs, though the right one just barely. My hands burned and my foot and lower leg had gone numb. Using all my energy, I hefted her to her feet. As bad as it might be to move her if she were seriously injured, it had to be worse to leave her outside in a blizzard or anywhere near Aidan.

He shouted from inside the shed.

I staggered up the steps, stopping twice because I felt unsure of my footing with my numb foot. Finally, I got us in the way we'd come out. Legs shaking, I eased Lauren onto the floor near a maintenance room door between the outside doors that led to the stairs down into the marina and the inner door to the reception area.

"I'll hide." Lauren nodded at the door. "Find Rani."

"Aidan could get free," I said.

"Lock me in."

"What if he has keys?"

She shook her head. "He'll go straight for Rani. And I'm already feeling less bad."

I didn't like it.

Her face was stark white and her arm at an odd angle. But if Aidan freed himself soon she'd be safer here than staggering around with me in the open. The only other option was the management office, and Aidan would surely look for her there if he were intent on finding her.

"Keep trying to call Carole," I said. "And the Immigration Rights Center. And anyone else you can think of."

I fumbled with Debbie's keys, finally finding the ones marked maintenance. The third one I tried opened the door. Lauren crawled in and sat against the wall next to a shelving unit, legs outstretched.

"I'll be okay," she said. "Find Rani. Before Aidan gets out. I'll go get Ty or Jeff if I can."

"Just be careful. And quiet."

I locked the door after we checked to be sure Lauren would still be able to open it from the inside. Shivering, I pulled off my soaking wet sock, shook the water out of the boot, and dried the inside of it with my fleece. The spilled water washed away the footprints that had led to the maintenance room.

I put the boot on again, minus the wet sock. By the time I reached the Security counter and grabbed the last flashlight my toes felt a little less numb but still icy. I paused at the top of the escalator. I could run for Jeff or Ty. But I felt sure Aidan's next stop had been the health club. He'd been headed in that direction, not toward the grocery store.

At the health club door for a moment I thought I'd lost Debbie's keys. Swearing and sweating, I groped through my coat pockets and finally found them in the coat lining. They'd slid through a hole in the pocket.

Once inside, I did my best to shield the flashlight beam with my body, but the wall that bordered the hall was glass, and there was no way the light wouldn't be seen.

The concrete floor had been painted off-white or gray. Probably it was meant for the weights or workout machines, but for now it was empty and clear. A doorway to my left led further into the club.

I clicked off the light and crept forward in blackness that smelled of plaster and sawdust. I felt pins and needles in my right foot when I stepped, which I figured was an improvement though it forced me to move slowly for fear of losing my footing.

Fifteen years ago, I'd been in an experimental production where I'd been on stage in the dark for over an hour. It was the sort of thing that once I became a lawyer I realized could have gotten a lot of people sued, but thankfully none of the actors or audience members got injured. I learned through that to listen carefully and feel my way. I pretended that was what I was doing, imagining the room in my head as I inched toward the doorway.

From the hallway beyond the health club I heard creaks and groans, but I felt sure — almost sure — they were the aging building shifting in the wind. What seemed like endless minutes later my outstretched palms hit a wall. I shuffled sideways until I reached an open area that must be the doorway.

This health club was meant to have a pool. I couldn't risk stepping into an excavated space, so I clicked on the flashlight. I stood a few yards from an unfinished Olympic-sized pool area.

Two doors to my right in the middle of a long wall probably led to what later would be locker rooms. I clicked off the flashlight again, held my breath, and listened. Nothing new.

My right shoulder and arm pressed against the wall, I slid sideways in the dark.

Once inside the next room where I knew I couldn't be seen from the outer corridor I turned the flashlight on.

Two-by-fours and other boards had been stacked everywhere. Paint cans, bags of cement, and other construction supplies and equipment had been piled against the wall opposite me. The workers must be using this area for storage while they worked elsewhere. In the far corner boards had tumbled at odd angles near a large red metal toolbox the size of a steamer trunk.

Ammonia permeated the air, but nothing worse, nothing like when I'd found Marco's body. I still awoke sometimes with that smell in my nose.

"Rani?" I kept my voice low, not wanting Aidan to hear if he were prowling the halls.

I picked my way around the boards askew on the floor and shone the light into the corner beyond the giant toolbox. Rani lay on the concrete floor on her side. A heavy board lay across her shoulder and back and smaller ones all around her.

A dark puddle under her knees and gummy patches on her jeans and under the side of her head suggested blood.

"Rani?" I hurried around the trunk to kneel beside her. I felt her neck with two fingers. She had a faint, slow heartbeat. My shoulders dropped, and I let my breath out.

In the flashlight beam her face looked pale but not chalky. A two-inch cut slashed across her right cheek. Blood had crusted along it. I felt under her head, barely grazing her skull with my fingers. Her hair felt sticky with blood over a small bump.

Her eyelids fluttered.

I spoke into her exposed ear. "Rani, it's Quille. Quille Davis. Carole's been looking for you. And Shanda."

I studied the board lying on top of her. Surely it was better to get its weight off of her. I couldn't imagine how that could hurt her.

"I'm going to move this board." It was heavy, but I was able to shift it bit by bit off of her and onto the floor.

She shifted her legs. Her lips moved but no sound came out. I bent so my ear was close to her mouth.

"Thank...you," she said.

I wanted to ask what hurt, but I feared wearing her out. And wasting time. We needed a doctor and more people to defend against Aidan should he find us.

"The power's out," I said, "and hardly any phones are working, so I need to leave you to get more help. I'm sorry. But I'll be back as soon as I can."

I wasn't about to tell her how unavailable emergency personnel were or that I'd dropped the first aid kit somewhere near the marina.

She grasped my arm, but her fingers made no impression through the triple layer of my parka, fleece, and blazer sleeves. "Aidan."

"I know," I said. "I'll be careful."

I stood and listened for a moment for Aidan or for anyone else who might be in the hallway. Nothing.

Flashlight shining on the floor ahead of me, I hurried toward the pool area. In my other hand I gripped a two-by-four. A door banged somewhere outside the health club, and I froze. It could be Lauren or someone else coming to help, but I couldn't be sure. I also couldn't just stand here. I'd seen another exit on the opposite side of the pool, but I didn't know if that would bring me closer or farther from whoever was out there. My mental map of the building told me it should bring me out near the grocery store. I decided to risk it.

Flashlight off, but keeping the tip of it against the wall as a guide so I didn't stumble anywhere near the dug out pool area, I moved away from the main room that fronted the corridor. I lifted each foot and set it down centimeter by centimeter so as not to make noise. Time slowed and every instant felt sharp, as if it were all in slow motion and high definition at the same time.

I'd gone what I thought was halfway around the pool when footsteps sounded from the corridor. A few quick ones, then dragging, then nothing, then more steps.

I heard the sound of a door swinging open and shut. It seemed to come from the direction of the common area restrooms down the hall from the health club. I moved a little faster until the flashlight hit open air. Keeping my side against the wall, I slipped through the open doorway.

My right toes smacked into something. I dropped the flashlight, stifled a yell, and swore in my head at the pain shooting through my foot. Dizziness washed over me. I kept ahold of the two-by-four and crouched down, a hand against the wall, in case I passed out.

The sound of breaking glass came from the main room. Aidan must've gotten a hammer or some other tool. If it had been Lauren, she would have called out to me. I forced myself to stand, my stomach heaving.

Moving as quietly as possible with my throbbing foot I reversed course and felt my way along the wall, skirting the pool again. I couldn't leave Rani at Aidan's mercy. More shattering sounds, then feet crunching on glass.

Through the doorway I saw a tiny flashlight beam. The noisy footsteps from that direction gave me cover to move. I neared the doorway to the main room. Judging from the bobbing and swinging flashlight beam, Aidan's gait was uneven and he was shivering from being trapped in the shed.

While his flashlight made it easy to pinpoint his location, it also operated as it did when you go hiking in the woods. You see what's illuminated by the beam, but everything else goes black because your irises have dilated.

I again imagined the main room and the entire health club as if it were a stage set. Based on my memory, Aidan was heading for the doorway that led to the pool area.

Shifting a few feet put me out of the flashlight beam but near enough to hit him with the two-by-four if he came through the doorway. Taking him by surprise might give me enough of an advantage.

44

———————

December 14, 4:44 a.m.

I heard clicking sounds. It took a moment to realize it was Aidan's teeth chattering.

As he came through the doorway he turned in my direction and his flashlight blinded me. I swung the board like a baseball bat, aiming for where I thought his head was. The board connected with what felt like his shoulder or upper torso. He grunted. The flashlight banged against the wall, fell to the floor, and rolled away, its light creating spinning circles on the opposite wall and leaving us in shadow.

The balance training I'd done when rehabbing from an injury during the summer helped me stay upright despite the jolt when I hit Aidan. He crumpled against the wall and slid to the floor, but I couldn't see well enough to trust he'd stay down. I swung the two-by-four again.

He must barely have been hurt. He dove forward out of the way. I hit drywall. The impact with the wall jarred my arms and shoulders.

As I got my bearings, I heard rustling behind me. Aidan's icy fingers grabbed my shoulder and spun me toward him. His punch glanced off my cheekbone when I tried to duck. Darts of pain shot through the side of my face. Rather than fighting the momentum from his punch, I threw myself backward and sideways, jolting my head and setting off nauseating hot pokers of pain behind my eyes. I lost my grip on the two-by-four. Allowing my knees to buckle, I dropped to the floor the way I'd learned to do to fake passing out on stage. I landed on the flashlight. It jabbed my right hip.

The migraine that had been threatening roared to life, stabbing into my brain. My vision blurred.

With the searing in my head I barely felt my hip, but I maneuvered the flashlight out from under it. Darkness is better for a migraine. As Aidan staggered toward me, an idea broke through the swirling fog of pain. I found the button and shut the flashlight off. Unless he had some sort of special training I didn't know about I'd have the advantage in the dark.

I drew my knees to my chest, held my arms close, and rolled sideways along the wall, farther from him. My entire head and neck throbbed, but I concentrated on listening. I waited as long as I thought I could and thrust both feet out toward the movement I heard. I felt only air but quickly pistoned my legs. This time I connected.

A whoosh escaped Aiden as he hit the floor, making me think he'd landed face down with his weight on his diaphragm. I scrambled along the floor on my hands and knees, gritting my teeth against the pain coursing through my head, and doing my best to keep in mind where I was in relation to him and to the excavation. At last I found the two-by-four. His labored breathing helped me find my way back. I'd hoped to find the flashlight, too, but didn't take the time to keep feeling for it.

As I rose to a kneeling position and raised the board over my head, his arm shot out and smacked my thigh. I brought the two-by-four down.

The board thunked as it hit flesh. Aidan howled. I swung

lower, aiming for where I thought his knees might be. He squealed and shifted position, probably curling around himself. I wanted to make sure he couldn't come after Rani or me, not kill him. Yet as I swung again the exaltation I felt frightened me. My whole body hummed as I brought the board down twice more, breathing hard and yelling as I hit him.

I caught my breath and gripped the board with both hands to stop myself. Aidan was sobbing and it sounded real, not like fake crying for sympathy. But he'd fooled everyone about who he was, so I kept a tight hold on the board as I felt for the flashlight.

At last I found it and turned it on.

Aidan lay curled on his side, arms around his stomach, gasping for air. Blood ran down the side of his face from a gash on his forehead. He looked woozy and disoriented. I didn't trust that he'd stay that way. I staggered to the room where Rani lay, checked that she was still breathing, and snagged a roll of duct tape from the metal shelves.

Fighting dizziness, I bound Aidan's hands first. He struggled but looked to be in too much pain to do very much about it. I wrapped duct tape around his ankles until I used the entire roll.

Getting help for Rani and Lauren had to be my next action, but I couldn't help feeling that if Aidan had gotten out of the shed he might somehow get out of that duct tape. Fighting the hot jabs of pain in my head and my aching body I staggered up the escalator shouting for help and that it had been Aidan all along.

December 14, 4:55 a.m.
Near the top of the escalator I misjudged the height of a frozen stair, stubbed my toes, and fell forward. The ridged steps scraped my hands as I grabbed at them. The pressure in my head ballooned, and I lay half on the steps, half on the lobby's tile floor, the world swirling around me.

When it began to stabilize, I struggled to a sitting position on the floor. The pain in my head receded as if it had been stunned by the fall. After another minute I crawled to the Security counter, moving gingerly to avoid setting it off again. I pulled myself to my feet and started down the hall toward the stairwell. As I rounded the curve, though, two bobbing lights came into view.

It was Lauren and Ty. Lauren limped on the right side, and her pace was half her usual walking speed, but she was walking. I spilled out what had happened.

Ty grabbed my arm, steadying me, and turned to Lauren. "Go get anyone else you can. I'll go downstairs with Quille."

Lauren wore Ty's leather jacket. She gave it to me for Rani and headed back the way she'd come, hugging the wall for support.

In the health club again, Aidan's duct tape looked wrinkled and frayed as if he'd been struggling with it, but it had held. Ty stood over him, flashlight in one hand, two-by-four in the other while I went to Rani. I was afraid to move her, but I covered her with Ty's coat and found bottled water in a kitchen area in one of the other rooms. She revived and drank a little, then drifted in and out of consciousness. I sat next to her, drank water, and held her hand until Ty came in.

He'd brought blankets that another neighbor had collected. He told me someone else was knocking on doors to find someone with medical training. He covered Rani and wrapped a blanket around me as well.

"Lauren?" I said.

"In the other room. My next door neighbor went to go tell Shanda and Carole."

What seemed like hours later, but was only about fifteen minutes according to Ty, a paramedic arrived who lived on the seventh floor. He set multiple flashlights around Rani and examined her without moving her.

He cut away the leg of her jeans and found a deep cut above

her knees. He cleaned it out and bandaged it, saying she might need stitches and would need to be evaluated for head injuries.

After disappearing to tend to Aidan and check on Lauren he returned and felt around my head for lumps. There were none, but he had me follow his penlight with my eyes and touch my nose anyway. He cleaned my cuts and bruises with alcohol and put on bandages. He said I'd been smart to take off my wet sock.

"You'll live," he said. "But you should see your doctor."

Ty gave me thick wool socks someone had brought for me. As I pulled them on, shouting came from the main room.

~

December 14, 5:15 a.m.

"How could you?" Janelle loomed over Aidan, her feet inches from his head. Jeff Chang stood to her right, a hand resting on her shoulder. "I can't believe I...how could I have fallen for you? Evil. You're evil."

I paused in the doorway between the locker room and the pool room, gripping the doorjamb for support. The paramedic and Ty had stayed with Rani. Lauren sat against the wall near the door to the main room, one knee drawn to her chest, her injured leg stretched in front of her. Her right arm was in a makeshift sling.

Eliza Driscoll hovered in the doorway from the main room. I'd forgotten about her and was relieved to see her. While pale and hunching her whole body, otherwise she looked injury-free, at least in the light from multiple flashlights and one lantern set around Aidan.

"Don't...know...what...talking...about."

Aidan spoke as if squeezing the words from his lungs. A wool blanket covered him as well, and it trembled as he shivered under it. The paramedic must have put it over him to help keep him from going into shock.

"Patryk was a good man," Janelle said.

"Never hurt anyone. Never." Aidan coughed and his eyes shifted to me. "She's wrong...confused. Locked me up."

"Rani, Novia, what was that, clean up? Get them out of the way?" Janelle said. "You thought I'd marry you after you killed Patryk?"

"Love you," he said. "Never hurt anyone."

Janelle's foot twitched as if she wanted to stomp his head. Jeff gently drew her away.

"Rani's alive," I told Aidan. "The truth will come out."

He said nothing.

45

―――――

December 14, 6:13 a.m.

Police and paramedics arrived on snowmobiles an hour later. The sky still looked pitch dark. Snow plows had finally gotten a few main streets cleared. Rani was put in a sled and pulled by snowmobile to an ambulance waiting on Clark Street. Ty had gone on foot with Shanda, who'd been unable to stop crying when she'd seen Rani. Service had been restored on the Red Line, which ran underneath downtown. They hoped to get to the Northwestern Emergency Room that way.

Detective Sergeant Beckwell, the lead investigator into Marco's death, interviewed me in Eliza Driscoll's office. She'd slept through all the events on the chairs in Shanda's office. She'd awakened but paramedics had sent her, too, to the emergency room to see if she'd been drugged.

The power was still out on our side of Wells Street. Detective Beckwell had brought an emergency fluorescent lantern that cast a whitish-blue light around the room. Behind him snow still drifted down. I could see it under the streetlights on the other side of Wells, wide flakes spaced far apart. The snowmobiles had made straight lines in the heavy snow that still covered the street.

The detective wore a tan suit and fiddled with his glasses as I told him the entire story.

"I'm not sure if you're very bad luck or very good luck for those around you," he said.

I took a long drink from a paper cup of water from Eliza's water cooler. "Not good luck for Patryk, Novia, or Debbie."

"I can't say for sure yet, but from what you told me it sounds as if those deaths would have happened regardless," the detective said.

I disagreed with him about Debbie. If she hadn't seen the ticket stubs on my phone, she wouldn't have questioned Aidan and might still be alive.

~

December 14, 6:48 a.m.

"She would totally have questioned Aidan," Lauren said when I relayed the conversation to her.

We were waiting for the front residence elevators. Power had come on as I'd been talking with Beckwell. Lauren's lower lip was swollen, she limped, and her arm hurt. She'd refused to go to the emergency room, though, saying she'd rather see someone at her own doctor's office later that day. Her parents had a concierge plan where they paid extra each year for anyone in the family to be seen quickly if needed.

The elevator doors slid open and we stepped inside. While Lauren moved slowly and favored her good leg, she said she wasn't in too much pain.

I pressed Fifteen. "But if Debbie hadn't heard Carole and me talking about the tickets, she wouldn't have connected Novia and Rani and called Aidan."

"I only knew her for a day and I could tell she liked to poke into all her neighbors' business," Lauren said. "You didn't tell her to call Aidan. You didn't ask her to listen in on your conversation with Carole. I'm as sorry as you are about what happened, but it is not your fault."

Carole answered the door immediately and hugged both of us. We filled her in on everything that had happened over a breakfast of bagels, cream cheese, and grapes.

"You should listen to Lauren," Carole said when we'd finished.

~

December 14, 9:15 a.m.

Shanda called Carole to let us know that Rani had been pronounced out of immediate danger but admitted overnight for observation. She had a broken leg and a possible concussion. Shanda discouraged us from coming to see her, saying everyone was exhausted and it would be better if we came tomorrow.

I napped on Carole's couch and Lauren slept in Carole's guest room on the King-sized bed. After we awoke Lauren iced her leg and arm. By that time enough streets had been plowed that we could walk to Lauren's doctor's office four blocks away in Dearborn Station. She'd finagled a visit for me as well, insisting I needed to be evaluated.

Traffic downtown was non-existent, something I'd never seen before.

~

December 15, 11:21 a.m.

We visited Rani late the next morning.

Getting to Northwestern Hospital posed a challenge. We took the Red Line. Since its trains ran underneath downtown, they stood a better chance of getting through. I nearly slipped on the concrete stairs going down to the subway platform. We had to exit at Chicago Avenue and State Street and hike over half a mile east toward the lake to reach the hospital. Parts of the way were unshoveled, leaving us to trudge through knee-high drifts and reroute to avoid deeper ones. Lauren needed to rest several times because of the pain in her arm and knee, but we made it.

Rani was sleeping when we reached her room. Shanda stepped into the hall to talk with us.

Her black hair hung around her shoulders. The ends looking ragged, and dark areas underscored her eyes. "I feel I brought this on Rani. I hired Aidan. I called his references, but I didn't truly dig into his background. If I had, I would never have hired him."

"Why?" I said.

"The detective who interviewed Rani. He said there were warrants for Aidan in Arizona for passing bad checks. To parents of a friend who let him stay temporarily with them. Also a conviction in Pennsylvania for a real estate scam."

An orderly wheeled a patient past us in a wheelchair.

"How long ago?" I said.

"Ten years ago on the checks, and it took over a week for them to bounce. In the meantime, he opened a new checking account and credit cards using their address, then took off. They got notices for months for bad debts. At least he didn't steal anyone's identity, I suppose."

"And in Pennsylvania?" I said, struggling to ignore the alcohol and disinfectant scents in the hallway. The mix threatened to set off another migraine.

"More sophisticated. Five years ago he married a woman with an online travel agency catering to golfers. Using her money, he started a real estate company with a partner. Got people to pretend to buy as homeowners and get mortgages, then flip the properties. Something didn't resell fast enough and they got caught. But the prosecutor couldn't pin much on Aidan. He'd never met any of the fake buyers or the mortgage brokers. He got off with probation and the partner went to jail, though he swore Aidan masterminded everything."

Lauren shifted her injured arm, now in a neon pink sling, to adjust the angle. "His wife wasn't involved in the scam?"

"No, but she'd trusted him to handle the money, and guess where most of it went. I feel for her. I liked him a lot. Thought he was a good guy."

"Seems like everyone did," Lauren said.

46

———

December 15, 12:15 p.m.

At the Starbucks on the ground floor of the hospital I got a Chai Latte and Lauren ordered an espresso. We both bought giant chocolate chip brownies. I felt both hungry and unable to eat anything substantial. That morning I'd had only a half a protein bar.

As we settled at a center table far from the windows, Janelle entered. I waved her over.

She joined us after she got a cup of black coffee. Her blond curls had strung out into ragged waves and gray hairs sprang from around her part. Bags weighed down the skin under her eyes. She'd come to visit Rani, who was still resting. Shanda had told her where to find us.

She told us the police had questioned her first at River City and a second time at the station with Danielle in attendance. I'd referred her. I didn't think she'd done anything wrong, but the idea that only the guilty need to be wary when dealing with police is a bad one.

"Thanks for the referral," she said. "I felt a lot better

answering with Danielle at my side. Not that anything can really make me feel better."

Lauren touched the back of Janelle's hand. "Did they believe you?"

"I think so." She stared down into her coffee. Its dark almost bitter scent filled the air. "He understood me so well. Aidan. It seemed like he did."

"He was good at manipulating people," I said.

"How did it start?" Lauren said. "Unless you don't want to tell us."

Janelle glanced through the glass wall toward the building lobby with its soaring ceiling and shiny reception counter. "No, I'll tell you. It helps a little to talk. I met him at a Tenants Association meeting. Someone introduced us. I don't remember who or why, but when he heard what I did he mentioned having money to invest from a business he and his ex-wife had owned. The amount he named was below what Patryk and I handled, but we met for coffee the next day and I gave him some general advice."

"Do you do that often?" I bit off a corner of the brownie.

"If someone seems nice. It's good to help people out. And you never know who they might refer. Or someone Aidan's age might come back ten years later and become a client. It's a long game."

It was something Joe often said to me about his business, and it was true in law as well. Maybe in everything in life.

"So you had coffee...." Lauren said.

"And I had a good time. He asked a lot about how Patryk and I had started our firm and why I'd chosen finance. He seemed so interested in everything I said. When he asked if we could meet again after he'd followed up on my suggestions, I said sure. That time he told me about his travel business with his ex-wife. Said they'd gotten married young, like Patryk and me. That he'd tried to stay out of loyalty to his ex because they'd been high school sweethearts, but they'd grown apart over the years. It was exactly how I felt with Patryk, but for us it had taken decades."

"Had you been having problems with Patryk before you met Aidan?" I asked.

Janelle's hair had swung forward into her eyes as she spoke. She brushed it aside. "Yes. And no. I guess we were and I didn't realize it. Aidan's words, they hit me. I felt this envy. Not that I wanted to be with him, not then. Envy that he'd made this change. Hadn't felt tied because of what the marriage had once been."

"And you felt tied to Patryk?" I said.

Setting aside his criminal activities, I wondered if the story of Aidan's marriage had any grain of truth and that's why he'd recognized a longing he could exploit in Janelle. As an actress I'd often found a hook, however small, in my own life that allowed me a way into a character's world no matter how different she might be from me. As a lawyer, I used the same technique to connect with witnesses.

"Maybe tied is the wrong word. But we'd become our business. That wasn't bad. I love what I do. Love to help people. My clients are ones typical investment firms find less appealing because they have less to invest, but they're driven to make the most of their lives. Patryk and I shared that vision. And it's not as if we only worked. We bought a summer home in Lake Geneva. We rehabbed that together. We met friends there. But once I got to know Aidan, I realized how long it was since Patryk and I truly spent time with one another. Not at a networking event or community function or with six of our closest friends."

Janelle's cup was still half-full but she started bending the brim and tearing off tiny chunks.

Lauren finished her espresso. "Did you talk to Patryk about that?"

"He didn't see any issue. He asked me did I think we should have long heart-to-heart talks like we had when we'd first met and if we did, what would we talk about." She twisted a chunk of the paper cup and dropped it on the table. "I feel terrible saying these things. It's not that he didn't care, he was just very practical. But when I thought about his response, the world got grayer and grayer. Because it was like saying there was nothing more for the two us."

I hoped she hadn't blurted those feelings out to the police. I was sure Danielle would have cautioned her to answer only what was asked and no more if she answered at all.

"The conversations with Patryk were after you met Aidan?" I said.

"A week or two after I met him. We were barely friends yet."

Tiny pieces of cardboard coffee cup lay on the table in front of Janelle.

"How long before you got involved?" Lauren asked.

"About another month. Before that there was a little flirtation. Harmless, I thought, especially since Aidan's almost twenty years younger than me. Patryk and I both knew sales sometimes involves a little chemistry with the prospect. I'd never had it get out of hand. But it felt so good to have a man admire me. Excited to see me."

I thought of Marco. We'd been in that exciting phase where everything was new and thrilling. I'd never know what sort of life we would have had together, what that phase of our relationship would have turned into.

My Chai had gone cold and the dregs tasted too sweet, but I drank them.

"I made the first move," Janelle said. "After he said something in passing about too bad I was already married. I knew I was too old for him, but he said age didn't matter. That no one would think twice if it were reversed, if he were twenty years older than me. I kissed him right outside the Dollop across the street. Anyone could have seen us, but nobody did."

Aidan had taken Janelle, too, to many of the same concerts and events we'd discovered he'd gone to with Novia and Rani. She and Aidan had often met in the vacant apartment where

Debbie had been found. He'd told Janelle he and Novia were good friends and that he'd gotten the keys from her but not to mention it because Novia was worried about getting in trouble.

"He's the one who broke it off." Janelle had dismantled nearly half of her paper cup. Shreds lay everywhere. "After six months. Said it was too hard seeing me when he knew he could never be with me. That's when I thought about whether I could divorce Patryk, and eventually I told Aidan I couldn't. That I wouldn't, but there was this little part of me that hoped he'd try to convince me."

"Did he?" I said, guessing the answer was no. Someone like Aidan would want Janelle to feel she'd made the decision all on her own, that he'd had nothing to do with it. He'd want her to long to be with him again. Either that or he'd already decided that a widow was a better deal than a divorcee. Janelle likely would inherit Patryk's share of the business, their home, and their investments. Had she divorced Patryk, she would only have had half of that.

She shook her head. "No. He said I was doing the right thing, that Patryk was a good man and I'd be foolish and cruel to end things with him. I was devastated."

"How long ago was that?" I said.

"That Aidan ended it? August 1."

Maybe Aidan had shifted gears after that and decided to focus on weaseling into Shanda's business through Rani instead. Or he'd simply been biding his time with Janelle and Shanda was the back up.

The trees outside whipped in the wind. Janelle shivered. "All these people dead. All because of my affair with Aidan."

Lauren slapped her hand down on the table. "Stop. Just stop. The only one responsible for the deaths is Aidan. Not you, not Quille, not Shanda. Only Aidan."

～

ecember 15, 2:20 p.m.

Rani was sitting up in her hospital bed when we returned, sipping apple juice from a plastic cup through a straw. Her hair was plastered back away from her face. Her round face looked thinner than before, and the space under her cheekbones sunken in.

Janelle stopped in for a moment, saying she only wanted to see for herself how Rani was doing and to apologize for her role in all that had happened.

After she left, Shanda took a walk to the cafeteria for lunch. Lauren sat in the green vinyl reclining chair so she could stretch her injured leg and settle her arm more comfortably. I drew a metal chair that looked like it had come from the cafeteria near the bed.

"You don't need to talk if you don't want," I said. "We don't want to wear you out."

Rani shook her head. "No, I'm bored out of my mind here. Talking's better than lying around thinking about my leg hurting. These pain pills — not doing much."

I asked how she'd come to be in the health club.

She set the juice cup on her metal tray. "I noticed something odd about the photo I'd taken of the homeless man. After I posted it on the Tenants Association site."

Lauren leaned forward. "Women's boots, right?"

"Were they? I just thought they looked too new and stylish. Like you might get them at an upscale resale shop or on eBay, not from Goodwill. I couldn't see the boots very well, but I had a weird feeling, you know? Plus I wanted to help if he really was homeless. I started carrying info on homeless shelters with me and watching for him."

"And you saw him again," I said.

"Yeah." She glanced at the ceiling. "Today's Friday, right? So I saw him three weeks ago yesterday. Near the grocery store. He came in from the parking lot, asked someone for money, and left. All I had on were sweats and gym shoes, but it was dark and I followed him out. Thought maybe he'd go to the construction site next door. Instead he went up the stairs outside, past Eliza Driscoll's office, and in that side door down the way from her office."

"Did you talk to him that night?"

Rani shifted in the bed. I helped reposition the pillow under her injured leg, which was in a cast. "No, but he dropped a glove on the stairs. I grabbed it. When I got inside, though, I didn't see him. I tried all the doors on the offices and they were locked."

Rani told us she'd watched for him over the next few nights, this time staying down the hall from Eliza's office in an alcove. Finally one night he came in that same side door.

"He used a key to open an office. I quick slipped in behind him before the door shut all the way. And it was Aidan. He'd taken off his scarves, so I saw his face."

"You weren't afraid following a strange man into a room? Before you knew it was Aidan?" I said.

With my family's history about strangers, I couldn't imagine doing that. I'd have tried to talk to him out in the open somewhere.

"Now I would be." She rubbed her hands over her arms, bare under the hospital gown. "But I figured I'd return the glove, ask if he needed help."

"How did Aidan react?" Lauren said.

"Laughed. Like it was a joke we'd planned together. He told me it was for his University of Chicago class. He was in their Graduate Student At Large program."

I knew the program. I'd looked into it once.

It allows students with bachelors or advanced degrees to take undergraduate and graduate level courses for credit, though the credits never lead to a U of C degree. It's a way to fill in gaps in your education or to use as a bridge to another program. It costs over four thousand dollars for a single class, though, so I hadn't done it.

Aidan told Rani he was taking GSAL classes to flesh out his humanities, as he had a bachelor of science degree. He claimed he was dressing this way for a paper about how people might react to a homeless person, or seemingly homeless person, who appeared in their midst.

Rani drank more juice and twirled the straw. "It didn't seem right, but I thought maybe it was some weird U of C thing. When I was looking at grad school programs, everyone told me the students there are brilliant but odd. I asked if his professor knew what Aidan was doing. He said not yet, he was going to explain the methods in the introduction to the paper."

"But the health club?" I said.

"Last week Novia found my envelope with all my ticket print-outs and programs from places I'd gone with Aidan. She kept asking who I'd gone with. I didn't tell her because Aidan didn't want Shanda to know we were seeing each other. But I started wondering if Novia was why Aidan had tried to discourage me from volunteering at the Center."

I moved my chair a little closer. "Discourage you how?"

"He said it was better to meet more people outside the building, better networking. That I already met other immigrants through Shanda's non-profit and just living here. But now I thought maybe he was seeing Novia, taking her the same places he'd taken me. Which made me wonder about what else he might be lying about. I looked on U of C's website. The quarter was over. So how could he still be working on a paper for it? Also, the description of the class he'd said he was taking — none of it fit with his supposed project."

"And you confronted him?" Lauren said.

"Wednesday morning. I wanted to catch him early before Shanda got in. Aidan was almost always in by six."

"He was?" Shanda said from behind us. I twisted around. She

stood in the doorway holding a can of Diet Pepsi. "He told me he usually got in a few minutes before me, about eight. After getting coffee with you."

"No, for the last few months he's been in really early."

Shanda perched on the long, narrow couch built into the wall beyond the bed. "So what happened Wednesday morning?"

"I texted to meet me at five-thirty. That way I was sure no one would be around. I didn't want to embarrass him in front of Shanda or get him fired, I just wanted him to tell me the truth. As soon as he walked into the office I confronted him."

"I'm guessing he came up with some explanation," I said.

"He told me I was wrong about everything, and he'd prove it to me."

47

December 15, 2:30 pm.

"First he claimed he was just friends with Novia," Rani said. "That she wanted something more, and she'd gotten mad when he said he wasn't interested. He admitted he sort of used her to get the keys to the empty apartment where he let me in to take photos. He'd told me he'd gotten permission from management for me. He was super apologetic and begged me to give him another chance."

"And the homeless man outfit?" I said.

"He wanted me to come with him to what he called his 'second office.' He said it was that vacant office where I'd found him. Novia had also given him keys to that, supposedly so he could study in peace."

"But it was empty," I said.

"Right, but I didn't know that. When I walked in on him before he hurried me out, I was so caught up in why he was dressed the way he was, I didn't look around. We talked in the hall mostly."

"Why that office?" Lauren said. "I mean, I know why he wanted you in an empty office but what did he tell you?"

"He said he had his laptop and other work there. That he hadn't wanted Shanda to know about the course because she might think he wasn't dedicated to his job. It sounds so stupid that for a minute I believed him." She twisted around and adjusted the pillow under her knee again. "But you had to know Aidan. He seemed so sad that he'd upset me and caused me to doubt him."

"But why would going there explain dressing as the homeless man?" I said.

"He said he'd turned in the paper but he'd decided to expand on it for a personal essay. Claimed he had a magazine interested. He wanted to show me his draft article, and he didn't have it on his work computer."

"He couldn't email it to you?" I said. "Or pull it from the cloud?"

Rani shifted again to lie partway on her side, obviously uncomfortable from her injury. We'd need to leave and let her rest soon.

"He said he had handwritten markings on it from the editor, on a paper copy, that would prove what he was saying," she said. "I wanted to believe him, I really did. I started to follow him up the side stairwell. But it didn't feel right. Who sends paper back and forth these days? And I thought about what you told me when I moved here." She gestured toward me.

"Me?" I said.

"You told me trust my instincts."

"About?" Lauren said.

"Anything that feels off. If an elevator comes and you don't feel good about someone in there, don't get on. Take the next one. Or someone's on the street that you feel nervous about, duck into a building with a doorman even if you feel like you'll look foolish. That kind of thing."

"I'm glad it helped," I said.

"It maybe saved my life." Rani gripped the hospital sheet with both hands. "I slowed down so I was a few feet behind him when he opened the office door. I looked past him and saw there was nothing inside. So I ran. He caught me and threw me against the wall. Or tried to. His foot slipped. I hit the wall and hit my head, but somehow I got to the stairwell. Then I twisted my ankle when I came down wrong on a stair. I felt like I was going to throw up from pain. I can't believe I didn't fall down the stairs. But I kept going. I wanted to exit at the lobby, but I got disoriented and got out on the Marina Level by mistake.

"I was stumbling and yelling for help, but no one was in yet, and I barely got out of the stairwell. I didn't think I could make it to the elevators or climb the escalator, but I had a key to the health club. I'd just started taking photos of the construction there, part of an independent project over winter break. I had to sign all kinds of waivers to get access, and Aidan didn't know anything about it. So I let myself in."

"Why not the grocery store?" Lauren said. "It's not that much farther."

"It's a lot farther if you're injured and practically crawling. And I thought Aidan might expect me to go that way. I crawled to the storage room. I figured the workers would find me when they came in. But I banged into those boards and one landed on me. And no one came to work because of the expected blizzard, I guess. I'd dropped my camera on the stairs, and I was hoping someone would find it."

"No one did," I said, surprised. Maybe Aidan had snatched it and gotten rid of it.

"What about your phone?" Lauren said.

"I passed out before I could call anyone. When I woke up, I tried, but I couldn't get any signal down there. After that I drifted in and out until Quille found me."

〜

December 15, 2:45 p.m.

Rani wanted to keep talking, but Shanda nodded when I suggested she rest for a while. Lauren and I sat in the waiting room, drinking hot chocolate I got from a vending machine and dozing.

When we returned an hour later Shanda sat in the recliner, and Rani was watching a documentary on PBS and eating pudding. She waved us in and told us how things had started between her and Aidan. Lauren and I sat next to each other on the couch.

"We got to be friends right when he started working for Shanda. I felt like he really got me. He asked about my studies, and he picked up right away that I didn't want to go into computer science as a profession and why."

Shanda opened her mouth, but before she could speak, Rani turned and shot her a look. "I just don't, all right? It was something I only figured out last year. Too late to change, I thought. Aidan told me he was doing the U of C program partly to figure out what he wanted to do next.

"We started hanging out more, and eventually it just turned into seeing each other. He asked me not to say anything because Shanda might think he was using me to get in good with her. I was so busy, I figured who cared if he wanted to keep it quiet. It's not like we could see each other that much. And he was a great boyfriend. Always listened whenever I was upset about anything, always sympathized. Ran interference with Shanda."

"Interference?" Shanda shifted the recliner into the upright position. "What?"

"Are you serious?" Rani scraped the last of the pudding from the cup with her plastic spoon. "All you ever do is criticize me, and the closer I got to graduation, the worse it got. Oh, and Aidan helped me research graduate programs."

Shanda gathered her long hair in one hand, twisted it, and

clipped it in the back with practiced motions. "I'm sorry. I never meant to be so hard on you. I just worry about you."

"Did he use your computer password?" I said to Rani. "When he helped you research?"

"For the work computer? Yeah. That way he could call up my automatic entries on different applications. He filled some out for me."

"Is that when he started going in so early?" I said.

Rani nodded.

I imagined Aidan busily searching through Shanda's files, copying her client list, looking at whatever he didn't have access to so he could squirrel it away and use it later.

"I bet he also researched overstayed student visas under your name," Lauren said.

As Rani and Shanda compared notes, it became clear that while Aidan had claimed to be trying to make things better between Shanda and Rani he'd been doing his best to undermine their relationship. The day that Rani had stayed late at the library, she'd told Aidan where she'd be and called and left a voicemail for Shanda at the office. Shanda had never gotten it. No doubt Aidan had deleted it, and he'd only said Rani was at the library after Shanda complained about her not showing up. It made it seem as if he were simply covering for her.

Shanda grasped Rani's hand. "I'm so sorry I didn't see what was happening. But I don't understand it. Why set us against each other?"

"Maybe so you wouldn't believe Rani if she told you anything bad about Aidan," Lauren said.

"Or so Rani would be less likely to tell you how close they'd gotten, which might make you worry about his access to your files," I said.

"You're probably right." Shanda smoothed Rani's hair. "I don't guess we're ever going to hear the truth from him."

48

December 18 through December 20

Aidan's ex-wife contacted Shanda a few days later after a police detective interviewed her.

Contrary to what he'd told Janelle, they hadn't been high school sweethearts. He'd met her at a digital business conference and claimed he wanted to enter the travel business. He'd started with her company as an intern, learned everything about it, and became the perfect employee and, eventually, husband and business partner. Any number of potential investors and clients told her later that they'd believed he'd been on board from day one and had a decade of experience in the field.

She agreed that his goal likely had been to copy and steal from Shanda as much as he could, possibly to start a competing business or to run some type of scam involving her clients. When he'd met Janelle, Shanda had likely become his back up. With Janelle, after killing Patryk, he could start seeing her again after a respectful time, marry her, and become a co-owner of her home and business as he'd done in his first marriage.

Aidan's claim on LinkedIn that he had a degree in physics turned out to be true. He'd once considered further coursework in meteorology. One of his significant contributions to the travel business had been a deep understanding of weather and climate that enabled him to make last minute changes in golf plans for clients so they could still play if the weather turned bad.

The blizzard must have been, for him, a golden opportunity.

It almost guaranteed the hallway outside the grocer would be deserted when he attacked Patryk. I guessed that had there been no blizzard, Aidan would have waited in the parking lot as many nights as it took to attack Patryk in one of the shadowy areas where few people parked or walked. But the extreme weather had made Patryk a far easier target.

The camera on the ATM in the grocer had been working. The security footage eventually was released. It showed Patryk exchanging what looked like heated words with a man dressed the way Aidan had been in the photo. The two got into a shoving match. The man grabbed Patryk by the front of his coat and slammed him repeatedly against the wall, then dropped Patryk on the ground, rifled through his pockets, and took his wallet. He appeared to struggle with the doors to exit, making it look like he dropped the glove by mistake.

The man's back was to the camera most of the time, making it impossible to see his face.

I wondered how many times Aidan had videoed himself and practiced to make it work.

At Novia's funeral, her best friend, whom she'd known since high school, told Leslie Jones that Novia had confided that she was seeing a man she'd met through work. She'd promised the man she'd keep it a secret so she didn't share his name. The friend knew that he was in his mid-thirties, worked for a business in River City, and was in the midst of a complicated divorce and didn't want word of him seeing someone new to get out. He claimed his ex simply wouldn't let go and he was trying to let her down easy.

The man had to be Aidan.

Detective Beckwell unofficially told me the prosecutor and police thought it unclear whether Aidan would have gotten rid of Novia absent the blizzard. While she knew he had keys to different parts of the building through her, no evidence suggested she'd put that together with the homeless man. After a time, they thought he likely would've broken it off with her and resumed the relationship with Janelle after a waiting period following Patryk's death. But I thought he worried that she and Rani might have talked, and that's why he'd taken advantage of the deserted garage to eliminate her.

As for Rani, the prosecutor's theory was that she had sealed her fate the instant she learned Aidan had been disguising himself as the homeless man. Before that, it appeared that Patryk was the only target.

~

A lot of people think you can't convict someone of murder on circumstantial evidence. You can, but there are some challenges. Danielle tells me that jury members are so used to seeing detailed forensic evidence on TV shows like CSI that they expect to hear about fingerprints and fibers and DNA.

If the prosecutor can't produce all of that and more, the absence alone sometimes raises doubts. And Aidan had been careful. Other than the single glove, the clothes and boots he'd worn to disguise himself were nowhere to be found, nor was Rani's camera.

The gray scarf around Debbie's neck and the red scarf around Novia's had no DNA evidence other than theirs. I suspected they were duplicates of the ones in the photo, and that Aidan had never actually worn them himself.

The vacant apartment and Novia's car had no fingerprints or other forensic evidence that pointed to Aidan. His DNA was on her body, but we'd all seen him perform CPR, so that didn't prove anything.

All the same, Aidan was charged with multiple counts of attempted murder for Rani, Lauren, and me, and first-degree murder for Patryk, Novia, and Debbie. If convicted on more than one of the murders, he'd without question be sentenced to natural life, meaning he'd die in prison.

Danielle thought Aidan would eventually plead to second degree murder. In Illinois, second degree murder means either a crime of passion or that the murderer killed someone while having an unreasonable belief that it was necessary to defend himself or someone else.

I didn't believe either applied, but he'd need to make a statement as part of the pleas. At least that way his victims' loved ones would get some confirmation of what had happened. And he'd be in prison for a very long time.

49

———————

Decmber 21 though December 31

Three days before Christmas I emailed Kendra and declined her invitation to Christmas dinner. Kendra emailed back faster than I expected saying she understood and that my niece and nephew would still come to my place for the weekend of New Year's Eve. It had been a tradition since they were old enough to take the train to Chicago by themselves. We played games on New Year's Eve along with many of my friends. Joe would be absent, but Marco's son Eric would be back from Alaska and was joining us for the first time.

I called Gram to tell her what I'd decided. The conversation was short, and she was disappointed, but I assured her I'd be fine for the holiday.

I'd made a reservation at the Palmer House Hotel downtown for Christmas Eve and two nights after. It's a beautiful historic hotel with hand-forged bronze doors, arched ceilings, and chandeliers everywhere. I'd told Marco that when I'd been an actor on a limited budget, it had always been my image of somewhere I'd like to stay if I had money. He'd promised we'd go there on a long weekend, but we hadn't gotten the chance.

Lauren wasn't satisfied. "If you want a vacation," she said, "come with me to Park City."

We were sitting in her place near the fireplace.

"You're missing the 'alone' part." I poured myself a little more Cabernet. "I want some quiet. Solitude."

"You'll get depressed," she said. "Post-holiday wallowing in grief will make it worse. You'll just sit around and think about Marco."

"It's okay," I said. "Christmas will be sad no matter what I do. I've been keeping busy all year. It doesn't keep me from thinking of Marco. It just wears me out. So I'll rest for a few days, feel however I feel, and in a few days I'll be hanging out with everyone on New Year's Eve."

I was being overly optimistic. Overstating so my friend would leave me alone. But I'd get through it, and I felt sure it'd be better than being around a lot of cheery people.

"Then I'll stay too," Lauren said. "I'll get a room there too."

"No. Seriously. Go skiing. Have a lovely time."

She hugged me. "I'm going to call you every day."

The Harmoniums had four concerts the weekend before Christmas. Danielle, Joe, and I had fun and were exhausted. Joe and his girlfriend left for Aruba the next day.

Marco's mom made dinner for herself, Eric, and me the night before Christmas Eve. We exchanged gifts. Eric gave me a magnifying glass a la Sherlock Holmes. He also gave me a beautiful leather-bound accounting journal. "I know you do everything on the computer, but I thought this was cool."

Marco's mom gave me a gift basket of homemade cookies, cheeses, wine, and cold meat she'd put together from Macy's. She was always worried I wasn't eating enough. I decided I'd take it with me to the Palmer House.

I gave Eric a new skateboard, one I'd seen him eyeing when we'd gone to Uprise, a skateboard store on Milwaukee Avenue late in the summer. He left for Alaska early the next morning, and I checked into the Palmer House.

On Christmas Eve, Danielle and her daughter and I went to see Hamilton — she'd gotten tickets in the lottery — and had dinner afterwards in the Palmer House's marble lobby area with a soaring Christmas tree. I thought of last year's Christmas Eve with Marco, but I still enjoyed the evening. On Christmas Day I ordered room service and then watched streaming movies. It took a while to find something after skipping holiday fare, romantic comedies, and horror films. I settled for superhero action films with lots of special effects.

Later in the day I went to the Starbucks in the Palmer House and read. Reading at coffeehouses was something I'd loved to do whenever I could squeeze it in during law school and my early years as a lawyer. It had been a half hour I'd carve out for myself once a week where I shut off my phone and told no one where I was. The feeling of relaxation came right back to me.

The beauty of a city like Chicago is that no one looked at me oddly for sitting alone and reading on Christmas Day. No one looked at me at all.

Late in the day I talked to Lauren and called Gram to wish her a Merry Christmas. I checked in with my niece and nephew and sister, and my dad called me. He put my mom on the phone. As usual, she said hello and went into a litany of what had gone wrong with the dinner my dad had made for himself, my mom, and my aunt who always spent Christmas Day with them though they didn't celebrate it.

In a way it was a relief. My mom had run through the same complaints in her holiday call to me last year and the year before that and every year since I was fifteen and my parents had moved without me back to Edwardsville.

The next day I texted Ty to thank him for his advice about getting through the holiday. He sent back a photo of a beautiful sunset from his hotel in Maui.

On New Year's Eve Gram and my niece and nephew came to my place to play games. Lauren was still in Park City, but Danielle and her daughter joined us and so did Marco's son, Eric.

We ate pizza around the kitchen island. Gram put away leftovers. I laid out the board for Settlers of Cataan with the expansion set on the dining table near my sliding glass door. My niece had started placing her first two blue roads and houses when a text came in.

It was from Ty:

Happy New Year. Hope this one is less eventful & I get to see you again. In better circumstances.

"C'mon, Auntie Q," my niece said. "It's your turn."

I placed my roads and houses. Eric groaned and bent over the board, holding his pieces in his hand.

"Sorry," I said.

I sent Ty a quick answer that I'd like that.

Danielle's wine glass was empty. I refilled her glass and mine. Before I could sit down again, though, someone knocked at the door. I figured it must be a neighbor stopping by since the doorman hadn't rung me to tell me anyone had arrived.

But when I opened the door, Joe stood on the other side. He wore his dark cashmere coat. His cheeks glowed from the cold. "Happy New Year."

I opened the door wide. "Thought you weren't home until next week."

He shrugged. "I came back early. I wasn't going to let you ring in the New Year without me."

He handed me a bottle of my favorite Pinot Noir, hugged me, and joined us at the table.

The End

Want more?

Would you like to hear why Quille's sister Kendra became so angry with her? See what happens next with Joe and Quille?

Join the author's email list at LisaLilly.com to receive Free Q.C. Davis short stories, a monthly e-newsletter, and updates on sales and new releases.

ABOUT THE AUTHOR

In addition to *The Worried Man (Q.C. Davis 1)* and *The Charming Man (Q.C. Davis 2)*, Lisa M. Lilly is the author of the bestselling four-book *Awakening* supernatural thriller series. The books in the series, *The Awakening, The Unbelievers, The Conflagration,* and *The Illumination,* have been downloaded over 80,000 times.

A member of the Horror Writers Association, Lilly also is the author of *When Darkness Falls,* a gothic horror novel set in Chicago's South Loop, and *The Tower Formerly Known As Sears And Two Other Tales Of Urban Horror*, the title story of which was made into the short film *Willis Tower*. Her stories and poems have appeared in numerous publications.

A resident of Chicago, Lilly is an attorney and a member of the Alliance Against Intoxicated Motorists. She joined AAIM after an intoxicated driver caused the deaths of her parents in 2007. Her book of essays, *Standing in Traffic,* is available on AAIM's website.

She is currently working on The Fractured Man, Book 3 in the Q.C. Davis series.

To learn more or join her email list, visit LisaLilly.com, email her at Lisa@LisaLilly.com or connect on social media.

ALSO BY LISA M. LILLY

The Q.C. Davis Series

The Worried Man (Q.C. Davis 1)

The Charming Man (Q.C. Davis 2)

The Fractured Man (Q.C. Davis 3) Coming Soon

The Awakening Supernatural Thriller Series:

The Awakening (Book 1)

The Unbelievers (Book 2)

The Conflagration (Book 3)

The Illumination (Book 4)

Standalone Occult/Horror:

When Darkness Falls (a supernatural suspense novel)

The Tower Formerly Known As Sears And Two Other Tales Of Urban
Horror

Writing as L.M. Lilly:

How The Virgin Mary Influenced The United States Supreme Court:
Catholics, Contraceptives, and Burwell v. Hobby Lobby, Inc.

Super Simple Story Structure: A Quick Guide to Plotting and Writing
Your Novel

Creating Compelling Characters From The Inside Out

The One-Year Novelist: A Week-By-Week Guide To Writing Your Novel
In One Year